Turning The Page

To CJ —

Turning The Page

This is an oldie, but a goodie
I hope you like it
Thanks
Georgia Beers

Georgia Beers

Yellow Rose Books
a Division of
RENAISSANCE ALLIANCE PUBLISHING, INC.
Nederland, Texas

ISBN 1-930928-51-3

First Printing 2001

9 8 7 6 5 4 3 2 1

Cover design by Linda A. Callaghan

Published by:

Renaissance Alliance Publishing, Inc.
PMB 238, 8691 9th Avenue
Port Arthur, TX 77642

Find us on the World Wide Web at
http://www.rapbooks.com

Printed in the United States of America

Acknowledgements

My first ever trip to a women's bookstore took me to a little shop in Rochester called Silkwood. I was in awe! That was many years ago and though I'm very sad to say that Silkwood closed recently, it has a permanent residence in my memory. Although the shop in this book is by no means a replica, Silkwood was definitely an inspiration.

Thank you to Stacy, for reading the same paragraphs over and over again and still catching the boo-boos and inconsistencies. Even when I was making her crazy, she remained supportive and encouraging, which means more than she knows.

Thank you to Tonya, for giving me a loving kick in the pants and assuring me that this story was indeed good enough to publish. Without her encouragement, you wouldn't be holding it in your hands. I don't think I thanked her nearly enough when I had the chance, but I hope that wherever she is now, she knows how grateful I am.

Thank you to the two women who had the most influence on my life as I grew up:

My mother, Roseann, for always being there, no matter what...

My Aunt Joyce, for always believing in my ability to write—even when I wasn't using it.

Lastly, to the woman who has the most influence on my life now...the one who keeps me strong when I'm about to cave in, the one who nudges me along gently when I've lost my confidence, the one who tells me I'm beautiful when I'm feeling my most unattractive, the one who loves me every minute of every day and makes sure that I know it all the time...my Bonnie, the one who makes all things possible.

Chapter
1

"I always thought you were smart, Mel, but this is undeniably the dumbest move you've ever made." Dale Radcliffe was dashing, as always, in his custom-tailored, double-breasted, gray pinstriped suit. A red silk tie added the finishing touch, like the cherry atop an ice cream sundae.

Hearing his grating voice behind her, Melanie Larson rolled her blue eyes heavenward as she continued to pack up her office. Most women—and some men, for that matter—would visibly swoon as Dale breezed past their desks, leaving a hint of Calvin Klein's Obsession for Men hanging provocatively in the air. After all, he was devastatingly handsome. From his perfectly highlighted blond hair and year-round tan down to his spit-shined wingtips, he was an impressive representative of the human male.

It was only after a disastrous night together, which Melanie now labeled an extremely gross error in judgement on her part, that she saw him for what he really was: a pompous and arrogant jerk who would step over his own grandmother if it would get him a promotion.

"Contrary to what you believe, Dale, I think this was a smart decision for me." She sounded less convincing than she'd intended, as if she were trying to convince herself as well as him.

He snorted. "If you say so. Call me in six months. I guarantee you'll be singing a different tune." He breezed out as smoothly as he had breezed in, tossing an insincere "Take care of yourself, Mel," over his shoulder.

"Thanks," Melanie replied, then under her breath, "Asshole." She was well aware of the fact that Dale was thrilled with her departure, knowing he'd have the chance to slither into the hole she left. She also knew he'd never make it. He put on a good show, but he would never be able to handle the pressure. It wouldn't be long before the Powers That Be realized it. She smiled at the thought of his inevitable demise.

There was a quiet knock. Melanie turned to see Angela Benetti, her soon-to-be-ex-secretary standing in the doorway.

"Hi. Can I come in?"

"Absolutely." Melanie smiled at her.

Angela was a plump, Italian woman in her late fifties. Her dark hair was streaked with gray and pulled back into a tight bun, the severity of which was offset by the pleasantness of her face. Her navy skirt and sky-blue blouse were simple and neat, and her reading glasses hung from a chain around her neck. Of all the people Melanie had worked with throughout her career, Angela had been the most dependable. Not only was she quick, organized, and efficient, she was also loving, caring, and nurturing. She looked after Melanie—with and without her knowledge or approval—like a mother would. During the hectic days and late nights, she made sure Melanie ate, often bringing leftovers from home and literally standing in front of Melanie's desk until she consumed every last bite of macaroni or eggplant parmesan or chicken cutlets or whatever her family had had for dinner the previous night. When Melanie hit her third cup of coffee, Angela began pouring her decaf. She watched proudly as Melanie rapidly ascended through the ranks of Rucker & Steele. With each promotion—three in four years—Melanie was offered a new office and secretary. Each time she accepted the office and declined the secretary, insisting that Angela stay with her. They were a great team.

"Have you eaten this morning?" she asked her boss.

"I had some coffee," Melanie replied sheepishly, knowing what was coming.

"No, I asked if you've *eaten* this morning." She set a foil-wrapped package on the desk. "Cranberry nut muffins I made last night. *Mangia.* Now."

Melanie knew better than to disobey Angela, the roles of boss and employee nearly non-existent between them. Mother and child were more adequate titles. She opened the package and popped a piece of the sweet cake into her mouth, immediately making the inevitable "oh my God, this is delicious" sounds that seemed to appear all on their own whenever she ate something Angela made.

They stood in companionable silence, eating muffins and looking out at the Chicago skyline. Angela spoke after several minutes.

"All packed?"

"Yup." Melanie gestured to the half-filled banker's box sitting on the rich mahogany desk. She took a deep breath. "I hope I know what I'm doing."

"You listen to me," Angela said sharply, startling Melanie. "You are doing the right thing. I heard that weasel in here a few minutes ago." She rolled her eyes in disgust. "I don't know what you were thinking when you hooked up with him. What he said? Bullshit. He's salivating over your job so much, he's in danger of drowning himself."

Melanie burst into laughter over the visual that had formed in her head, Angela joining in. When they were able to regain their composure, Angela continued.

"Honey, I love you like you were my own, and even though I'm going to miss you like crazy, I know you made the right decision."

"The Decision" referred to leaving her high-ranking, very well paid position at Rucker & Steele. She remembered it like it was yesterday, and she equated it with being hit by a sledge hammer.

Just two months earlier, on April third, the upper management had announced Rucker & Steele's successful merger with a large international company. They would be relocating to Seattle by the end of June. It really was a big thing, a huge financial plus for R&S, virtually ensuring the future success of the company and all those who had helped it reach its upper-class status, including—and especially—Melanie, head of their marketing department. The announcement had come around lunch time and, although she had been trying to work, she'd been bodily dragged out of her office by coworkers and forced to join the celebration. R&S had spared no expense to thank the entire building: champagne all around and caterers with amazing hors d'oeuvres. There had been an incredible sense of pride and accomplishment hanging in the air, and everybody had felt it. R&S was paying the moving expenses of all those who wanted to stay in its employ and the excitement had been evident.

The party had gone on well beyond five o'clock, and when Melanie had tried to return to her office, she'd been met by Angela, as well as Thomas Rucker, who'd both admonished her for her long hours. When she had tried to brush off their concern as a joke, Rucker had blocked her office door, refusing to let her in. "Go home, for Christ's sake. See a movie. Watch TV. Get some sleep. You deserve a break. You're a big part of why this merger was possible, and I want you to pamper yourself, at least for one night." Angela had smiled and nodded in satisfaction. Finally, someone who saw things her way.

After accepting the fact that there was no arguing with a slightly tipsy Thomas Rucker, particularly when backed by a bossy Angela Benetti, Melanie had given in, and headed home to her top floor loft apartment. It had been just after seven—a very early evening for her—and she was not used to having time on her hands. She'd stood in the center of the sparsely furnished living room feeling a bit disoriented.

Deciding to cook for herself, she'd opened her refrigerator and sighed at the old jar of mustard with a fuzzy green top layer, a half-empty bottle of seltzer water and a stick of butter. She hadn't been able to remember the last time she'd been in a grocery store.

No problem, she'd thought. *I'll call somebody and go out to eat.* After twenty minutes of staring at the phone, she had sighed heavily. Not a single name would come to mind. There had been no one to call, and the idea of sitting in a restaurant alone had seemed far too pathetic. She'd sat back on the blue and cream striped couch which, along with the oak coffee table, was one of the only two pieces of furniture in the room, and let out a long, slow breath.

It was over her meal of a Quarter Pounder with cheese, large fries, a Coke, and an apple pie that she'd made up her mind. She'd looked around the apartment as she chewed. It was a beautiful place—high ceilings with wood ceiling fans and wood beams, rustic wood trim and molding, huge windows overlooking the city, large, modern kitchen. It was gorgeous. It was also empty. Aside from the couch and coffee table in the living room, there was a queen-size bed of wrought iron and wood and a matching dresser in the bedroom. In the corner of the living room, which Melanie lovingly thought of as "the den," was an old beat-up desk holding a computer, printer, and papers and files, which seemed to flow like a river from the top of the desk down and around the legs and across the floor. There were no pictures on the walls or table. There were no plants. There was a top-of-the-line television and VCR, neither hooked up nor plugged in. The cardboard boxes they had come in were stacked nearby. The place had the feel of somebody just moving in.

She'd been renting the apartment for over two years.

She'd swallowed hard and set down her burger. The sledgehammer hit, and she had suddenly felt sick to her stomach. She had a great job she was damn good at and lots of money. She had no friends. No hobbies. No furniture. She'd swallowed again, blinking rapidly as her solitary existence stared her in the face.

"God," she'd whispered, "I have no life."

"Did you hear me?" Angela was saying, clasping her hands tightly. "You made the right decision."

Melanie snapped back to the present. "You think so?"

"You better believe it. Look at this place." Angela gestured around the plush, rich-looking office at the thick, gray carpeting, mahogany furniture, leather chairs, beautiful view. "Where's Melanie?" she asked meaningfully. "Look in your box. What have you packed? What are you taking from this place that's you?"

Melanie looked into the banker's box, half-full of meaningless items. Pens and pencils, ten books on marketing, several computer disks, and a thriving plant in a deep purple pot. She held up the plant hopefully.

Angela glared at her. "The only reason that plant is alive is because I give it water once in a while."

Melanie set it down in defeat.

"There's no Melanie here," Angela continued softly. "Know why? Because you don't even know who Melanie is. You work, work, work, and you're good at it, and so what? Who cares if there's nobody beyond the work?"

"You're right," Melanie sighed. "I know. You're right."

"You take that severance package, and you go on vacation or something. Get to know Melanie." She smiled warmly. "I think you'll like her."

She wrapped her arms around Melanie and squeezed hard, blinking back tears. Melanie hugged her back, knowing Angela was what she would miss the most.

"What about you?" Melanie asked, wiping her own eyes. Angela was not moving to Seattle either. She had too much family in Chicago, and did not want to uproot herself so close to retirement age. "What will you do?"

"You think I can't find a job without you?" she chided Melanie with a grin. "I can find a job anywhere. You watch. I'll be working in a new place next week."

"I believe that's probably true," Melanie laughed.

Chapter
2

The phone call from Melanie's uncle couldn't have been more perfectly timed. Melanie was just beginning to absorb the fact that she was now out of a job and had been wondering exactly what she would do with herself, when the phone rang.

Phillip Richter was a soft-spoken, kind man, who had always held a special place in Melanie's heart. The two of them had much in common, the most predominant being their work ethic and business savvy. Phillip was the Vice President of Marketing at a very large training firm in Philadelphia. He and Melanie shared long conversations about their work, Melanie attributing much of her success to her Uncle Phil's advice.

Phillip and his wife, Darlene—Melanie's mother's sister—had only one child, their daughter Samantha, who was two years older than Melanie. Despite their distinctly different personalities, the cousins had grown up quite close to one another. Each was an only child and knew the other was the closest to a sibling they were likely to get.

Melanie was pleasantly surprised to hear her uncle's voice.

"Hi there, Red," he said with a smile in his voice.

Although her hair had gone from the strong red of her childhood to a softer, more mature auburn many years ago, Phillip Richter still used the pet name he had given his niece when she was three.

They breezed through the pleasantries, inquiring about the weather and each other's families. Then Phillip became serious.

"There is a specific reason I called, Red. I need your help, if possible."

"Sure, Uncle Phil. What's up?"

"Well, it's your cousin, Samantha. I'm afraid she's gotten herself into an unfavorable situation that I can't seem to get her out of."

"Really." Melanie knew Samantha all too well. She was probably in a situation she found very favorable, but Phillip wouldn't give her any more money.

Samantha Richter had been a wild, spoiled rotten teen-ager who blossomed earlier than most girls her age. Boys fell all over themselves to be near her, and she quickly learned to use that to her advantage. In school she drank, smoked, screwed around with everybody and their brother, and barely got her diploma. Melanie used to watch her in awe, sometimes disgusted at Samantha's behavior, some-times envious of it. She helped her cousin with her studies, often actually doing papers and assignments for her. Samantha, in turn, took Melanie under her wing socially, allowing her to tag along to parties and gatherings. Mela-nie was a quiet, shy, late bloomer, and having somebody as popular as Samantha vouch for her kept her from being picked on.

At parties, Melanie would stand near a wall or in a corner, invisible to everybody through the loud music and smoke of various substances. She would watch in amaze-ment as her beautiful blonde cousin worked the room. It was almost artistry, the way she commanded attention. Everybody—guys and girls alike—wanted to talk to her or bring her drinks or simply stand near her. She absorbed the desire like a sponge, and when she had had her fill, she would float in Melanie's direction, grasp her fifteen-year-old hand, and make her grand exit. That was the moment Melanie loved, the looks of jealousy and disbelief on the faces of the party guests, because of all the worthy people in the room, Samantha chose to leave with the scrawny, flat-chested little redhead. Samantha had been invaluable to Melanie's fragile, teenage self-esteem.

"You knew she and Jeff split up, right?" Uncle Phil asked.

"I think Mom mentioned it around Christmas," Melanie replied. She'd been surprised by the wedding in the first place. Neither Samantha nor Jeff had ever been faithful to anybody. Had they really thought getting married and moving to Rochester would solve the infidelity problems?

"Well, since he's been gone, Samantha's been having trouble with the bookstore. I think he must've run it, and since he's taken off with his little snow bunny, he's kind of left Sammy high and dry."

Melanie loved Phillip dearly, but his naivete when it came to his daughter—or maybe it was just plain blindness—was a bit frustrating. Samantha had never been "left high and dry," would never *allow* herself to be "left high and dry." If Jeff had left with his snow bunny, Melanie was sure that Samantha most likely had a little pet of her own. As for the bookstore, if Samantha was having trouble running it, that was probably because she didn't want to.

Phillip had given them the little shop for their first wedding anniversary, saying he knew Samantha had always loved books. There was already strain in the marriage, and Melanie deduced the store was probably Phillip's attempt at stabilizing it. Jeff couldn't hold a job; Samantha didn't want a job. Maybe dropping a source of income in their laps would help the situation.

"Red, do you think maybe you could give her a call, talk to her about the business end of things? I've tried to do it myself, but she won't listen to me. I know she listens to you. She always has. I'd hate to see such a nice place go under because she doesn't know how to prevent it."

"And I'm sure you'd prefer she didn't completely throw your money away without at least trying to make the place work," Melanie said with a smile, voicing the truth her uncle wouldn't.

He laughed heartily. "You got that right."

"Sure, Uncle Phil. I'll give her a call. I can't guarantee it will make a difference, but for you, I'll give it a shot."

"I have never gotten a favor out of Samantha that quickly. Would you be my kid?"

"I'll call her tonight. Love to Aunt Dar."

"You're the best, Red. Take care."

Chapter
3

From the road, Rochester seemed like a nice place. The plan had been to call Samantha and pump her for information on exactly what was going on with the bookstore. Instead, they got caught up in reminiscing and gossiping. When Samantha found out Melanie had some free time on her hands, she begged and pleaded with her cousin to come and stay for a bit. Deciding that a road trip would be less depressing than sitting around in her empty apartment, Melanie finally agreed.

As Melanie cruised along in her Jeep Grand Cherokee in the warm June sunshine, the expressway took her directly through the heart of the city, which seemed to have everything—tall buildings, a baseball stadium, a river, even a brewery. According to Samantha, very few of the suburbs were that far from downtown. *A nice set-up*, Melanie thought as she followed Sam's directions to Webster.

Thirty minutes later, she pulled into the driveway shared by Samantha and the Rhodes family—her landlords.

The main structure was a big, yellow farmhouse, complete with white pillars holding up the open front porch and white shutters on each of the many front windows. Large, full trees, mostly maple, adorned the property, and

Melanie couldn't help thinking of the Waltons. A brick walkway curved around from the porch to the driveway, which led to a matching two-car garage with a red Honda parked in front of it. Just beyond the garage and off to the right a hundred or so yards away was a small, cottage-like structure, decorated in the same colors and design as the main house. She followed the driveway around to the cottage, as her cousin had instructed her.

As Melanie pulled the Jeep to a stop in front of the small house, the front door flew open and Samantha bellowed, "Mellie!"

She caught Melanie in a hug before she even got both feet out of the Jeep. "God, it's been a long time," she said, squeezing her cousin hard. "Let me look at you." She held Melanie at arm's length and looked her up and down. "My God, Baby Cousin, you look terrific."

"I bet," Melanie scoffed, running a self-conscious hand through her rust-colored hair. "Ten hours in a car always brings out the best in me." She smiled lovingly at her cousin. "It's good to see you, Sammi."

Samantha was a classic example of somebody able to get by on looks alone, although she was by no means dumb. Melanie was an extremely attractive woman, but she always felt mousy next to Sam. Standing two inches taller than Melanie, Samantha was blonde and tanned and could have easily blended in on the set of *Baywatch*. She was the stereotypical Blonde Bombshell, but rather than try to fight the brainless beauty stigma, she embraced it and taught herself to manipulate it. As much as Melanie despised the idea of somebody who didn't work for what they wanted, there was the tiniest hint of admiration for the way Samantha just flat out used what she had to get what she desired. She had become very good at it.

"I'm so glad I was able to talk you into visiting. How long do you want to stay?" Sam asked as she helped unload the Jeep.

"I'm not sure yet. Let me know if you get sick of me before I make up my mind."

"Nonsense. You're welcome to stay forever. Come on in and I'll show you around."

Taylor Rhodes watched from the kitchen window as the black Jeep pulled into the driveway and around to Sam's place. She dried her hands on a flowered towel, vaguely remembering Samantha saying something about her cousin coming to visit, and put away the breakfast dishes she'd left behind earlier. Saturday morning breakfasts had become sort of a tradition between Taylor and her father, Ben, since she moved back home two years previously after the death of her mother.

She wiped down the counter and folded the towel over its rack. Picking up a can of Pepsi, she leaned back against the sink and looked around the open, sunny kitchen, allowing herself to be transported back to simpler days when her mother baked cookies and Taylor had nothing to worry about except coming in from her woodland fort in time to scrape the bowl of batter.

There was so much of her mother in this room. True, the entire house reflected Anna Salvaggio Rhodes, but the kitchen had been her domain. From the white, ruffled valences on the windows to the various knick-knacks and framed prints on the walls, the kitchen was pure Anna. Taylor could still see her bustling around, humming Neil Diamond or Barbra Streisand completely off-key, her unruly dark hair trying desperately to escape from the clip fastening it behind her head, wiping her flour-covered hands on the apron she wore faithfully every day, like a uniform. It infuriated Taylor, the talk these days that criticized women without a career, women who chose to stay home with their children. *Housewives.* Taylor hated that word. Keeping the household running smoothly, being available for either Taylor, her big brother Frankie, or Ben, cooking, cleaning, laundry, shopping, sewing, gardening. How could anybody say that wasn't a full-time career?

Anna was President and CEO of Rhodes, Inc. That was all there was to it. Taylor was fiercely proud of what her mother had represented. She just wished she had taken the time to at least mention it to Anna when it would have mattered.

Trouble was, Taylor had been on the side of those hurling the criticism for a long, long time. She knew it wasn't uncommon for a woman of the 90s to be embarrassed by a woman of the previous generation who chose family and home over education and success in business, but that didn't make it any easier now that her mother was gone.

She sighed, the sad, weary sigh of one that knows she never said the things she should have while she had the chance.

The jingling of the telephone cut through Taylor's guilt and brought her back to the present. She picked it up, watching out the window as Samantha and her cousin unloaded the Jeep. "Hello?"

"Tay?"

Taylor closed her eyes, cursing herself for not just letting it ring. "Maggie."

"Hi." The voice on the line was soft and unsure, with a slight crack, as if the speaker could burst into tears at any moment. Taylor knew the tone well. She had dubbed it the Morning After voice. It was the inflection Maggie's voice took on when she had tied one on, said or done something stupid the night before, and was trying to make up for it. Although they hadn't been together the night before, or in several weeks for that matter, it was still obvious to Taylor that Maggie had been drinking recently.

"Hi."

"How are you, Tay?"

"I'm fine." Taylor chose her words carefully, not wanting to invite a prolonged conversation.

"Good. That's good." There was a long, awkward pause. "I miss you. I miss you so much."

Here we go, Taylor thought. "Maggie..."

"Honey, I know I screwed up. I can change. I can."
Maggie's voice was pleading now, pathetic. "You were
right. I know that now. I just miss you so much. I love you.
I need you. Please, Taylor."

Months ago, even weeks ago, conversations like this
would cut right through to Taylor's soul, corralling all the
possible guilt and hope available within her and combining
it into forgiveness and willingness to give it another shot.
And another. And another. Again and again, she would
agree to allow Maggie another chance to stop drinking, get
some professional help for her depression and make their
relationship work. It had taken almost three years, but Taylor had finally realized that no matter how much she tried
to help, no matter how much she hoped or prayed or
begged, nothing would ever change with Maggie. After
several failed attempts, she had finally managed to make a
clean break, at least in her own mind.

"Maggie," she said firmly. "We've been through this a
hundred times. You have got to stop calling me."

"I can't." Maggie was crying openly now. Instead of
sympathy, Taylor could feel her anger building and worked
hard to push it back down.

"Pull yourself together," she ordered. "This is ridiculous. You're not hurting anybody but you here, Maggie. We
are no longer a couple, do you understand me?"

"Taylor, please."

Taylor shut her eyes against the pain in the voice
imploring her for another chance. This pitiful, childlike
begging was something Taylor always had a difficult time
fighting. It was usually at this point that she gave in and
took Maggie in her arms, crying with her, holding her,
rocking her, murmuring reassurances that everything
would be okay. She swallowed hard, barely able to find her
voice.

"I have to go." She hung up the phone quietly. After a
couple of seconds, she took the handset off the hook and
let it dangle, the dial tone changing to an angry beeping as
she went out to the backyard and slid back into an Adiron-

dack chair with a weary sigh.

"This place is really something, Sammi." Melanie was pleasantly surprised by the taste and class with which her cousin had surrounded herself. "When you said you were living in a carriage house on somebody else's property..." She left the sentence unfinished, mildly embarrassed by her initial expectations.

"You were thinking run-down trailer park, weren't you?" Samantha accused with a grin.

"'Fraid so. Sorry."

"No problem, Baby Cousin. Beer?"

"Absolutely."

Samantha's carriage house was cozy and comfortable, small, but not stifling. Melanie took in the earthy colors, smiling at the warmth they created. The front door opened into the small living room where a natural-colored couch sat against the front wall beneath a large picture window, through which the afternoon sun shone in all its brilliance, making the room seem much bigger than it actually was. Soft, fluffy pillows of rust, yellow, and various shades of brown were strewn about the couch, as well as the hardwood floor and the matching oversized chair that sat against the opposite wall. There was a handmade afghan folded neatly over the back of the chair, and a halogen floor lamp stood commandingly behind it. Melanie immediately pictured herself tucked under the afghan, her feet stretched onto the chair's ottoman, a cup of tea on the end table and a good book in her hand.

"Here ya go."

Melanie was brought back from the lazy Sunday afternoon in her mind by a stinging cold bottle against her bare shoulder. She took it from her cousin and swallowed a healthy swig of the ale.

"The colors in here are beautiful," she commented.

"Aren't they? Ben's wife was quite the decorator, from

what I understand."

"Ben?"

"Yeah. Ben Rhodes. My landlord." She pointed out the window toward the main house. "He lives there."

"So, you didn't do this?" Melanie gestured at the room, trying to hide her disappointment. She should have known that Samantha hadn't done the decorating. Too time consuming for her.

"Are you kidding? I don't have the patience for interior design," she snorted, as if reading Melanie's mind. "Ben's wife did it just a couple months before she died."

"His wife died?"

"Yeah. Couple years ago. Car accident, I think."

"So he lives in that big house all by himself?"

"No, his daughter Taylor lives there, too. She moved back home after her Mom's death to look out for him. Wait 'til you meet him. He's a doll." She gently tugged on Melanie's arm. "Come on, I'll show you the rest of the place...what little there is."

There was no denying that the carriage house was small, but Melanie continued to marvel at the decorating. The tiny kitchen, the cozy bedroom and even the bathroom each radiated its own personality and charm. The colors all blended perfectly, from the deep greens of the bathroom to the lighter sage of the bedroom. Nothing stood out on its own. Everything blended into the rest of the items in the room as if they were not separate objects, but simply pieces of something on a grander scale. The effect was beautiful and incredibly calming. Melanie felt immediately at ease in this place, so far from the hustle and bustle of her office, not to mention her barely furnished apartment.

"That's it. Tour's over."

"It's beautiful, Sam. Really."

Samantha smiled, showing perfect white teeth. "Thanks. The couch pulls out into a bed, so that will be your room."

"What, I don't get to have a slumber party in your bedroom like when we were little?" Melanie joked.

"Not if I've got company, Baby Cousin." She winked. "I'm up for almost anything, but a threesome with you isn't one of them."

Taylor was just about to head inside when she noticed Samantha and her cousin rounding the back corner of the garage, walking in her direction. They were both laughing, carrying half-empty bottles of beer. Samantha stopped in mid-sentence when she saw Taylor lounging in the red-wood chair.

"Hey, girl," she called, scrambling toward Taylor and plopping sideways into her lap, her feet dangling over the arm of the chair. Taylor couldn't help but smile. "Take me away from here. Please," Samantha drawled in a painfully bad southern accent, laying the back of her hand across her forehead in mock woe.

"You tell me where and when, my little sugar dumplin'," Taylor drawled back.

"Ah, you couldn't handle me," Sam laughed with a wave of her hand and climbed back to a standing position. She held out her beer. "Sip?"

Taylor took the offered bottle and chugged the remainder of the contents, handing it back to Samantha empty.

"Bull dyke." Sam sneered.

"Hardly."

At the sound of a discreetly clearing throat, they both turned. Sam smacked her hand against her forehead. "Duh. Where are my manners? Taylor, this is my cousin Melanie Larson. Mel, this is my friend and pushover, Taylor Rhodes. She lives here."

They shook hands, both impressed by the firmness of the other. Melanie smiled warmly at the dark-haired young woman. "Pushover?"

"Just because Sam can have anything she wants from me at any time, no matter what, she thinks that makes me a pushover. Frankly, I don't see how."

Melanie laughed, tucking her hair behind her ear. "Pleased to meet you. This is a beautiful place you've got here."

"Thanks. How long are you staying?"

Melanie and Sam exchanged glances. "We're not sure yet," Samantha offered. "She just left her job, and I'm going to try to convince her to hang out for a while and enjoy the summer."

"Really. What do you do?" Taylor asked.

"Well, I was in marketing for a pretty large firm—" She was cut off by Samantha's upheld hand.

"No. Don't even start with the job talk, 'cause I'll never see the two of you again." She pinched Taylor's cheek. "Let me have her for a while. Hey, wait. Why don't you come to dinner tonight? Rob's coming. We'll have a foursome. 'Kay?"

"Rob?" Melanie asked.

"Flavor of the Month," Taylor confided.

"Hey." Samantha slapped Taylor playfully on the arm. "I just invited you to dinner. Be nice."

Coming to the realization that if she were not home, she wouldn't be forced to field any more phone calls from Maggie, Taylor accepted, promising to bring wine. She left the pair to continue their tour of the Rhodes property and went inside, watching them out the kitchen window.

Melanie was nothing like her cousin, but Taylor liked that. Physically, she was smaller and seemed to have a more classic look. Where Samantha was very Hollywood, with the blonde hair, big breasts, year-round tan, and constant make-up, Melanie seemed more sophisticated, almost a level above what Hollywood said was attractive. Her hair was a very unique shade of rust and cut in a simple, professional style...one length, reaching about to her collar. She didn't have the voluptuous figure Sam did, but she was definitely feminine in all the right places. Her curves and shapely legs hadn't escaped Taylor's attention. Next to Sam, Melanie seemed paler than she actually was, and Taylor was willing to bet she'd never even seen a tanning bed.

Her soft, pretty face had been virtually free of make-up, but her big, blue eyes had stood out just the same. Taylor guessed she was around the same age as Sam—although she seemed years more mature—which would put her in her mid-thirties or so. Sam had never given Taylor an exact age, claiming it would destroy the mystery. Melanie was definitely more professional, and Taylor was surprised to find herself looking forward to dinner. It would be nice to talk to somebody in a similar field of employment.

Feeling infinitely better than she had an hour before, she bounded upstairs to gather her workout paraphernalia and headed to the gym.

Chapter
4

Rob was exactly what Melanie expected him to be. She expected him to be dark and incredibly good-looking with a rough, dangerous edge. He was. She expected him to paw at Sam most of the evening and to appraise Melanie with a predatory up-and-down-very-slowly, animalistic look. He didn't disappoint her...he might as well have licked his lips. She expected to dislike him immediately. She did.

Taylor and the delivery boy from the Chinese restaurant arrived at the same time. Taylor looked fresh and vibrant in khaki shorts and an olive green T-shirt. Her dark hair was pulled back in a ponytail, she wore brown leather Teva sandals on her feet, and Melanie thought she smelled like soap and sunshine. Taylor winked at Melanie, who was paying for the food.

"I see Sam spent the day slaving over a hot stove again."

"Honestly, I don't know how she does it," Melanie joked back. "She's a regular Julia Child." She smiled her thanks as Taylor helped carry the bundles to the tiny kitchen.

"Hey, get a room, you two," Melanie scolded Samantha and Rob, who were joined at the tongues, leaning against the kitchen counter. They pulled apart, showing no embarrassment whatsoever.

"Rob," Taylor acknowledged coolly.

"Taylor." He nodded back.

She doesn't like him either, Melanie thought with a grin, mentally giving Taylor points for good taste.

It was such a beautiful evening—not to mention the carriage house was so small—that they opted to sit and eat at the picnic table behind the house. Taylor poured three glasses of the Merlot she'd brought; Rob preferred his Bud Light.

Samantha and Melanie played catch-up, updating each other on mutual friends and family, pausing every now and then to give Taylor or Rob background on the person they were talking about. Taylor sat smiling quietly, enjoying the interaction between the cousins. Rob made various noises to indicate how bored he was, absently peeling the labels off his beer bottles.

As dusk settled, Melanie finally decided to broach the subject she had promised her uncle she would. "How's the bookstore doing?"

Sam rolled her eyes. "Ugh. Damn waste of time."

"Not good, huh?"

"Jeff always took care of it. What do I know, or want to know, about running a business?"

"But, didn't you help Jeff with it?"

Sam shrugged. "At first, yeah. Then...I don't know. I got bored, Mellie. You know how I hate to be stuck in one place all the time. Jeff seemed into it, but with *Barnes & Noble* down the street and *Borders* around the corner, it's hard to make it work."

Melanie sighed. This would not be good news for Uncle Phil. "What's the deal with it now?"

Sam took a large gulp of her wine. "Well, since Jeff decided to take off with our only employee, I closed it indefinitely."

"You closed it?"

"Yup."

Melanie tried to hide her frustration. "You mean, it's just sitting there, full of inventory and costing rent and it's not even open for the *possibility* of customers?"

Taylor and Rob glanced at each other in an unusual silent agreement to keep their distance from the conversation. Both swigged simultaneously from their drinks.

Sam shot Melanie a warning look. "Don't you go getting all preachy on me, Baby Cousin. I didn't ask for the damned shop, and I don't want it."

"Sammi, your dad was just trying to help you and Jeff get on your feet. He thought you loved books."

"Yeah, well, I love cars, too. Doesn't mean I want to be a car dealer."

Rob snorted a laugh at that, earning a searing glare from Melanie.

"The fucking thing's like an albatross around my neck, Mellie. I wish I could just sell it, but of course, it's in Daddy's name."

Melanie rubbed her forehead with her fingertips, hoping to stroke away her frustration with her cousin. She remembered her promise to her uncle. "Okay, look. How 'bout if I take a look at it? I'll check out the numbers, the inventory, all that, and see where you're at. Then we can look at your options."

With that simple suggestion, Samantha's entire demeanor changed. Her face lit up, and she reached across the table to throw her arms around her cousin's neck. "You are just the best, Mellie. Rob and I have plans, but I'll leave you the keys and directions, and you can go tomorrow. It's not hard to find."

Taylor rolled her eyes at the look of disbelief on Melanie's face. She was very fond of Samantha, but also found her very frustrating at times, her priorities so far out of whack it wasn't funny. Here, her cousin had been with her for barely half a day, and she was bailing on her already. To be with her white trash boyfriend. "I'll take you, Melanie. I'm going to the gym in the morning. I can drop you off on the way and pick you up when I'm done. If you want."

Melanie smiled with gratitude, then glared at her cousin. "That would be great. Thank you, Taylor."

If Sam noticed the look, she didn't react to it.

"Come on, baby," Rob ordered as he stood. "Let's go for a ride."

Sam jumped up, downed the rest of her wine and followed Rob's leather-clad bulk. "Don't wait up." She winked at Melanie and Taylor, leaving them to clean up the remnants of dinner. From the front of the carriage house, they heard Rob's Harley roar to life and Sam's squeal of delight as they sped away.

"She is a piece of work, isn't she?" Melanie sighed, shaking her head.

"That's the understatement of the year." Taylor held up the wine bottle. "Just enough for two more."

Melanie held her glass out and Taylor replenished them both, emptying the bottle.

"So. Tell me about you," Melanie suggested, taking a sip of wine. "What do you do?"

"I'm in sales," Taylor answered.

"Really? I wondered about that. You seem so easy-going, I figured if you weren't in sales, you should be. What do you sell?"

Taylor felt a warm flush rise up her neck at the compliment. Thankful for the near-dark that she hoped would prevent Melanie from seeing her new pink tint, she launched into a speech about the wonderful world of radio advertising sales.

Melanie studied Taylor as she spoke, loving the smooth, relaxing sound of her low voice. She was sure Taylor had blushed over the compliment Melanie had paid her, something Melanie found inexplicably endearing.

A few stray locks of dark curls had escaped her pony-tail and fluttered gently in the night breeze, like feathers on the wind. Even in the late dusk, Melanie could see the flash of adrenaline in Taylor's dark eyes when she spoke of landing a big client. Melanie was concentrating on Taylor's full, moist lips when she realized they had stopped moving. Her blue eyes snapped up to meet smiling brown ones, framed by impossibly thick, dark lashes.

"I'm rambling, aren't I?"

"What? No. Oh, no. Absolutely not." Melanie finished her wine in one gulp, mortified that she'd been caught staring. What was wrong with her?

"What about you?" Taylor asked, graciously overlooking Melanie's embarrassment. "Sam said you left your job. Why? If you don't mind my asking, of course."

Melanie met Taylor's gaze for a long moment. She felt so...what was it?...at home in those eyes. She couldn't remember ever being so comfortable with somebody. She hadn't told anybody but her secretary her real reason for leaving Rucker and Steele, not even her own parents, but she felt so safe with Taylor. So secure. It was strange and comforting at the same time.

She took a deep breath and told Taylor the whole story, from beginning to end, leaving nothing out.

"Wow," Taylor said when Melanie finished.

"Yeah. Crazy, huh?"

"What? No. I admire you."

"You do?"

"I admire somebody who has the guts to make a change. Most people wouldn't realize what you did until they were in their forties or fifties and had already wasted most of their lives on their job. By then, it's almost too late. Or, they realize they're unhappy, but are too lazy or scared to do anything about it, so they stay unhappy forever. I think you did the absolutely right thing."

"You do?" Melanie repeated.

"Without a doubt."

Melanie felt a great burden lifted from her shoulders at Taylor's words. She didn't understand why the approval of this young woman was so important to her, but it was. She'd only known her for several hours, but her opinion already meant a great deal to Melanie. *What a strange day,* she thought with a smirk.

Taylor stood and began clearing the table. "It's getting late. You must be exhausted from your drive."

"Now that you mention it..." Melanie stretched and stifled a yawn.

They cleaned up in companionable silence, Taylor showing Melanie where various dishes and utensils belonged.

"So," she said when they finished, "I'll come get you on my way to the gym in the morning? Is nine o'clock too early?"

"That's perfect."

Taylor turned back as she stood in the doorway. "Thanks for dinner."

"Thanks for the wine and the company. I really enjoyed myself."

"Me too. Good night."

"Good night, Taylor."

Melanie watched as Taylor made her way across to her own house, the moonlight bathing her in a soft glow. She had finally managed to close the door when she was struck by the realization that she was actually focused on the gentle sway of Taylor's hips.

Chapter
5

It was precisely nine a.m. when Melanie reached for
the doorknob to answer the brisk knock. Taylor smiled
brightly, looking fresh-faced and sunny in her navy blue
gym shorts and bright yellow T-shirt. Her white socks
accentuated the beginnings of a tan on her legs, and Melanie noticed Taylor's hair was still slightly damp when it
had been pulled back and fastened behind her head.

"Do you always shower *before* you work out?" she
asked.

Taylor's smile faltered slightly, and the pink tint from
the previous evening returned in full force, creeping
slowly up her neck. "Um...no. Not always." She decided an
immediate subject change was in order. "Ready to go?"

"Well, I have a small problem. Sam didn't come home
last night."

"Surprise, surprise."

"I can't get into the bookstore."

"Sure you can." Taylor slipped through the doorway
and into the kitchen, Melanie on her heels. She opened one
of the cupboards to reveal several hooks supporting various sets of keys. Each had its own label, neatly printed in
block letters. "Jeff Mason may have been an idiot, but he

was an organized idiot." She handed the keys marked STORE to Melanie with a grin. "Ready now?"

"You're a lifesaver."

"Nah. Just observant."

Sunday morning traffic was minimal as they tooled along in Taylor's Honda Civic with the sunroof open, the sun reflecting off of their sunglasses.

"How'd you sleep?" Taylor asked.

"Great, once I actually closed my eyes. It's so quiet, nothing like the city."

Taylor nodded her dark head in agreement. "I know what you mean. I used to have a studio right downtown. It didn't matter what time it was, there was always some sort of sound. I'm still not used to being back in the suburbs yet. So, need coffee?"

Melanie's eyes lit up. "Do I."

They were sitting in line at the *McDonald's* drive-thru when Melanie noticed the small, metal ring dangling from the rearview mirror. It had some sort of design carved into it, accented by light blue dots. "What's this?"

"It's a chakram."

"Chakram?"

"Ever watch Xena?"

"Xena? Is that the sword-fighting Greek god show? I think I caught a glimpse of it once or twice, but I couldn't figure out what all the hype was about. This is that round thing she throws around, right?"

Taylor shook her head in mock-disappointment, tsking as she pulled back onto the road. "Melanie, Melanie, Melanie. I see you're in need of enlightenment."

"I am?"

"I'm afraid so. It's important that you understand the phenomenon that is Xena."

"Really." Melanie grinned. "Why is it important?"

"Because I say it is."

They grinned at each other for several seconds, before Melanie nodded.

"Okay. Enlighten me."

Loving the flirty, albeit unintentional, tone of Melanie's voice, but deciding she wasn't going to touch that one with a ten foot pole, Taylor stayed on the subject. "Tell you what. I have every episode on tape—"

"*Every episode?*" Melanie's eyes widened.

"As any good Xenite does."

"I see."

"I'll lend you the first few so you can get a feel for the story. After that, I'll leave it up to you. If you want to see more, say the word."

Melanie laughed heartily. "You've got yourself a deal."

Taylor smiled with satisfaction as she pulled the little red car to a halt alongside the curb. "I believe this is your stop, young lady."

Melanie looked up, surprised. The ride had been much quicker than she'd expected, but she had a feeling it was due to the company and not the distance traveled.

The short block held just one long building, which was subdivided into three individual shops—the bookstore being in the center. Its storefront was not exactly eye-catching, although it was sandwiched between two shops that were, making it look even duller than it actually was. The large wooden-framed glass door stood alcoved between two oversized display windows facing the sidewalk. The trim, and essentially the front of the store, was in dire need of a paint job. What used to be a chocolate brown was badly chipped and peeling, revealing a frightful shade of yellow underneath. A crooked, wooden sign, obviously hand-lettered by somebody who was *not* a sign painter, announced that this was *Mason's Books*.

Now there's a creative name, Melanie thought to herself, the marketer in her shaking its head in disgust. *Yup, makes me wanna run right in and buy a whole stack of books.*

Her gaze rested on a sheet of paper taped to the door from the inside. It read "Closed Due To Cheating Husband."

"Oh, that's good for business," she sighed, opening the car door.

Taylor chuckled. "Hell hath no fury, blah, blah, blah. Your key fits both the front and back doors. Do you need anything before I head to the gym?"

Melanie smiled gratefully at this woman she'd known for one whole day, sorry to see her go. "No. I'll be fine." She got out and shut the car door, leaning down to peer into the open window. "Thank you, Taylor, for carting me around. You've been great."

Taylor pulled her sunglasses down to the end of her nose so Melanie could see her smiling eyes. "It's been my pleasure." They held each other's gaze for several long seconds before Taylor pushed the shades back into place with her finger. "I'll be back in about an hour and a half."

"I'll be here."

Melanie watched the car pull away, then turned toward the task at hand.

Melanie was pleasantly surprised by *Mason's Books*, despite its lackluster first impression—which was not improved by the musty smell that assaulted her when she opened the door—and its unimaginative name. The inside was bigger than she'd expected, with big rays of bright sunshine pouring through the front windows and lots of rich, dark wood, which gave it a great deal of character; it actually bordered on charming. The marketer in her perked up and took notice.

The door opened into the center of the shop, which, in total, wasn't much bigger than a large, two-car garage. Directly forward, at the back of the shop, she could see a small, electronic cash register on a wooden countertop jutting out from the rear wall in an L-shape. All of the bookshelves, Melanie counted four rows—including the two outside walls—and half the back wall, were made of the same polished wood as the floor and the doorframe. There

were two overstuffed burgundy chairs tucked away in corners like naughty children. She realized the little shop
actually had a library feel to it. She was immediately comfortable there, much to her surprise.

Unsure exactly where to begin her task of "checking
the place out," she decided Sam and Jeff's paperwork was
probably the best starting point. She followed one of the
two freestanding bookshelves to the back wall in search of
an office of some sort, leaving a very noticeable finger
mark in the thick dust along the way. She wasn't sure if
Sam never dusted, or if the shop had been closed much
longer than she originally thought. Knowing her cousin,
either explanation was possible.

The office—which seemed to double as a stock room—
was located at the very back of the shop, behind the cash
register, and smelled of dust and fast food leftovers. It was
small, with barely enough room for an undersized desk that
was littered with a half-eaten cheeseburger and fries, a two
drawer filing cabinet, and several boxes of apparently new
books. A miniscule rest room containing the very barest of
necessities was squeezed into a back corner. It looked as
though it hadn't been scrubbed in months.

A handful of three ring binders was lined up on a shelf
above the desk. Upon quick examination, Melanie found
them to be inventory and ordering records. The filing cabinet revealed receipts and check stubs, as well as accounts
payable records. She pulled several folders, cleaned the
top of the desk of the food remnants, as well as four half-
consumed cans of Diet Pepsi, and sat down with the information.

Noticing a small clock radio, she tuned it to the first
station that came in clearly. Tapping her fingernail to
Madonna's *Like A Prayer*, she opened the binder labeled
Inventory.

Much to Taylor's own dismay, it seemed she had

become one of those women she used to laugh at, the kind nearly addicted to working out. It hadn't been a planned thing. Maggie hated the gym, and when things were falling apart between them, the gym was simply a place of refuge where Taylor could go to be alone with her thoughts. Or— as was more often the case—it was a place she could go to crank up her headphones so she couldn't hear her thoughts.

After several months, though, she noticed subtle changes in her body. Pleasing changes. The tightening— not to mention the definition—of muscles, the higher level of energy, the increase in overall strength. She was surprised to discover that she actually liked working out. Craved it. Once she had made the break from Maggie, she still found herself at the gym three times a week, using the visits to work her body, as well as clear her mind.

Today, the thoughts filling her head to the point of spilling out her ears were all orbiting around the same subject: Melanie. Taylor shook her head with a wry grin as she pushed against the steps of the Stairmaster, sweating as she climbed her way to nowhere. It had been quite some time since she had clicked so easily with somebody. Melanie seemed just as comfortable with her, judging from dinner last night and this morning's ride. Was Melanie flirting with her on purpose? Was she even aware that she was flirting? For that matter, was she gay? Taylor didn't·think so. Samantha had made Taylor's sexuality painfully clear yesterday when she'd first introduced them and it would be just like her to out Melanie in a similar, immediate fashion, for shock value, if nothing else. The fact that she hadn't done so told Taylor that Melanie was straight.

I'll just have to watch myself, she thought with determination. It was such a lesbian cliché—the gay girl falling for the straight girl she could never have...a cliché that Taylor would like to avoid at all costs.

What was it about Sam's cousin anyway? Sure, she was very attractive. She was very, very attractive, but so what? So were a lot of women Taylor had contact with almost every day. Aside from the occasional fantasy, she didn't find herself spending her workout analyzing what it was about them that she found so attractive.

It wasn't like she'd had so much experience with women that she had no trouble reading them. She hadn't actually come out until her senior year in college, a mere five years ago. Other than a few casual flings, Maggie was her only real relationship, and what a disastrous model to follow. Truth be told, she hadn't the foggiest idea how tell if a woman was interested in her, unless, of course, they used the old neon-sign-on-the-forehead trick. Taylor was pretty sure she'd catch that.

Before she could dwell more on the subject, her mind shifted to focus on the ad playing through her headphones. A young man and young woman were discussing the benefits of a nearby community college. Both sounded painfully like they were reading from a piece of paper, coming off so incredibly scripted, that it left a bad taste in Taylor's mouth.

Ugh, she grimaced, making a mental note to mention the ad to Jason tomorrow. He was the newest sales rep at the station, and Taylor had more or less taken him under her wing. He had great sales potential—he was a very likable guy—but he was still leery of being firmer with the talent when they didn't deliver. The local college was his account, and she was amazed that his client had approved the ad before it aired.

With the onset of that train of thought, Melanie was quietly transferred to a back burner while Taylor wasn't paying attention.

Chapter
6

"Hey."

Melanie nearly jumped out of her skin at the sound of Taylor's voice. She hadn't heard the door or her approach to the tiny office in the back of the store, so absorbed was she in the paperwork she was studying.

Recognizing the shock on the older woman's face, Taylor immediately apologized.

Melanie smiled, embarrassed. "It's okay. I tend to tune out the rest of the world when I'm working. Has it been an hour and a half already?"

Taylor looked around with amusement. Files, books, and binders were strewn all over the tiny office, Melanie in the center like a floating buoy in a sea of paper. "Actually, it's been two. Sorry I'm late. How's it going?"

"Well, I'm not quite sure yet." She gestured to the mess she had made. "You were right. Jeff's a pretty organized guy. All his records are well-kept and in order. No thanks to me."

Taylor nodded, not surprised.

"However, I don't think he made one red cent the whole time he's had this place."

Taylor chuckled, again not surprised. "That's because

he didn't listen to me."

"What do you mean?"

"I told him he needed to specialize."

Melanie furrowed her eyebrows, an expression that made Taylor smile.

"Come here." Taylor reached for Melanie's hand and pulled her out of the office and into the store itself. She made a grand gesture with the sweep of her arm. "Take a good look at this place."

"Okay. I'm looking." She paused for a minute. "What am I looking at?"

"Size, my dear Melanie. Contrary to popular belief, when it comes to retail, size *does* matter."

Melanie blinked with understanding. "You're right. You're absolutely right. This is a tiny shop...much too small to be a general interest bookstore. You can't compete with *Barnes & Noble* when you've only got four book-shelves. The only way a place this size could be effective is to specialize in something."

Taylor touched her nose with the tip of her finger. "Bingo."

"And you suggested this to Jeff?"

"More than once."

"Apparently, he didn't agree."

"I told you. Organized idiot."

"He must have been getting killed by the big chain stores."

"Yup. *Barnes & Noble* is just a ten minute drive from here."

Melanie shook her head. At least she had something to tell Uncle Phil. He'd given his daughter and son-in-law a business with potential. They just hadn't known what to do with it. Too bad. It really was an enchanting little place.

When Taylor and Melanie pulled into the driveway at Taylor's house, there was a distinguished-looking man watering the flowers out front with a gentle spray from the hose. He was very handsome, with a thick head of salt-and-pepper hair and familiar, smiling, dark eyes. Melanie guessed him to be around fifty, although his athletic build suggested he might be a bit younger. He was dressed in a smart pair of khaki shorts and a forest green polo shirt, a brown braided belt cinching the shorts around his waist. He smiled and waved as they coasted past him to a stop.

"Come on," Taylor said to Melanie as she exited the car. "I want you to meet the gardener."

Ben Rhodes shook hands firmly with Melanie, holding on a split second longer than necessary, something not lost on Taylor. *And we're off,* she thought.

"It's a pleasure to meet you, Melanie. I hope you're enjoying your stay so far."

"Your daughter's been a fantastic tour guide. This is a beautiful place you have. Sam's very lucky to have found the carriage house. It's wonderful."

Taylor was used to losing attention to her father. After all, he was a handsome, charming guy, and, although they never actively competed against each other, it wasn't unusual for Ben to ease a woman's intentness from his daughter to himself. They had never really discussed her preference for women, but Taylor was sure that there were times when he intentionally sought out a woman she had been interested in or whose company she happened to be enjoying at the time. It was a little game he seemed to find amusing. Most of the time, Taylor let it slide, gracefully excusing herself.

This time was different. She wasn't sure why. It just was. Losing Melanie's attention to him irked her, and rather than say or do something stupid, she made a quick and quiet exit. Neither Melanie nor Ben seemed to notice, which annoyed her even more.

In the kitchen, she got some orange juice out of the refrigerator and poured herself a glass, trying not to hear the soft, lilting laughter as Ben Rhodes put his wit and charm to work on their guest and Melanie ate it up.

She chided herself for acting like a jealous teenager. After all, she had no claim on Melanie. So what if she was attracted to Ben? Lots of women were. Lots. He was a good-looking, successful, single guy. Why wouldn't Melanie want to be with him?

In the year and a half since Anna Rhodes had been killed, Ben had dated a number of women. At first, Taylor had been angry, which was to be expected really. Once she'd gotten past the feeling that he was cheating on her mother, she'd decided it was good for him to date. She didn't want him to be alone for the rest of his life. Plus, she was getting antsy living at home and was anxious to find her own place again. She'd begun to rethink her approval, however, when the front of the house had become a revolving door, and Ben had seemed to date a different woman every month. Finally, Taylor had snapped, and the two of them had had it out in the middle of the living room. To an outsider, it would have looked like a strange game of role reversal, with the child scolding the parent about his poor dating habits and lack of responsibility and how about acting his age? In the end, Ben had seemed to take his daughter's words to heart, and the endless stream of women had slowed to a trickle. Taylor absolutely did not want Melanie to become another drop in his bucket.

She sat down at the kitchen table and slowly banged her forehead on the tabletop. How had this happened? She'd known Melanie all of two days, and already she was playing protector. She had always been this way, ever since she could remember. She developed a "crush" on a woman and became her self-appointed bodyguard, making sure nobody hurt her. It had started at summer camp with Theresa, her camp counselor. Taylor was fourteen, Theresa was sixteen. Taylor had no idea what was going on. Hell, she hadn't even known what the word sexuality meant. All she had known was she wanted to be near Theresa all the time. She'd followed the older girl around like a puppy dog, always ready to help. Theresa had been flattered by the attention. One rainy day, the camp had organized a mud war. It was something they often did when the lake activities were rained out, and it was loads of fun for the kids. How often were you allowed to just get absolutely, irretrievably filthy? It had been noon and the war had been in full swing, various cabins trying to stay cleaner than their rivals, when twelve-year-old Danny Jenkins had thrown a fistful of mud that had caught Theresa in the side of the head. At her yelp of pain, Taylor hadn't even stopped to think. She'd been on Danny like a heat-seeking missile, slamming his face into the mud-covered ground, screaming at the top of her lungs. It had taken three counselors to get her off the poor kid. She often wondered where Theresa was now, if she remembered her from camp. Did she have any idea then—or now—that her little shadow had been a lesbian-in-training with a serious crush on her?

She shook her head, disgusted with herself. Why couldn't she fall for a nice, available girl who would fall for her in return? It didn't seem like a lot to ask. She sighed, finished her orange juice, and headed upstairs to shower.

Melanie returned from the grocery store that evening still in awe. She'd wanted to stock Sam's kitchen, since there wasn't much more in it than some Saltines and an old jar of peanut butter, and Ben had given her directions to a place called *Wegmans*. Never had she seen such a gigantic grocery store. It was like a giant warehouse full of food and sundries. The seasonal aisle alone had boasted enough summer items to stock a small drug store. She'd spent nearly two hours in there, gaping at the enormity of it. She'd also spent way more money than she had originally intended.

Waiting for her at the door of the carriage house was a small bundle. Picking it up, she realized she held three tapes, six episodes, of *Xena: Warrior Princess*, as promised. She smiled to herself. *Now, I have something to do tonight.*

Her thoughts returned to Ben and the unexpected lunch invitation he had extended for the following afternoon. It had been so long since she'd gotten such attention from a man—so long since she'd taken the time to accept it—that she had sucked it in like life-giving fluid. He was charming and handsome, familiar with the corporate world, and she liked him immediately. She had been talking a little about the bookstore, and he mentioned a nice little place across the street. As long as she was planning to be there tomorrow anyway, would she be interested in joining him for a bite? Although her initial reaction to his invitation had been refusal—what would Taylor think? Sam?—as she turned it over and over in her mind, she decided to go. Why not? He wasn't asking for her hand in marriage. He wasn't asking for a relationship. It wasn't even dinner, for Christ's sake. It was lunch. That was all. And when she looked at it that way, the fact that he was more than ten years her senior didn't seem to bother her quite as much.

Her thoughts shifted focus with a sudden jolt. Where the hell was Sam anyway? She'd been gone since the previous evening. Here it was, almost twenty-four hours later, and she had heard nothing. Not that it was unusual for Sam to disappear without telling anybody, but a little bit of goddamned consideration would be nice. *I'm her guest, for crying out loud.*

She proceeded to put the food away, guessing where things should go. She had purchased a lot of fresh summer fruits—peaches, plums, and nectarines—and filled a big, round, wicker basket she found in one of the cupboards with the sweet-smelling delights, placing them in the middle of the tiny breakfast table. A loaf of bread and a package of English muffins on the counter and the kitchen almost looked lived-in...certainly more lived-in than the kitchen she was used to.

The sun had set a while ago and Melanie was changing into her sweats when the phone rang. She hesitated, not being one to answer the phone in somebody else's house. After four rings, the answering machine picked up, Samantha's flirty, sexy voice breathily asking the caller to leave a message at the beep.

"Mellie? You there? Pick up," came the same voice as was on the tape.

Melanie snatched up the receiver. "Sam? Where the hell are you?"

"Hi, Mellie. How's it going?"

"Where are you?" she repeated. "Do you realize you've been gone for twenty-four hours?"

"We're in Toronto. We just kept driving, ya know? This is where we ended up last night, but we're heading out again soon." The connection crackled, and Sam said something indiscernible to somebody close by.

"Toronto? Sam, what the hell?" Melanie sighed her frustration. It was so like Sam to just go where the wind—or a good-looking guy on a motorcycle—took her. "When are you coming home?"

"Oh, not for a few days, at least. Rob wants to drive through Canada for a bit. Everything's so cheap up here, Mellie. Our dollar is worth almost two of theirs. Their money looks fake." She giggled. It was obvious that she wasn't entirely sober.

"A few days?" Melanie had trouble keeping the hurt out of her voice. "Sammi, I came to spend time with you."

"Oh, I know, sweetie, and we'll do something fun when I get back. I promise. Just keep an eye on things for me, okay? I'll call again soon. Bye, Mellie."

"Bye." She said it even though Sam had already hung up. She hadn't even asked about the bookstore. Damn her. She was always pulling this shit. She was thirty-five years old. When was she ever going to grow up? And what the hell was Melanie supposed to do now? She sure as hell wasn't going to sit around and twiddle her thumbs, waiting for her cousin's return. For reasons she couldn't explain, she felt no desire to return to Chicago...at least not yet. Her thoughts shifted quickly to the bookstore. She could spend some more time there, she supposed. At least she knew how to get there now.

Her eyes dropped to the bundle Taylor had left for her, the three tapes secured with a rubber band. She picked it up and noticed for the first time that there was a note attached. She smiled as she slid it out from under the band and unfolded it, noting Taylor's very smooth and beautiful handwriting.

Hi, Melanie—

Are you ready for your enlightenment? As promised, here are some Xena tapes for you to start with. I recommend you watch Sins of the Past first, because that gives you the history behind Xena's background and how she first meets Gabrielle. Then, I suggest Altared States and then Is There A Doctor In the House. There are three other episodes, feel free to watch them or don't, but if you like these, let me know. There are many others. I'll stop by tomorrow to see what you think.

Enjoy!
Taylor

Melanie smiled warmly, feeling an unfamiliar flush in her body. What was it about Taylor that affected her in such a weird way? It was something she couldn't quite put a finger on. Attraction, maybe? Melanie had never been with a woman sexually, although the thought had crossed her mind once or twice during her life...usually when a boyfriend or potential boyfriend was pissing her off. She'd often thought being with a woman would be so much easier. A woman would understand the shifting moods and hormonal swings that a man just couldn't seem to grasp. But she'd never actively pursued that line. She'd just never thought to look for an opportunity.

Maybe the fact that she knew Taylor was gay was what was giving her these weird vibes. But she was so *not* what

Melanie pictured when she thought of a typical gay woman. When she thought of the word *lesbian*, Melanie automatically pictured the stereotype, and she was embarrassed to admit that to herself. To her, a typical lesbian was masculine, tough-looking, with short hair, carried her wallet in her back pocket, drove a truck, swigged beer, shot pool, and wore men's clothes. Taylor was so...not that. Just for giggles, she tried to conjure up a picture of herself and Taylor in a sexual embrace, and was horrified to discover such a vision presented itself much easier than she had expected, in a matter of mere seconds. She swallowed hard, and shook the image from her head, literally, pushing the entire train of thought from her mind.

She pulled the sofa bed out, retrieving Sam's thick, cozy comforter and pillows from the bedroom. *Hell, if she's not gonna use them, I will.* She made up the sofa bed, creating a sea of pillows in which one could very well drown, retrieved a pint of Ben & Jerry's Pistachio Pistachio ice cream from the freezer, and popped *Sins of the Past* into the VCR. Then she hopped onto the bed with the remote and a spoon, a small giggle forcing its way through her lips. She couldn't remember the last time she'd spent an evening like this, and she snuggled down on top of the covers, surprised that she was actually looking forward to it. She sighed contentedly as she sat back and hit the play button.

The gently probing tongue was like velvet in her mouth and she sucked on it greedily. Her eyes were closed tightly, and she sank into the kiss, holding fast to the naked body above hers. She wrapped her legs tightly around the waist positioned just over her own, pulling it down more solidly onto her, the weight causing her to groan with pleasure into the mouth devouring hers. She'd never felt such sensation from a simple kiss...well, okay, a positively soul-searing kiss...but a kiss just the same. She slid her hands up the

muscled and surprisingly smooth back to tangle in hair—
lots of it—soft and silky and smelling of citrus and sun-
shine. Suddenly, the hips above her—they felt different
than usual...why?—ground gently into her center, and she
thrust up into them, pulling her mouth away and arching
her head back, allowing a sensual moan to escape from her
throat. The questing mouth fastened itself to her offered
neck, its owner humming with delight, as the soft tongue
circled her pulse point. She thrust her hips up a second
time, whispering her desire to her lover. "Please, Taylor.
Please..."

Melanie sat up with a jolt, breathing heavily, sweat
covering her body. There was a familiar, pulsing ache
between her legs, and she was immediately aware of the
fact that the crotch of her panties was stuck to her body.

"Oh my God," she whispered, running a shaking hand
through her tousled auburn hair. She'd had erotic dreams
before, even a couple involving women, but never one that
was so real. And never one that her body had responded to
with such vigor. "Holy shit."

She fell back against the pillow, heaving a final sigh
that brought her breathing back to normal.

"Oh my God," she repeated. She wondered how the
hell she was going to look Taylor in the eye tomorrow.

Chapter
7

Ben wasn't kidding when he said right across the street. Melanie could see *Aladdin's Natural Eatery* from the window of *Mason's Books*. She'd been there for nearly three hours, going through more papers, as well as scanning the shelves to see exactly what kind of inventory with which Jeff had stocked the store. It was easy to tell who his personal favorites were. There was a section of John Grisham novels that spanned almost three feet, as well as the entire series of Sue Grafton's Kinsey Millhone novels, from *A is for Alibi* all the way to *N is for Noose* Melanie smiled at these, enjoying them herself, and waiting anxiously for the next letter. The remainder of the mystery section, however, was sorely lacking.

She sighed. Jeff had obviously tried to put a little bit of everything on the shelves, and by doing so, had inadvertently limited his stock tremendously. Taylor was absolutely right. This needed to be a specialty bookstore. But, specialize in what?

She pulled out a sheet of paper, and made a list. Lists were her friends, she'd been heard to say; she used them every chance she got to help clear her mind, and organize

her thoughts. In what subjects could a bookstore specialize? She tried to think of every single little shop she'd ever
visited, and scratched words onto the pad.

Computers, pets, feminism, business, mysteries, classic literature, used, science fiction...

Eight choices, right off the bat. Not bad. She smiled to
herself. Then, a sudden thought came to her, and she made
a second list, right next to the first. She looked thoughtfully at the eight subjects, then transferred four of them to
the second list: computers, business, feminism, and mysteries. She leaned her chin in her hand, and studied the
paper for several minutes before the alarm on her watch
beeped, signaling lunch. She grabbed her keys and wallet
and, locking the store behind her, crossed the street.

Aladdin's was a charming, albeit busy, little place with
two levels and an outdoor seating area on the roof. Melanie
stopped inside the door, and faced a small flight of stairs
that would take her to the second floor. The restaurant was
small and bustling, with patrons and wait staff warring for
space. The tables were small, mostly seating two or four,
and draped in salmon-colored tablecloths, which blended
nicely with the earthy colors that accented the rest of the
restaurant.

Her blue eyes did a quick scan, and she saw Ben waving to her from the top of the stairs. She smiled, trotting up
the steps to meet him. "Hi," she said pleasantly. "Have you
been waiting long?"

"Just got here." He smiled, and Melanie noticed again
how much Taylor's eyes looked like his...color, shape, and
the way they sparkled when he smiled. He looked incredibly handsome in his navy suit, complete with red power tie
and a gold golf club tie clip. He led her to a small table for
two in the corner, holding her chair as she sat.

"This is a nifty little place," she commented, looking
around. "And busy."

Ben chuckled, a deep, rumbling sound Melanie could
feel in the pit of her stomach. "Yeah. It's usually like this
at lunch. It's in a good location for business people who

work in the city. It's a hop, skip, and a jump away, and the service is pretty fast."

As if on cue, their waitress appeared to take their drink orders, and was gone just as quickly.

"Don't let the subtitle of 'natural eatery' fool you," Ben added with a smile. "It's healthy stuff, but good...not all tofu and rice cakes. Lots of great salads and soups."

She grinned. "Salad will be good for me. I ate way too much junk food on the run in Chicago, that's for sure."

"So, what brings you to Rochester? Are you on vacation?"

"Sort of, but not exactly. The company I worked for was purchased by a larger one, and they're relocating to Seattle. I didn't want to go, so I took the severance package and decided to take some time off." She left out the fact that it had been the most difficult decision of her life.

"Seattle, huh? That's a long haul."

The waitress returned with their iced tea, asking if they were ready to order. Ben nodded politely in Melanie's direction.

"I think I'd like the fruit and nut salad, please."

"I'll have the gazpacho and a side salad."

The waitress took their menus, and Ben looked sheepishly at Melanie. "Since Taylor's been home, I've been indulging a bit too much." He patted his belly. "She's a very good cook. I usually try to be a good boy during lunch."

"Taylor can cook?" Melanie asked, somewhat amused by the fact, but not sure why.

"Amazingly well."

"She's been very sweet to me, helping me get to the bookshop, lending me her tapes."

Ben chuckled. "She trying to make a Xena convert out of you, too? Careful, she'll have you doing back flips and battle cries in the middle of the yard." They were both laughing when their lunches arrived. Ben looked at Melanie sincerely. "Taylor's a good girl. She's been a godsend for me, since Anna died." His voice softened. "Moved right in and took over the household. Refused to let me be alone. Much as I may have acted like I resented it then, it was just what I needed. I don't know what I would have done without her." He nodded, then spoke as if to himself. "She's a good girl, my Taylor."

Melanie was touched. It was obvious from his quiet tone and lack of eye contact that Ben didn't often talk this personally. "I like her a lot. I'll have to get her to cook for me."

Ben's face brightened. He was mildly embarrassed that he had strayed into such emotional territory so soon, and he was relieved to have the subject shifted away from it. "You'll be hooked, I warn you. And before long, you'll have one of these." He patted his belly again.

"And I'll have to order salad and soup for lunch, right?"

"Every day."

"That must earn you some harassment from your coworkers."

"You have no idea."

They fell into an easy mode of conversation. Melanie felt quite comfortable with Ben, considering she hardly knew him. *Must run in the family*, she thought. He was a broker at Merrill Lynch, and had been for the past fifteen years. Stocks and bonds and CDs and mutual funds were things that Melanie had a hard time grasping, but Ben didn't go into long and boring detail. Instead, he asked about her marketing experiences, and over mouthfuls of deliciously fresh food, they traded corporate war stories, laughing over the glaring similarities that existed from big business to big business.

Regrettably, Ben noticed the restaurant had begun to clear out, and he spared a glance at his watch.

"Time to go back to work?"

"I'm afraid so. Melanie, thank you so much for joining me. I've had a wonderful time." He quickly snatched up the bill, ignoring the redhead's protests.

"Thank you for inviting me. It was very sweet of you,

considering my cousin seems to have left me to my own devices."

He shook his head with a chuckle. "That Samantha. She's something else, huh?"

"That's one way of putting it." Melanie was still a bit stung over her cousin's sudden departure.

"To be that free, that immune to responsibility..." Ben sighed wistfully. "Ah, well. Some of us have to be practical. Shall we?"

Melanie stood, and they walked to the door. "Thank you again, Ben."

"It was my pleasure." He squeezed her upper arm gently, then inclined his head toward the bookstore. "Don't stay cooped up in there too long. It's a beautiful day, and you're on vacation." With a wink, he turned and headed for the parking lot behind *Aladdin's.*

She grinned, and carefully crossed Monroe Avenue. When she got to her side of the street—no small feat; the traffic seemed endless—she stood, and regarded the storefront with distaste. "What a godawful color," she mumbled to herself. "Why would anybody be drawn to this place?" She stared for several more minutes, before making a decision to find the nearest paint store as soon as possible. How could Sam get mad at her if she made the store look better? Certainly, once she saw it, she would forgive her cousin for overstepping her bounds, right?

The sun was just disappearing over the horizon when Melanie heard the soft tap at the door. She put down the one of hundreds of paint swatches strewn over the little breakfast table, rubbing at her eyes as she got up. Something in her stomach fluttered when she opened the door and saw Taylor's smiling face.

"Hey, you," the brunette said playfully, almost seductively. *Seductively? Where the hell did that come from?*

"Hey, yourself. Come on in." She stood aside, allow-

ing the taller woman to enter, noting with approval that she
definitely preferred Taylor's hair down, as it was now, falling in big, dark, fluffy waves around her shoulders. Her
dream from the previous night came unbidden into her
mind, and she swallowed hard.

"I'm not interrupting anything, am I?"

"Absolutely not. I was just looking at some colors."
She gestured to the swatches.

"What are you painting?"

"I can't stand that brown any longer. If Sam wants to
kill me, she can. Serves her right, anyway, for leaving me.
How long does she think I can sit around and do nothing?"

Taylor plopped down on the couch as Melanie
retrieved some Pepsi from the fridge. "Have you heard
from her?"

"Oh, didn't I tell you?" Melanie called from the
kitchen. "She and Rob are biking across Canada."

"What?"

"Yup." She handed a glass to Taylor. "Who knows
when the hell she'll be back."

Taylor hated to see the disappointment in the older
woman's eyes. Although the move didn't surprise her, she
was angry at Samantha for hurting her cousin. "Well, that
was a lousy thing to do." A sudden thought struck her,
causing her to nearly choke on her Pepsi. "You're not leaving, are you?"

A corner of Melanie's mouth quirked up at the barely
veiled panic in Taylor's voice, and a warmth she couldn't
explain filled her. "No. I don't think so. Not right away."

Taylor's sigh of relief was audible, and she blushed.
"Good. I haven't gotten to show you around my city yet."

"I'd like that."

There was a long, comfortable silence.

"Hey," Taylor said suddenly. "Did you get a chance to
watch the tapes?"

It was Melanie's turn to blush.

"You didn't?" Taylor guessed.

"Actually, I did. All six episodes. I stayed up way too

late." She studied her glass, waiting for the inevitable.

"Ha! I knew it. You liked them, didn't you?"

Melanie blew out a breath in defeat, and grinned. "Okay, you win. I liked them...a lot." She'd actually been thinking about the show quite a bit throughout the day, surprised by how it had affected her. She startled herself by sitting down on the couch right next to Taylor, their legs touching. "Let me ask you something."

"Fire away," Taylor said, trying not to notice the heat her own body was generating from having Melanie so close. She watched the blue eyes search the ceiling for what she wanted to say.

"Are Xena and Gabrielle...um...together?" She wasn't quite sure how to word it. *Oh, for Christ's sake, just say it,* her head screamed at her. *What the hell's the big deal?* "I mean, like...more than friends?"

A huge grin split across Taylor's face, and she nodded appreciatively. "I'm impressed. Not a lot of straight people pick that up right away. Good catch."

"You mean, they are?" She was actually surprised by this.

"Well, it depends on who you ask." Taylor launched into an entire Xena education, explaining to Melanie the whole concept of the "subtext" that portrayed Xena the warrior princess and her sidekick, Gabrielle, as lovers, how it came about accidentally. The creators of the show decided to have a little fun with it—never solidly admitting to it, of course, lest the censors get wind—and before long, Xena had become a lesbian icon.

Melanie was not only impressed by Taylor's knowledge and charmed by her obvious passion for the show, but she realized that the relationship between the two characters was exactly what she had liked so much. Sure, the action was fun, and it was great to finally see a female lead character on television who didn't take any shit from anybody *and* could kick their ass if they didn't like it, but it was definitely the chemistry between Xena and Gabrielle that had roped her in from the very first episode.

"I wish there had been something like Xena on when I was fourteen or so, you know?" Taylor said. "I think it would've made the confusion about my sexuality a lot easier to deal with if there had been something to relate to."

"Yeah, I see what you mean." It was unnerving how aware she was of Taylor's bare thigh resting against her own. It was more unnerving to realize Melanie herself had no intention of moving away. "There were a few, though. Wonder Woman. The Bionic Woman."

Taylor chuckled. "I watched them both faithfully. Looking back, I wish they hadn't made Wonder Woman quite so femmy, you know? She threw like a girl and ran like a girl."

"You wished she was more butch?" Melanie nudged her with an elbow.

Taylor laughed. "Yeah. Exactly. Now, Lindsay Wagner. Boy, did I have a crush on her."

"I watched that one. Every week. Jaime Sommers was cool."

"Oh yeah."

They sipped their sodas, enjoying the closeness of the other, but unwilling to say so out loud. Taylor broke the silence.

"Do you miss Chicago? Your job and your friends and stuff?"

Melanie thought about it for a moment. It would be easy to say yes. That was the answer that was probably expected anyway. But, there was something inside, deep inside, something completely unfamiliar that wouldn't allow her to lie to Taylor. "I guess a little. The hustle and bustle of the big city has always fascinated me." She hurriedly put her hand on Taylor's arm. "Not that Rochester isn't a big city..."

"Understood." Taylor nodded, trying desperately not to look at the hand burning her skin.

"But, I'm very surprised to say, I don't really miss my job." She sat there in awe, shocked by the admission. She looked at Taylor in disbelief. "I mean, I miss it a little. I don't miss the politics or corporate bullshit, that's for sure. But, I didn't like the person I was becoming there. An executive shark. Like I told you the other day, nothing mattered but the company." She was quiet for a moment before looking up to meet the soft, warm, brown eyes that were silently regarding her. "You asked if I miss my friends. Honestly, the only friend I had was Angela, my secretary. I didn't have time for anybody else." She grimaced sadly. "Pretty sad, huh?"

"At least you realized it before it was too late. Like I said before, it took a lot of guts to do what you did. I admire you. I do have to say that I can't see somebody like you with no friends, though. That is sad."

Melanie blushed at the compliment. "Thanks."

"I've worried about the same thing where I am. Sales is tough, and people can be so damned phony."

"You can say that again."

"I don't hang out much with anybody from work because it's hard to tell who's really my friend, and who's pretending to be because they want something from me."

Melanie nodded in agreement, tucking a strand of hair behind her ear, feeling Taylor's eyes on her as she did so. "I got used to not trusting anybody but Angela. I came to the understanding that almost anybody who was nice to me was just gunning for my job."

"The business world has become a frightening place." Sitting so close to Melanie was making it hard to breathe, but Taylor couldn't bring herself to move away. Their thighs were still pressed together, neither of them choosing to break the contact, a fact Taylor digested with delight, and filed away. "So, you want to see more of Rochester, then?"

Melanie shook her head in confusion. "Whoa, hang on. I think the subject just shifted drastically."

Taylor laughed. "Sorry. Corporate shit bums me out after a while."

"Me, too. I'd love to see more of your city."

"You busy tomorrow for dinner? We could drive

around a little and go out. Or we could come back here. I'm a great cook."

"So I hear. Your dad says you've fattened him up."

"Does he?"

"Yup. I had lunch with him today, and he had to order a salad."

"Really."

Melanie wasn't sure what that particular tone meant, nor how to respond to it. She swallowed, and decided on avoidance. "I just happen to be free. When should I expect the sight-seeing taxi to arrive?"

Taylor was glad to have the invitation accepted. She wanted nothing more than to spend time with Melanie. "How 'bout five-thirty? I'll come get you, and we'll play it by ear."

They stood up together, both reluctant to end the physical contact neither one of them had acknowledged. Melanie handed the Xena tapes over to the taller woman. "And you'll have to show me more of these. Soon."

Taylor took them, their hands brushing, and Melanie held on longer than she needed to. "You've got yourself a deal. I'll see you tomorrow night, then?"

"Yes, you will."

Melanie stood under the pounding spray of the shower. The water was much colder than she liked it, but she felt so hot and flushed after Taylor left, this was the only way she could think of to get her body temperature back to normal. She stood in the tub with her hands on the wall and her face directly in the spray, analyzing her two "dates" today, and trying to figure out why they felt so different.

Ben was a great guy. He was handsome. He was very handsome. He was successful, polite and considerate. He certainly must have been interested in Melanie; he had asked her to lunch even though she was a virtual stranger. That made him bold. It took guts to ask somebody out you've only just met. The risk of rejection is huge. Guts were good. She silently gave him a point. He was a business executive, so they'd had plenty in common to talk about. That was another point. It was a very pleasant lunch, and she would do it again, given the opportunity.

Taylor. Where to start with Taylor. Melanie bent her head down, letting the icy spray pound against the back of her neck. When Taylor was near her she felt...nervous. And jumpy. And she got butterflies in her stomach. Taylor was attractive. She was very, very attractive. She was successful, polite and considerate. She was attentive, Melanie realized. She always felt like she had one hundred and ten percent of Taylor's attention. She liked that. She gave Taylor a point for it. She remembered how they had sat on the couch, their thighs touching innocently. Innocently? Ha! Hardly. Melanie had sat in that spot on purpose, just to see what Taylor would do. She could admit that now, though at the time, she had shocked herself. When Taylor had spoken, all Melanie could do was watch her mouth. Her mouth and her hands. Taylor had great hands, she realized now. They looked strong, yet feminine at the same time. Her nails were devoid of any polish, but were filed neatly to a length not long or short. And her lips...

"Oh my God," she said out loud. "What is going on with me?" Was it possible for a woman to be a lesbian, and have absolutely no inkling until she's thirty-three? No. That was silly. If she were gay, she would have gotten a clue before now. Wouldn't she?

She forced her mind back to Ben. She concentrated on any and all of the things she had felt as she sat across the table from him this afternoon. She tried to picture his hands. She shut her eyes tightly. No good. Nothing. How about his voice? He had a very deep, commanding voice. She'd felt it in the pit of her stomach, but not in her groin like she did Taylor's.

What? Good lord, where did that come from?

Melanie cranked the water off and stood dripping, banging her head against the wall of the shower. *That's it. I can't think about this any more. I'll go insane.*

She toweled herself off, and slipped into a pair of flannel boxers and a soft, green T-shirt. In the living room, she pulled out the sofa bed, retrieved the pillows and comforter once again from Sam's room, and clicked on the television, looking for something mindless, preferably a horror movie, to save her from the madness in her own head.

Across the lawn, only a football field away, Taylor sat in her room, the remote in her hand stopping on HBO. A madman with a knife was chasing Neve Campbell through a big house, toppling furniture and breaking knick-knacks. Taylor ran a hand through her still-wet hair, and pulled the covers up around her, chilled from her shower. What the hell was she supposed to do about this? She'd never had such as aching attraction to anybody in her life, and she was at an absolute loss over how to deal with it.

It was pretty clear to her that Melanie was straight. Or was it? She'd thrown the word out there for Melanie to jump on, actually referring to her as a straight person, but she hadn't bitten. That didn't mean anything, of course. She'd only know Taylor a couple days. Why on earth would she suddenly blurt out something as personal as her sexual preference? On the other hand, she knew Taylor was gay, so she had to realize she was in friendly territory.

She'd had lunch with Ben. Taylor grimaced. She hated that this little fact bothered her so much. *So, they had lunch. So what? Didn't mean anything.* Of course, there was the tiny little fact that Ben Rhodes had known Melanie for all of fifteen minutes before he'd asked her to lunch. That definitely meant he was interested. She swallowed hard, knowing that it would be very difficult for her if Ben and Melanie began seeing each other.

She lives in Chicago, for Christ's sake. She's not going to be "seeing" either of you. Jesus, Rhodes, get a grip.

On that not-so-pleasant note, she pushed all thoughts of Melanie Larson as far away as possible, and concentrated on the screen, hoping two hours of Neve would take her mind off this mess.

Chapter
8

Melanie was perfectly content, her head resting against the seat, sun warming her face, Taylor at her side. She stole a glance at her companion, who was tapping the steering wheel to the Latin beat of the Ricky Martin tune on the radio. Tapping it with those hands. Melanie caught her bottom lip between her teeth. She let her gaze wander down to the smooth, muscular legs, up to the khaki shorts, and indigo long-sleeved henley. Her dark hair was down again, much to Melanie's delight, and round, black-framed sunglasses hid her eyes. The warm, musky scent she wore floated to Melanie's nostrils, and she breathed deeply, thoroughly enjoying it.

They had exited the expressway, and were now cruising through the city. "This is a pretty good time, with rush hour being just about over. You don't want to be driving around here at five o'clock." She made a left, and pointed out the window. "This is Frontier Field. It's only a couple years old. We have a minor league baseball team, the Red Wings, that play here. I'm not a big baseball fan, but it's fun to go to the games."

"I played softball in high school, but I can't seem to

get through an entire baseball game on TV. Bores me to
tears."

"Me, too," Taylor laughed. "There's no earthly reason
a simple baseball game should take four hours."

Melanie adjusted her sun visor. "It's been just gorgeous out. Is the weather always this nice here?"

"Ha!" Taylor spat. "You, young lady, must be a good
luck charm, because Rochester weather sucks much of the
time. The summer's not too bad, although it can get
awfully hot. And the winter? Ugh. Nasty."

Taylor had turned down a narrow, quiet street, and
found a parking spot. "Feel like walking a bit?"

"Sure. I'm up for anything you can dish out."

Taylor slid a glance her way, a challenging sparkle in
her eye.

Melanie swallowed, but was surprised to find herself
returning the look with one of her own.

Taylor arched an eyebrow questioningly, then smiled.
"Come on."   .

God, it's fun to flirt with her, Melanie thought.

They walked down a wide sidewalk, Taylor pointing at
different buildings. "This is called High Falls. It used to be
a very rundown, not-so-safe part of town, but our mayor
has been working really hard to fix it up, and get people
down here again. All these shops are fairly new. There's a
bunch of restaurants around here. The new baseball stadium has been a great draw for business."

They proceeded on and the sidewalk became a large,
wide bridge. They walked out to the middle, passing many
other people. There were benches and trash cans. The
whole area had a very clean, proud look. Taylor pointed to
the water flowing below them, splashing down from the
falls on the right.

"This is the Genesee River. And over there," she
pointed to their left, "is Genesee Brewing. Their beer is
very popular and plentiful around here." She dropped her
voice to a whisper. "It's not very good, though."

Melanie laughed. "Not very loyal of you."

"I know. I prefer Canadian. Don't tell anybody, though. They can make people disappear." She winked at Melanie, whose knees went weak.

They strolled casually back to the car, chatting about this and that. They drove a little more, and Taylor pointed out different things...the newly renovated and enlarged library, where Taylor claimed she could live, the Liberty Pole, which was turned into a Christmas tree with lights during the holidays, the War Memorial, now referred to as Blue Cross Arena, after the large, local health insurance organization. The brunette had grimaced at that. "I hate Corporate America. Everything's about money. I liked the War Memorial. But nowadays, a company can come along, flash enough money, and suddenly it's the Blue Cross Arena. Just like Frontier Field. Couldn't it be Red Wings Stadium or something? Frontier forks over enough money and now it's Frontier Field. It sucks." She made a turn, and headed back past the baseball stadium. "Okay, let's go this way."

Melanie leaned back, and closed her eyes, letting the warm evening air blowing in the sunroof caress her face. "Thank you for this. It's nice to have somebody to talk to."

"Well, you just happen to be great company, so don't thank me."

Melanie smiled at that, but didn't open her eyes. Taylor took the opportunity to alternate her attention between the road and the body next to her. Melanie was wearing denim shorts that hugged her curves perfectly, the first thing Taylor had noticed when the auburn-haired woman had walked ahead of her to the car. Her shirt was a short-sleeved white button down, which she had tucked neatly into her shorts and cinched with a brown belt. Brown boat shoes adorned her small feet. Taylor followed the sparkle of the gold watch on her left wrist as she lifted her hand and tucked a piece of hair behind her ear. The sun shining on her head was revealing golden highlights, and Taylor licked her lips nervously. *Goddamn.*

As they crested a hill and headed down the other side,

water came into view. "Hungry?"

Melanie opened her eyes, and smiled. "Yup."

"How 'bout a hot dog and a stroll on the pier?"

A grin lit up the face next to her. "And ice cream for dessert?"

Taylor laughed at the childlike quality of the question. "If you're a good girl."

"Oh, I'm very good." Melanie felt her face redden, mortified that the words had slipped out.

"We'll see," Taylor replied in a low voice that shot straight to Melanie's groin. *Jesus Christ. How does she do that?* Melanie asked herself.

They parked and locked up the car, Taylor grabbing a navy blue Gap sweatshirt from the back seat, and tying the sleeves around her waist.

"Is that Lake Ontario?" Melanie asked.

"Yup." She nudged Melanie playfully. "Maybe if we squint hard enough, we can see Sam."

"Maybe if we reach far enough, I can slap Sam."

Taylor purchased hot dogs for the two of them, and they wandered to the pier that stretched out onto the lake. It was busy, as the evening was pleasant, with various families out for a stroll and many a teenager just looking to hang out. The two women seemed aware only of each other. They wandered slowly, in no hurry, looking out onto the water, and eating their dinner.

"Taylor, can I ask you a personal question?"

"Sure."

"Do you look like your mom?"

Taylor caught her eye. "Where did that come from?"

"I just was wondering. Other than your eyes, I don't really see a lot of Ben in you. I just thought you must look more like her."

"Yeah. As a matter of fact, I look a lot like her. Almost like twins, as my grandma says."

"Were you close to her?"

Taylor hesitated, not used to the subject.

Melanie took it as annoyance and hurried to apologize.

"I'm sorry. You don't have to answer that. Never mind. I'm being nosy. It's none of my business," she said in a rush.

"No, no," Taylor reassured her. "It's okay. I don't mind. I'm just not used to talking about her." She took a deep breath. "Yes. We were very close. I could tell her just about anything, and she'd listen with an open mind and an open heart. I was terrified to tell my family that I'm gay, but Maggie and I were having problems and I was a mess...barely functioning, really. I made the decision to tell her, if for no other reason than I needed my mommy." She smiled at Melanie, and the older woman had a sudden flash of what Taylor must have looked like as a little girl. "She didn't even flinch—no small feat for a woman raised as an Italian Catholic. She came right over to me, put her arms around me, and just held me so I could cry, while she kept telling me that she loved me and everything would be okay. I think that was the single closest moment we ever had. There's nobody quite like my mom."

"Sam said you moved home to take care of your dad."

"Yeah. He was crushed, an absolute mess when my mom was killed. Not that any husband wouldn't be, but they had something really special. He hadn't the foggiest idea what to do. It was like he was in some kind of daze. My big brother Frankie came home and had to take care of the funeral arrangements. My dad was just too lost to do any of it. When Frankie had to go back to New York City, he and I decided we couldn't leave Dad alone in the state he was in. So, I moved out of my apartment and came back home to look after him."

"The poor man," Melanie whispered.

Taylor nodded. "It was pretty awful to watch. This big, strong man who's always been my hero was reduced to nothing more than a sobbing child." Even now, Taylor shuddered at the picture her father had presented. His grief was the hardest thing with which she'd ever had to deal, aside from the actual loss of her mother. "Luckily, he pulled himself through in a few months. But, it wasn't easy."

"You said you're not used to talking about your mom. Is that why? To spare him?"

"Yeah, I'm afraid so. I know it's not the best way to deal with things, but it seems to work. I just kept telling myself to give it a little more time, give it a little more time. It's probably been long enough, but I've gotten so used to not talking about her that I still don't."

Melanie nodded and said softly, "Well, she sounds wonderful. You must miss her."

"Terribly."

Taylor's dark eyes had misted, and Melanie laid a gentle hand on her arm. "I'm sorry. I shouldn't have brought it up. I didn't mean to upset you."

Taylor looked down at her, and tucked the redhead's hand under her own arm, as if walking her down the aisle. "Don't apologize. I haven't talked about her much at all since she died, and that's probably not healthy. I need to talk about her. It's good for me. She deserves to be remembered, and for some strange reason, I feel really comfortable talking to you. So, thank you for asking." Melanie smiled her relief and Taylor asked, "What about you? Are you close to your parents?"

"I guess you could say I'm pretty close to my mom, despite the fact that we don't have a whole lot in common. My dad's more of a passing presence in my life than a father." She said it with a half-grin, attempting to make light of the remark, but Taylor could see the faint shadow of old pain that shaded her pretty face. "My parents divorced when I was fourteen, and my father's been kind of a fleeting figure ever since."

"That's a rough age to deal with a divorce."

"Tell me about it. My mom had never worked—not full-time anyway—and suddenly she finds herself with no husband, no house, and a kid to support."

"Ouch." Taylor winced.

"Yeah. It wasn't easy for her. We moved to a suburb of Philly so she could be close to her sister Darlene...that's Sam's mom. Aunt Dar helped her find a job at a local bank.

I saw my dad on the occasional weekend or holiday here and there, but Sam's dad, my Uncle Phil, was much more of a father figure to me. We got a little apartment, just me and my mom. She did a damn good job with what was thrown at her."

Taylor smiled at the glimmer in the ocean blue eyes. "You're proud of her."

"You bet I am. She didn't let him destroy her life. It happens, believe me. I've seen it. But, she called up a strength she didn't think she had. I didn't think she had it, either, frankly."

"I think my mom and your mom would've liked each other."

"Me, too."

"No siblings?"

"Nope. Just me. Sam and I went to the same school, though. She was like a big sister."

"Except I bet you took care of her more often than she took care of you."

Melanie laughed at Taylor's nearly accurate assumption. "To a certain extent, yes. Let's just say that the majority of her school projects weren't hers."

"And term papers?"

Melanie poked herself in the chest.

"Figures."

"How 'bout you? Brothers or sisters besides Frankie?"

"Just him and me."

"Frankie. Nice Italian name," Melanie teased. "How'd you manage to get Taylor instead of Maria or Angela?"

"My mom named Frankie, so Dad got to name me. His mother's maiden name was Taylor."

"Nice compromise."

"Completely. Frankie's middle name is Jefferson and mine's Anna Maria."

Melanie raised her hand. "Lynn."

Taylor rolled her eyes. "White bread."

Melanie laughed, enjoying the feel of holding onto Taylor. She shivered involuntarily as a breeze blew in off the water. She inched closer to her companion.

"Cold? Here." Taylor untied the sweatshirt from around her waist.

Melanie held up her hands in protest. "No, no. I don't want to take your shirt. You need to be warm, too."

"I'm very warm-blooded, Melanie. I actually brought this for you. I thought you might get chilly. I'm fine."

Melanie gingerly took the offered shirt, softly thanking the taller woman, flattered that the shirt had been intended for her from the beginning. She pulled it over her head, inhaling deeply as she did so, the smell of laundry soap and Taylor invading her senses. It was very roomy, and she pulled on the sleeves until her hands popped out.

Taylor barely resisted the urge to brush Melanie's hair out of her eyes. "Navy looks good on you," she commented.

"Why, thank you," Melanie replied.

"Ready for ice cream?"

"Am I ever not ready for ice cream?"

They turned and headed back toward the beach.

"So, tell me about Maggie." Melanie shocked herself with her boldness, but she wanted to know as much as she could about this person with whom she walked arm in arm.

"Hmm. What do you want to know?"

"How'd you meet her?"

"College. She was a little bit older than me..." She turned her eyes toward her companion. "You sure you want to hear this? It's not very exciting, and I don't want to bore you to death."

"It's really none of my business, I know," Melanie said, lowering her eyes. "I just...I don't know." She shrugged. "I like talking to you. You are far from boring, Taylor."

Taylor smiled at her. "All right, but if you fall asleep and I have to carry you to the car, I'm going to be annoyed."

Melanie felt a tingle run through her body at the thought of being cradled in the arms of this woman, but shook it off. "No sleeping. I promise."

"All right. You asked for it." She thought for a moment, searching for a good starting point. "Like I said, Maggie was a little older than me. When I was a second-semester freshman, we lived in the same dorm, but she was a floor up. I first noticed her at a sorority party. She was loud and funny and the life of the party. People were just drawn to her. Kind of like Sam."

Melanie nodded, knowing exactly what she meant.

"I was just starting to realize my own sexuality. I mean, I'd had an inkling for a while, but college was really the first place where I actually interacted with other lesbians. Slowly, I started to understand just exactly why it was that I'd never quite fit in with my school friends, or why I was never quite comfortable with the guys I'd dated. I had no idea that Maggie was gay, too, not at first. She seemed to zero in on me and take me under her wing, like it suddenly became her responsibility to make sure I had a good time at college. We went to the movies together, she took me to parties, she introduced me to all kinds of popular people. She was terrific for me. Really brought me out of my shell."

"Wow. Couldn't we all use somebody like that in college?" Melanie asked wistfully.

"She was amazing. She was good-looking, with brown hair and these incredible green eyes that could burn right through you. She came from a pretty wealthy family, so she had lots of money, at least to the rest of us poor, starving college students. She was always buying me presents, taking me places. She treated me like royalty. The day she gave me diamond earrings was the day I realized that I was as in love with her as she was with me. We had been 'dating' for nearly six months, but I had refused to let myself just fall. I never had before and I was terrified, so I'd tried to prevent it from happening. I knew I was attracted to her sexually...she had a great body...but I was so scared to just give in to what I was thinking." She chuckled. "The first time I told Maggie I loved her, she let out this huge, relieved breath, flopped back in her chair and said, 'It's about fucking time. I've only been trying forever.'"

Both women laughed as they approached the ice cream stand. They took their cones to a nearby bench and sat watching the seagulls swoop and dive.

Melanie reached over and wiped a chocolate sprinkle off of Taylor's lip, ignoring the clouded look that passed over the brown eyes. "So, what happened?"

Taylor swallowed hard, her skin still tingling where Melanie's fingers had grazed it. "Oh, the usual," she said, somewhat evasively. "We didn't have a lot in common. Our relationship wasn't nearly as smooth as our courtship. It just ended up not working." She was unaccustomed to speaking frankly about the drinking problem she had refused to see, both out of embarrassment as well as respect for Maggie. "It didn't work," she added again.

Melanie nodded, sensing that Taylor wasn't telling the whole truth, but didn't feel important enough to push the point. Instead, she ate her strawberry ice cream and smiled at her newest friend. "This has been a great night."

Taylor returned the smile, grateful that the auburn-haired woman had chosen not to press the issue. "It has, hasn't it?"

"Thanks so much for the tour. Your city is beautiful."

"Thank you, ma'am. The company made the trip worthwhile, that's for sure."

They sat in companionable quiet, munching their cones and watching the waves, neither one able to remember when they had felt quite so comfortable with the silence of another.

Chapter
9

The next phone call from Samantha didn't come until Thursday evening. When Melanie heard the familiar voice on the answering machine, she snatched up the receiver.

"Sam?"

"Hi, Mellie!"

"Where are you?"

"On our way to Vancouver. Can you believe it?" Her voice was positively giddy, and Melanie was immediately taken back to their childhood.

"Vancouver? Sam, Vancouver's on the other side of the continent. What are you thinking? You've got no clothes, nothing with you..."

"Melanie, we don't all have to have things planned out, you know," her cousin scolded her. "Don't you ever want to just...I don't know...fly by the seat of your pants?"

Melanie made a face. "No. I don't. When are you coming home? You wanted me to look at the bookstore, remember?"

"Oh, that stupid thing. You know what? I really don't care what happens to it. Maybe you could just tell Daddy to sell it or something, okay?"

Melanie sighed. What Sam was really saying was, *You*

don't mind doing my dirty work for me, do you? Thanks. So
Samantha.

"Ooo. I gotta go, baby cousin. Hey, could you let Ben
know that the rent may be a little late this month. I'm not
sure when I'll be back. But stay as long as you want. Rob
says hi. Bye."

"Tell Rob to kiss my ass." Melanie sneered at the dial
tone in her ear. How the hell did Sam always manage to do
that? She'd breeze in, say what she wanted to say, and
breeze out before anybody could protest. She'd done it all
her life. People were usually so stunned that they didn't
realize what had been done or said until Samantha was
already gone.

Shit.

She flopped herself down on the couch and pushed her
hair behind her ear. The rent. Well, she wasn't going to
stay here without taking care of that. She got right back up,
and peeked out the window. Ben's Saab was parked in the
driveway.

A minute later, she was knocking on the back door of
the main house. Ben's face lit up when he opened the door.

"Melanie. Hi there. What a nice surprise. Come in,
please." He moved aside, allowing her to enter the spa-
cious kitchen.

"I'm sorry to disturb you, Ben."

"Nonsense." He waved her off. "Can I get you something to drink? I was just about to have a glass of wine
myself." He winked at her. "Been a long day."

"I think I could use a glass right about now."

He motioned her to sit at the table, while he retrieved
a bottle of Chardonnay from the refrigerator, then took two
crystal glasses out of the glass-front hutch in the corner.
Turning his sparkling eyes on her, he asked, "Everything
okay?"

She sighed, not wanting to say too much about Samantha and her bad habits, especially to somebody to whom
she owed money. She mentioned the unexpected trip and
the most recent phone call, unable to keep the disappoint-

ment out of her voice.

Ben pulled out the chair next to hers, handing her a glass, and sat. "She's quite the hostess, hmm?"

That got a chuckle from the redhead. "Oh, yeah. She's been great at showing me the sights, keeping me occupied..."

It was Ben's turn to chuckle. "What are you going to do?"

Melanie was silent for a long moment. Something about the bookstore had been scraping at the back of her mind since the first day she'd entered it. She shook the thought away. "I don't know. I'm enjoying myself, despite the absence of my irresponsible cousin, so...oh. Wait a minute." She slipped her checkbook out of the back pocket of her shorts where she'd stuck it on her way out the door. "Sam doesn't know when she's returning and she said the rent is due."

Ben held up a hand in protest. "No, no. Don't worry about that. She'll pay me when she gets back."

Melanie was having none of that. She ignored him, and continued filling in the blanks. "I refuse to stay here without paying for it. If it makes you feel better, Sam can pay *me* when she gets back." She winked at him. "How much?"

Ben sighed in defeat, and gave Melanie the figure. She handed the check over with a smile. He liked the spunk of this woman, he realized with a start, noting the quiet confidence present in her blue eyes. The invitation popped out before he had time to think. "Are you up for dinner?"

Melanie surprised herself by immediately accepting. "I'm starving," she said with a grin.

"Great. Let's go."

He ushered Melanie to the door where she ran headlong into Taylor, who was on her way in. "Oh. Sorry...hey, you." She smiled when she recognized the face.

"Hey, yourself." Taylor grinned back, until she noticed her father standing behind the redhead.

"We're just heading to dinner," he explained, the thought of inviting his daughter to join them coming and going.

The grin slid slowly away from her face, replaced by...what? Melanie wondered. "Would you like to join us?" she asked, hoping to bring the smile back.

"Um...no," Taylor answered, slipping past them into the kitchen, needing to be further away from this woman who affected her so. "Thanks. I had a late lunch. Have fun, though." She was gone from the kitchen in an instant, her footsteps echoing up the hardwood stairs, leaving Melanie standing in the doorway furrowing her eyebrows in confusion.

Ben seemed not to notice his daughter's rapid exit. "Ready?"

"Hmm? Oh. Sure."

He held the door for her, his warm hand on her back, guiding her out.

"God, I am so stupid," Taylor mumbled to herself, changing out of her work clothes and into a comfortable pair of soft, cotton gym shorts and a white Nike T-shirt. "Why do I always let this happen to myself?" She flopped backwards onto the bed, and pressed the heels of her hands to her eyes. "Boy, good ol' Ben certainly moves fast, doesn't he? Not that I'm surprised." She punched her pillow. "Wonder how long before he gets her in the sack." That thought came unbidden, before she could block its entrance into her brain, and her stomach twisted in revulsion.

Okay, relax. You don't even know her. She's been in your life for—what?—five days, Rhodes. You really need to chill.

She steadied her nerves with a deep breath. So what if she ended up in bed with Ben? Who cares? "Means nothing to me," she muttered. She got up, yanking the gold clip holding her hair back off, and tossed it onto the dresser. She headed down to the kitchen to find something to eat, her comment about the late lunch having been a lie to get her out of the impossibly awkward situation of dinner with her father and her latest crush ogling each other.

She poured herself a large glass of milk to go with her peanut butter and jelly sandwich. "I just need to stay away from her," she said aloud. "That's all. Pretty simple and basic. If it's going to make me this crazy, I need to stay away." The thought of Melanie's limbs entwined with Ben's was still doing a number on her, despite her best attempts to clear her head. "I need to stay away," she repeated.

She took her dinner into the living room, and popped in a Xena tape, not able to think about the situation for one more minute and still keep her sanity.

They stopped at the door of the carriage house, and Melanie toyed with the idea of inviting Ben in, not sure she was ready for what might happen if she did. And there was something about Taylor in the back of her mind that wouldn't leave her alone. Dinner had been very nice. The food was good and conversation had been steady and pleasant. It was comforting and familiar to be able to talk about the corporate world again, although the more she talked about it, the more Melanie realized she was happy to be out of it. This fact surprised her as much now as it had the other night when she'd admitted as much to Taylor. She'd been so afraid of being totally lost without her job, and she was shocked that she'd gotten along so well once it was gone. Ben was a great date, witty, charming, and fun to talk to, and the evening had been an agreeable one.

She turned to her companion, looking up at his handsome face. Faint lines of age were visible around his eyes, eyes that looked so much like his daughter's. "Thanks, Ben. I really had a nice time."

"Me, too." He smiled. "Thank you for indulging me. You're very good company."

There was a pause, and then Ben leaned his head down, softly capturing Melanie's lips with his own. The kiss was gentle, undemanding. Melanie could feel the roughness of his five o'clock shadow against her skin. He pulled back, and smiled at her, rubbing his thumb against her cheek. "Good night," he said quietly, then turned and strode across the lawn to his own house.

Melanie stood in the doorway for several moments, nibbling on her bottom lip, before slipping through and into the little house.

Whew. Benjamin, old boy, you're getting soft. When have you ever not pounced on the chance to be invited in?

He shook his head and chuckled to himself as he entered the back door of the dark house, and locked it behind him. Melanie was something else. It was so nice to have dinner with an attractive woman who could hold an intelligent conversation with him. How long had it been since that had happened?

He'd been attracted to her the minute he'd laid eyes on her last weekend, surprising even himself with his bold lunch invitation. He noticed light seeping out from under Taylor's bedroom door, deciding she must be reading, as he passed to the bathroom. Lunch was so much safer than dinner. There were time constraints, so if things weren't going well, there was always the excuse of having to get back to work. Melanie had passed that test with flying colors. He'd been thinking of the right way to ask her to dinner when she'd shown up at his door that evening. What luck. He returned the towel to its rack, capping the toothpaste and heading to his own room.

Dinner was wonderful, he thought, as he stripped down to his boxers and slipped between the sheets, knowing he had an early meeting in the morning. Melanie had listened intently to his stories about work, sharing a few of her own. He was amazed that she'd actually left her job, as successful as she had been at it. This was a businesswoman who knew her shit, he could tell just by the tone of her voice. She could go head to head with any number of hard-core corporate guys he knew, and beat the pants off them. She belonged in that world. However, she seemed strangely content with her decision, speaking about Sam's bookstore with a mixture of curiosity and possibility.

He sighed, reaching to click off the bedside lamp. There was something about her. His normal course of action would have been to figure a way to get into the carriage house, and then into her bed. But she was different, and he didn't want to take advantage of the situation. For some reason, he wanted to make sure that it would be *her* decision.

This admission momentarily stunned him. Since the death of his beloved Anna, he had dated several women. Never for very long, but several women, just the same. Sex was always the central focus of those relationships. Sex, physical attraction, blah, blah, blah. Emotion never once played a part. Not ever. That was the one thing he had had with Anna that he refused to share with anybody else. Besides, he'd never met anybody worth getting to know that well anyway.

Until now.

Melanie lost track of how long she'd stood with her back against the inside of the door. She was surprised by two things. One, Ben hadn't asked to come in. Two, she hadn't offered.

Why hadn't she offered?

God knew Ben was an incredibly handsome, charming man. God also knew it had been a very long time since she'd been with anybody. She scrunched up her face in concentration. Exactly how long *had* it been? The fact that she couldn't remember told her all she needed to know, and she rolled her eyes with a sigh.

She glanced at the clock in the kitchen. Nine-thirty. She wanted to get an early start in the morning painting the facade of the bookstore, so she decided that turning in early was a good idea.

Still smarting from Samantha's desertion, she decided to hell with the sofa bed, and dragged her bag into the bedroom. Thoughts of Sam and Rob assaulted her the second she stepped through the doorway, and she backtracked to the bathroom linen closet for fresh sheets.

Half an hour later, her nightly routine complete, crisp, clean sheets surrounding her, she lay in her cousin's bed staring at the ceiling. Sleep seemed as far away as it could possibly be.

Chapter
10

Ben was surprised to see his daughter at the breakfast table when he came down the stairs. She was spooning her usual brightly colored cereal—the name escaped him—into her mouth, grunting a vague reply to his greeting, seemingly absorbed in the morning paper.

He whistled as he poured himself a cup of coffee. "Looks like another gorgeous day," he remarked. "What's going on around here? It's never this nice, this long."

He sat across from Taylor, snagging the business section of the paper, and began to read. After a mere minute or two, he peered over the top of it at his daughter.

"What do you think of Melanie?"

Except for the fact that she had stopped chewing, it would seem Taylor didn't hear the question. She resumed her task, swallowing, and clearing her throat before answering simply, "She seems very nice." Hoping he would just leave it at that, she closed her eyes when he spoke again.

"She is. Very nice. We had a wonderful time at dinner last night."

"I'm glad."

"She really knows her way around a corporation. Did

you know she was the Vice President of Marketing at a big firm in Chicago?"

"Yup."

Ben narrowed his eyes at his daughter, who had yet to look up at him. "Something bothering you, T.?"

"Nope."

"Taylor..." Ben resorted to his don't-lie-to-your-dad tone, which brought his daughter's eyes up, finally, to meet his. "What is it?"

Taylor wasn't about to give away her secrets. *Gee, Dad, I'd rather you didn't date Melanie, because I want to.* Instead, she said matter-of-factly, "Don't you think she's a little young for you?"

Ben didn't know why he was surprised by the comment, but he was. "Well," he stumbled. "I...guess I...I hadn't really thought about it."

"You're nearly fifty, Dad. She's thirty-three," Taylor supplied.

He knitted his brows together for a moment, before bursting into a smile. "I couldn't even tell last night. She's so much on my level."

Taylor rolled her eyes, standing to brush off her skirt, and depositing her bowl in the sink. "I've gotta go." She knew if she listened to one more minute of her father carrying on like a schoolboy, she'd toss her Fruity Pebbles right there on the kitchen table.

Ben stared in bewilderment long after his daughter left the kitchen. She'd been acting a little strange since last night. Hmm. Maybe living with him again was getting to her. He sighed, and sipped his coffee. She'd been mothering him long enough. Anna had been gone almost two years now. He made a mental note to have a talk with Taylor about her getting her own place once more. Maybe that would ease her mind a bit.

The lunch hour traffic on Monroe Avenue was beginning to die down. Instead of speeding to various restaurants, hoping to make their business lunches on time, people were now in a hurry to get back to their respective places of employment, like worker ants returning to the anthill before they have a chance to be missed by the queen. Even the stream of hungry customers at the cafe next door to the bookshop—which had flowed steadily for over an hour—had slowed to a trickle.

The summer sun was warm on Melanie's rust-colored head as she chased away an itch on her nose with a paint-streaked forearm. Dressed in a faded pair of Buffalo Bills gym shorts and a torn red T-shirt she had salvaged from the bottom of Sam's dresser drawers, she'd been working nonstop since mid-morning. She set down her paintbrush, bending her aching wrist at various angles, trying to alleviate the cramping that had set in. *Not used to this physical labor,* she thought. *One of the disadvantages of a desk job.* She took a step backward on the concrete sidewalk to survey her handiwork, scrutinizing it critically, as an artist would her most inspired creation.

It was plain to see that it would take at least another coat—probably two—of the soothing azure blue before it thoroughly covered the ugly brown underneath. Even so, the vast improvement was remarkable. Melanie's intention had been to make the outside of the shop softer and more inviting. She knew that once people were through the front door, the warmth and charm of the interior would win them over. Judging from Jeff's sales records, the drab, mud-colored exterior wasn't exactly sucking in the customers. A new coat of paint seemed to be the simplest first step toward an image change. She'd spent nearly two hours sifting through colored rectangular swatches, pushing the normally patient young man behind the paint counter dangerously close to the brink of insanity, before finally settling on the soft blue, along with a deep cobalt for the trim. Melanie smiled as she remembered how he had been blissfully relieved to see her go.

Nodding with satisfaction at coat number one, she

knelt, prying the lid off of the smaller can of paint meant for the doorframe and trim. She submerged her flat, wooden stir stick into liquid the color of blueberry skins, using her left hand to do the work in an attempt to rest the aching right before subjecting it to more torture.

"Wow. What a difference."

The exclamation came from behind her, startling Melanie, so absorbed in her work was she, and causing her to jump visibly.

"Sorry," the friendly voice came again. "I didn't mean to scare you."

Melanie turned toward the source of the voice, and looked up into a pair of sparkling, smiling blue eyes. She stood, smiling sheepishly. "It's okay. I've been accused of becoming so engrossed in my work that I don't notice the world around me. I guess my accusers are right. That's the second time in a week somebody's gotten me."

"My name's Lynda Murphy. I own the café next door." She gestured to her left. "Thought you could use this. You've been out here for quite a while." She held a bottle of Snapple iced tea towards Melanie, who smiled widely, touched by the thoughtfulness of this woman she'd never met.

"Thank you." Melanie took several gulps from the bottle, blotting her lips on the back of her hand. "I didn't realize how thirsty I am. That was really very sweet of you. I'm Melanie. Melanie Larson." She offered her hand. The cafe owner shook it firmly.

Lynda Murphy was an athletic-looking woman, dressed neatly yet comfortably in khaki shorts, a white T-shirt, and black work boots. A white apron, smeared with various samplings of the day's specials, was cinched around her waist. She had close-cropped, salt-and-pepper hair, and sported four silver earrings in each ear. Melanie guessed her to be in her fifties.

Lynda gestured toward the bookshop. "This really does look a hundred percent better. That awful brown was just depressing. Are you the new owner?"

"Not exactly. My cousin and her soon-to-be ex-husband still own it. I'm just trying to fix it. Make it so maybe it will bring *in* some money."

Lynda laughed, a light, musical sound that was much more feminine than Melanie expected. "So, you're Sammi's cousin?"

Melanie smirked at the familiar term and nodded.

"How the hell is she? I haven't seen her in ages."

"Well, that makes two of us." Melanie made no attempt at further explanation, and Lynda didn't push.

"Tell her I said hello, would you?"

"Sure." She surveyed her handiwork, feeling guilty for being short with this kind woman. "I think I need a break. Can you come in for a minute?"

"Love to."

It took only a few minutes for Melanie and Lynda to forge an easy friendship. Lynda was cheerful and funny and Melanie liked her immediately. They chatted for nearly an hour and a half, trading stories about life and work, as comfortable with one another as they would be if they'd been friends for decades. Lynda was a recently single, very out lesbian, having broken up with her lover of eight years, and was only now starting to enjoy the single life. She'd purchased the Pita Paradise cafe four years ago. Specializing in unique and healthy sandwiches and creative salads had given her a niche, especially in the downtown location she occupied, and she was remarkably successful with her lunch business.

"You've really cleaned this place up," Lynda remarked, looking around the sparkling shop. "It looks like a different store." It was true. Melanie had spent the entire day Wednesday scrubbing, dusting, and straightening the little shop. It now shone like a new penny, and Melanie absorbed the compliment proudly. Lynda turned and winked at her. "I hope Sammi's paying you well."

Melanie chewed on her lower lip. "Um...she doesn't exactly know."

Lynda raised her eyebrows in question.

"I know, I know," Melanie argued. "She's out of town. See, Sam's dad actually owns it, and he asked me to look into why it's not doing so well." She shrugged innocently. "I decided the shit-brown exterior had something to do with it."

The older woman burst into laughter. "I've got to say, I'm with you on that one." She glanced at her watch. "Yikes! I'd better go before Julie issues an APB on me. She gets upset if I leave her with the customers for too long on her own." She held out her hand, and Melanie shook it warmly. "It was nice to meet you, Ms. Larson. I look forward to seeing you again soon."

"Thanks for the tea."

"Can't have you dehydrating in the middle of the sidewalk. Bad for business." With a wink, she was gone.

Melanie headed back out to her paint with a grin, deciding she liked Rochester very, very much.

By the time Melanie returned to the carriage house Saturday afternoon, her wrists were killing her. She'd applied the entire second coat, hoping that would be the end of it. No luck. A third coat was definitely a necessity. "If I never see another paintbrush as long as I live, it'll be too soon," she mumbled, stripping out of her stained clothing and stepping directly into the shower. She let the soothing spray ease her tired muscles. Luckily, it hadn't been that hot out, and she was able to complete her task without the danger of heat stroke.

Lynda had ventured over around noon with a chicken salad pita and another Snapple. "What did I tell you about dehydrating on the sidewalk?" she'd scolded the redhead with a smile, refusing to take any money for the food.

Melanie had been glad to see her. She'd been missing having somebody to talk to, unable to locate Taylor since they bumped into each other—literally—as she and Ben were on their way to dinner two nights before. She rephrased that in her own head as the water pelted her. No, she hadn't been missing *somebody*, she'd been missing Taylor. *Hmm. Interesting.*

Saturday was a light day for Lynda, so she'd spent much of her time popping her head out to chat with Melanie as she painted. "Benefit of owning the business...you're the boss." She'd grinned when Melanie asked her if her assistant would get mad that she was visiting. Having Lynda to chat with had made the day go by faster, and before Melanie realized it, coat number two was finished.

She'd decided to take the next day off, to rest and to think. The more time she spent at the little bookshop, the more attached to it she became. Today, she'd actually had a vision of herself as the owner. She'd changed it into a little specialty bookshop—the specialty still undecided—and it was hers. After all, Sam had said to sell it, hadn't she?

On the other hand, it was a huge change from the world of marketing. What did she know about selling books? Did she think she could just come along and make things work, after Sam and Jeff had failed so miserably? Still, she couldn't get the idea out of her head. Would Uncle Phil even consider selling it to her? She realized she wouldn't actually make a profit for quite some time, but she had enough money in the bank. That, plus her severance package, should keep her afloat for quite a while, allowing her to cultivate the business.

It was certainly a thought that had chewed at the edges of her mind all day. She had been surprised to realize that she really wanted to talk to Taylor about it. For some reason, she valued the younger woman's opinion, and was sure if this was a ridiculous idea, Taylor would find a way to tell her so without making her feel like a spanked child.

She changed into a pair of denim shorts and a pink T-shirt, then blew her hair dry. Taylor's car was not in the driveway, but maybe Ben would know when she planned on returning. She finished her hair, and headed out the door, strolling across the lawn towards the back door of the main house.

The grill was hot, and Ben came out of the kitchen just as Melanie turned the corner.

"Melanie," he exclaimed, obviously happy to see her. He held up a plate with two hamburger patties. "Join me?"

"Oh, no," Melanie protested. "I'm always interrupting your dinner. I'm sorry. I was actually looking for your daughter."

Ben flicked his eyes quickly over her, careful not to offend her, but pleased by what he saw. This woman had incredible legs. "Taylor's been working late on some project. I haven't seen much of her in the past couple days."

"Hmm."

"Please, Melanie, join me. Taylor mixed this ground beef up the same way she makes her meatballs...it's delicious. And I've got enough left in the kitchen to make one more patty." She was about to decline, so he gave her a pout. "You don't want me to eat alone, do you?"

She sighed, defeated. She'd really wanted to talk to Taylor, but she supposed she'd just have to wait. In the meantime, she really didn't want to eat alone, either. "Oh, all right. On one condition. You let me buy you dinner next week for a change."

"You've got yourself a deal, young lady." He grinned, hurrying off to flatten another burger.

Chapter
11

Melanie wasn't quite sure why she was so nervous. She twisted the phone cord around her finger and waited impatiently as the ringing continued in her ear. She was disappointed that she hadn't been able to talk to Taylor the night before, but she couldn't wait any longer. She had to find out if this crazy idea was even a possibility. She was about to hang up when a cheerful, albeit breathless, voice answered.

"Hello?"

"Aunt Dar?"

"Melanie." Her aunt was obviously ecstatic to hear her voice. "How are you, sweetheart?"

"I'm great. Am I interrupting something? You sound out of breath."

"Oh, no, dear. Your uncle and I were working in the yard and forgot to bring the cordless outside with us. I ran to answer it, and I'm so glad I did. Are you enjoying your stay? Is Sam being a good hostess?"

Melanie rolled her eyes, deciding to spare her aunt the dose of realism that was ready to shoot off her tongue. "She's being wonderful. I'm having a great time. Listen, is Uncle Phil around?"

"Sure is. Hang on, dear." There was a muffled sound, then her aunt's voice shouting, "Phillip! Melanie's on the phone."

Aunt Darlene was one of the sweetest women in the world. She would do anything for anybody and wouldn't hurt a fly. Her daughter was her pride and joy. If Uncle Phil had skewed vision when it came to Samantha, then Aunt Dar was simply blind as a bat. It used to frustrate Melanie, this false vision of the kind of person Sam was, especially when she was young and insecure. These were intelligent people. Why were they so oblivious to their daughter's shenanigans? As she got older and more comfortable in her own skin, she realized that making her aunt and uncle see the real Samantha would only cause them pain and give them reason to worry about their child more than they already did. Melanie had made a pact with herself to keep her mouth shut, and do whatever she could to keep their image of Samantha intact, preserving the happiness of the couple that had been so good to her while she was growing up.

"Hey, Red," her uncle's strong voice boomed in her ear. "How goes it in Ro-cha-cha?"

"Not bad, Uncle Phil. Not bad. I'm really starting to like it here."

"Good to hear. Sam's got a nice little place, huh?"

"It's adorable, really." They chatted about Melanie's drive and the weather, before she got down to business. "Uncle Phil, I want to talk to you about the bookstore."

"Uh oh. Don't like that tone. Bad, is it?"

"Well, no. Not so bad." She explained to him that the store was in good shape, but profits were not up, nor had they ever been.

"Son of a bitch," he muttered. "I knew that guy was a good-for-nothing...not a damn cent, huh?"

"Doesn't look like it. But, Uncle Phil, listen. I have a proposition for you."

"Okay."

"Sam doesn't want to run the shop herself. She really

wasn't much into the business end of it and now that Jeff's gone, she'd rather not deal with it at all." She waited to hear his reaction.

"Go on," he urged, his tone unreadable.

"She said to tell you to sell it."

Silence. Then, "She did, did she?"

"Yes."

"Can't say I'm surprised," he sighed. "All right. Let me—"

"Would you sell it to me?" She blurted the question before she had time to chicken out.

"What?"

"Sell it to me. I've been doing a lot of work on it, and some research, and I have some ideas I'd like to try. It's a great little place, it just hasn't had the right attention. I'd like to give it a shot, see if I can make a go of it."

"Sell it to you?"

"That's right. Look, work gave me a great severance package. I can afford it...I think...and I just..." She blew out a breath, trying to find the right words to express her desire to her uncle and make him understand this was something she *needed*. "I don't know, Uncle Phil. I just want to try this. It's been eating at me since I first walked in. I think I might be able to pull it off. If it doesn't work, I'll just sell it myself. Either way, you'll be rid of it." She listened to her uncle's breathing, almost able to hear the wheels turning, unaware that she was holding her own breath.

"Well, Red," he said finally, "I've never known you to make a business decision with your head up your ass. If this is something you think you want, let's do it."

Melanie expelled the air from her burning lungs with a whoosh of relief. "Thanks, Uncle Phil."

"I'll have to dig up some paperwork. I'm not sure about details, so I'll have to call you back tomorrow or Tuesday. That be all right?"

"That would be great. You're the best. You won't regret this."

"No, I don't think I will," he chuckled at his niece's obvious enthusiasm. "I'll be in touch."

"Okay."

Melanie sat staring at the phone for a long time. Did she just do what she thought she did? The bookstore was actually going to be hers. Hers. She had no idea why the fact excited her so. It couldn't be the responsibility. She'd had that at Rucker and Steele. She'd had a staff of fifteen that she oversaw, not to mention the clout she'd had with the Board. And it certainly wasn't the money. She didn't realistically expect to see a profit any time soon. There was too much cleaning up to do, restocking and liquidation of inventory. What was it? Why did the prospect of owning her own business make her giddy?

She poured herself a glass of iced tea and went out to the back yard. Sitting at the picnic table, she watched a cardinal poking at the grass. "Melanie Larson, Owner," she said aloud. It brought a girlish smile to her face, and she bit back the urge to giggle out loud. She'd never had anything that was just hers. She'd never allowed herself the time.

"Wow." She raised her eyebrows, suddenly realizing the scope of things. From now on, when it came to the bookstore, she was God. She was now responsible for the success or failure of it. Her. Melanie. Not Sam. Not Jeff. No bigwigs in upper management with the final say. Just her.

A little tiny piece of anxiety crept out from a corner of her brain, poking at her. She swallowed, suddenly nervous. What the hell had she done? Was she some kind of idiot? What kind of a moron buys a business they know nothing about? She tried to shake the doubts out of her head, realizing with a start that owning the bookstore meant relocating to Rochester permanently. She slapped herself on the forehead.

"Duh," she scolded herself, heading back into the carriage house with her empty glass. "I've got some moving to do. I need to find an apartment. And I've *got* to come up with a better name for the place. *Mason's Books.* Puh-lease." She rooted through the Sunday paper, yanking out the classified section. Hopefully, she peeked at the driveway, her face falling a little when she saw no sign of Taylor's red coupe. She hadn't seen the brunette in two days, and felt suspiciously like Taylor was avoiding her. The voice of reason took over. *Two days and that means she's avoiding you? Think pretty highly of ourselves, now, don't we?*

She heaved a frustrated sigh and plopped down in the chair with the paper, red pen in hand.

Chapter
12

By the end of the lunch hour on Monday, Melanie had the entire third coat of paint finished. She stood back, hands on hips, and surveyed her handiwork with a satisfied smile. Things felt a little different, now that she knew the store was going to be hers. She took a deep breath of the city air, feeling inexplicably victorious. Picking up the paint cans, brushes, and drop cloths, she entered the store.

There was so much to do. She knew Uncle Phil would take care of the necessary paper work, but she hadn't even decided what kind of books she was going to sell. She still had to figure out what to do with the books she didn't need any more. Should she sell them at a discount? Maybe she should call the local libraries and other bookstores to see if they'd be interested.

She entered the little office, her hands freshly scrubbed clean of the paint, and scanned all the paper strewn about. *I need my computer,* she thought. *This writing everything down is for the birds.* She had just sat down to make a list of things she needed to do or get and places she needed to call, when she heard Lynda's cheerful voice calling to her from the front of the store.

"Hello? Sherwin Williams, are you here?"

Melanie smiled. "In the office, smart ass. Come on back."

She heard the work boots clomping across the hardwood, and Lynda's smiling, food-smeared form appeared in the doorway a few seconds later. "All done? It looks great. Wait until Sammi sees it."

Melanie pressed her lips together and studied Lynda's face for a long moment.

"What?" the café owner asked, looking behind her, then back to the redhead.

"I bought the bookstore."

"You what?"

"I bought it. Sam said she didn't want it, and I asked my uncle to sell it to me."

"Just like that?"

"Just like that."

"Wow. Well, good for you, then." She narrowed her eyes at Melanie. "Why do you look less than enthusiastic?"

Melanie sighed, throwing up her hands. "Oh, hell, Lynda. I don't know. I'm on such a roller coaster right now."

Lynda's blue eyes twinkled, and she perched on the corner of Melanie's little desk, peering at her curiously. "Okay, come on. Talk to Auntie Lynda."

The gesture of friendship mixed with silliness made Melanie laugh, easing her tension just a bit.

"I just hope I know what I'm getting myself into. I don't even know what I'm going to sell."

"Well, I would think you'd sell books."

"Duh," Melanie said, slapping playfully at her neighbor. She rummaged through the papers spread across the desk until she came across the list she had constructed several days earlier. She handed it to Lynda. "What kind of books? Taylor was right. This is too small a place to sell books in general. It has to be some kind of specialty store." She pointed to the list. "Those are categories that interest me. Can't very well sell something I don't give a damn about, right?"

Lynda furrowed her brows as she studied the list.
"Hmm. Let's see...Computers? Boring. Plus, you'd have
mostly geekazoid computer nerds in here. Pets? A possibility. Would there be enough stuff to fill your shelves,
though? Feminism? Hmm. I like that one. We'll come back
to that. Business? Boring. Mysteries? Another possibility.
Classics? Nah. Old news. Used? Won't make much money.
Sci-Fi? You think the computer geeks are bad, wait 'til you
see what science fiction brings in the door."

Melanie nodded in appreciation at the insightful com-
mentary. Lynda brought up facts the redhead hadn't
touched on yet. "So, you like mysteries and feminism."

"Those would be the first two on my list. Can I give
you my opinion?"

"Yes, absolutely." Melanie had decided very quickly
that she liked Lynda and trusted her opinions. Lynda was a
successful businesswoman. More traffic in the bookstore
could only mean more traffic in front of her café. Melanie
didn't feel Lynda would intentionally steer her wrong.

"Okay. Please keep in mind that I am not saying this
simply because I'm a lesbian, not to mention a feminist."

"So noted."

"You are in a prime location to specialize in feminist
and lesbian works."

"I am?"

"You betcha. All these little streets that offshoot Monroe Avenue, most of the big houses on them are apartments. The population in this area is very
young...probably 18 to 30...and very gay or gay-friendly."

"Really." Melanie could hear her own wheels turning.

"If I was going to open *any* type of store catering to
the gay population, I'd put it right here. My assistant,
Julie, moved into her first apartment over on Oxford a few
years back. When her father realized where her apartment
was, he asked her if she was gay."

"Just because of where she moved?"

"Swear. This is gay central. Did Jeff keep a lesbian or

gay section here?" She headed out into the main store area and scanned the shelves.

"To the right, I think," Melanie offered.

"Ah. Here we go. Oooo, look. Seven whole books." She rolled her eyes and then scanned the miniscule selection.

"Anything worthwhile?" Melanie asked, honestly curious.

"Where the hell did he get this stuff?" the café owner queried, not recognizing the majority of the authors. "Oh, wait. Here we go." She pulled a book off the shelf and handed it to Melanie. "A classic."

"*Curious Wine* by Katherine V. Forrest. Classic, huh?"

"Every lesbian I know has read it. And some straight girls." She winked. "Seriously, it's a great book. Boy, it sure would be nice to have someplace with a large selection of gay books. *Barnes & Noble* has a section, but it's not very big. Hint, hint."

Melanie grinned. "I'll make a note. Lynda's vote: Feminist bookstore."

"You got it. Although, the mystery idea isn't bad." She glanced at her watch. "Shit. I've gotta run." She stopped in mid-step. "Oh. Wait. I almost forgot. Listen, Julie and I are going out Thursday night. It's Ladies' Night and we're going to hit Happy Hour. You want to go?" Melanie opened her mouth, but her response was pre-empted by an upheld hand. "Wait, before you say anything, yes, it's a gay bar, but don't worry. We'll protect you."

Melanie laughed out loud at that, playfully punching Lynda in the shoulder. "I'm a big girl and I can take care of myself, *Mom*. Yes, I'd love to go. Thanks."

"Great." Lynda headed out the door. "I'll come get you around five," she tossed over her shoulder.

Melanie turned back to the store, folding her arms and scrutinizing the overall space. "Well," she said out loud, "I'm definitely a feminist." She glanced at the book in her hand, taking it to the back office and slipping it into her bag. "Hi. I'm Melanie Larson. I own a feminist bookstore."

She smiled at the sound of it. *A feminist bookstore. Hmm.* She had noticed a library several blocks up the street and decided to see if it had internet access. It was time to do a little research.

Taylor was having a good week. First, she'd landed two major accounts at work, one of which she'd been working on for almost a year. Second, she'd helped Jason rework the ad for the local college and his clients were much happier with the result, making both Taylor and the radio station look good. Third, she'd managed to dodge any phone calls from Maggie and they were getting fewer and farther between, finally. And fourth, she'd managed to avoid Melanie for nearly five days. Of course, the only way to do that was to keep away from her own house, but, hey, whatever worked. She was proud of herself for sticking to her resolve.

It was when she drove down Monroe Avenue after a successful appointment with a potential new client that she noticed the new eye-catching and inviting blue exterior of the bookstore, and her resolve went flying right out the window of her Honda. She watched in horror as her hands and feet seemed to operate all on their own to steer her down a side street and park her within walking distance of the little shop.

"What the hell am I doing here?" she said aloud, staring at her hands on the steering wheel. When no answer appeared before her, she leaned her head back against the headrest and sighed. "I'll just go say hi. It's no big deal." The clock on her dashboard read four-fifteen. "She's probably not even there." It was several more minutes before she could get her brain and her body to focus on the same task, and she finally stepped out of the car, smoothing her red skirt, running a slightly trembling hand through her loose hair.

Melanie and Lynda were tossing names for the bookstore back and forth at one another with reckless abandon, but Melanie couldn't latch onto anything.

"Nothing's knocking my socks off," she whined, tossing her now-tanned legs over the arm of the overstuffed chair. Lynda sat the same way in the opposite chair, after they'd dragged the pair toward the back of the store. "Pita Paradise is unique. How'd you come up with it?"

Lynda shrugged. "I just always wanted my own little pita paradise," she deadpanned.

Melanie was quiet for a beat before bursting into laughter. "Ha! I get it."

"Took you long enough." Lynda smirked, shaking her head in mock-disappointment.

Their laughter ceased abruptly at the sound of the little bell that Melanie had hung over the front door. They exchanged questioning glances, wondering who would just wander in, despite the large CLOSED sign in the window. Lynda craned her neck to peer through the shelves blocking her view, able to make out only hints of bright red.

"Melanie?" a husky female voice called. "You in here?"

Lynda watched with amusement as Melanie's face took on a whole new expression at the recognition of the voice. She practically sprang up from her chair as a very attractive young woman in a red business suit cleared the shelves and came into view. Lynda recognized her face, sure she'd run into her at the occasional softball game or women's bar. Tina? Tammy? What was her name? She raised her eyebrows in quiet surprise when Melanie walked right up, and wrapped her arms around the woman's neck, hugging her like a long-lost lover. The woman in red closed her eyes, seeming to melt into the embrace, tightening her arms around Melanie's waist. For several seconds, Lynda felt as if she was invisible, as if the only people in the world were these two. The contact lasted longer than a typical hug between friends. *Isn't this interesting*, Lynda thought to herself, making a mental note to address this issue with Melanie later.

They parted slowly, and Melanie flushed an adorable shade of pink when she saw Lynda's raised eyebrows and twinkling blue eyes. She cleared her throat, consciously stepping a few inches away from Taylor. "I'm sorry. Lynda, this is my friend, Taylor Rhodes. I'm staying on her property, in Sam's house. Taylor, this is Lynda Murphy. She owns the Pita Paradise next door."

"Nice to meet you." Taylor reached out and shook the hand Lynda offered. The cafe owner had to make an extra effort to keep the smirk off her face when she noticed the barely disguised look of ownership Taylor had donned. *She might as well hang up a Posted No Trespassing sign*, Lynda smiled to herself, returning the too-firm handshake.

The three of them stood in awkward silence before Lynda made a move toward the door. "I'd better go check on Julie. She hates when I leave her to clean up by herself. It was nice to meet you, Taylor. Mel, I'll catch you tomorrow."

"Okay." Melanie watched the door shut, then turned to Taylor with a crooked grin. "It's good to see you. I've been keeping my eyes open for your car, but you're never around."

"Oh, yeah." Taylor waved her hand with an air of nonchalance. "Work's been really busy."

"That's what your dad said. I missed you."

"You did?"

"Yeah."

Taylor swallowed hard during the beat that followed, then took a deep breath. "This looks great. You've really done a lot." She wandered around, scrutinizing the shelves. "It's so much cleaner. And the outside...wow. Does that ever look better."

"You think so?"

"Absolutely. Great color choice. It looks very welcoming."

Melanie smiled, pleased at the compliment.

Taylor noticed the sparkle of the hardwood. "Good Lord, Melanie, did you scrub the floor, too?"

"Yesterday. After Sam called to tell me she was in Vancouver."

Taylor blinked at her. "Vancouver? They actually went all the way?"

"That's what she said."

"Well, she sure doesn't deserve all the work you're putting into her shop, after she deserted you like she did."

"It's not her shop anymore."

Taylor wrinkled her nose in confusion; Melanie was barely able to keep from smiling affectionately at the expression. "What do you mean?"

"She said she didn't want it, so her father sold it."

"He sold it? To who?"

"Me."

"You?"

"Yup."

Taylor blinked in disbelief, trying to take in all the implications of Melanie owning the bookstore. "How on earth did this come about?"

Melanie motioned to the chairs, and the two women sat. The redhead took a deep breath and recounted the appearance of her unexpected attachment to the little shop, which had begun the second she had set foot in the door. She explained how, at first, the cleaning and polishing were just to pass the time after Sam's sudden departure. However, after a few days on her own in the store, she'd started to visualize what changes she'd make and how she'd run it if it were hers. From there, she'd begun pretending it was hers. Taylor nodded with interest, her dark eyes fixed on the expressive blue ones before her.

"When Sam said she didn't really want it and could I just tell her dad to sell it, that's when the plan solidified in my head." She shrugged. "I just asked Uncle Phil if I could buy it from him."

Taylor sat back in the chair with a grin. "Wow. You

have got some balls, girl."

Melanie laughed nervously. "Is that what it is?"

Taylor scrutinized her carefully.

Melanie's eyes skittered away from the dark ones searching for contact.

Taylor reached out, catching the older woman's chin, and gently turning her face so their eyes finally met. "What is it? What's bothering you?"

Blue was absorbed by soft brown for several long seconds before Melanie felt Taylor slowly let go of her face. The redhead sighed. "This is hard. You have to understand that this is so hard for me. I'm not a worrier. I'm a go-getter. A doer. I always have been. But this…" She licked her lips and swallowed, making a grand sweeping gesture with her arm to encompass the whole shop. "I'm nervous, Taylor. I don't get nervous. I just don't. But…I'm nervous about whether or not I know what the hell I'm getting myself into. This is a big frigging step."

Taylor nodded slowly. "That it is. Okay." She kicked off her pumps and pulled her legs up to tuck them under her body, getting more comfortable, sinking into the soft fabric beneath her. "Let's talk it through then. You said you visualized the changes you'd make. Tell me about them."

Melanie watched Taylor shift herself into a cozy, red ball on the overstuffed chair, and decided to follow suit. She felt better already. She could almost feel the confidence oozing from the brunette across from her, making her own strength and usually ever-present assurance slowly seep back into her body. She closed her eyes for a moment.

Taylor watched as Melanie visibly relaxed. Good. That had been her intention. She knew in her heart that Melanie was more than capable of making the shop into a success. Now, she just had to make Melanie see it, too. Because once she did, everything would be okay and Melanie would be here, in Rochester, in *her* city, for good.

"First, I'd do what you said," Melanie began. "Spe-

cialize. You were absolutely on the money about the size
of this place. I was kind of leaning towards the feminist
market." At Taylor's raised eyebrows, she hurried on.
"This is a prime location. Feminist, woman-oriented stuff
would be popular, I think. I did some research at the
library the other day, just to see what's out there." She
widened her eyes. "Wow."

Taylor chuckled. "Wow is right. Okay. Feminist bookstore. Then what?"

"Image change. New paint for a more inviting exterior.
Clean and welcoming inside. I want people to think it's
okay for them to sit and relax for a bit." She waved her
hand. "Done."

"Very nicely, I might add. Then?"

"Computerize," Melanie said with conviction. "Everything is on paper right now and I hate it. It's messy. Jeff
did all right with it, but it's not how I do things. I've got a
PC in my apartment in Chicago that will do nicely. I'm
pretty knowledgeable when it comes to software. My
inventory has to be on computer. That's the only way to
keep track of things."

Taylor nodded in approval. "Good. What else?"

"Advertise." Melanie ticked off selections on her fingers. "Print, flyers, *radio*." She grinned at the brunette.
"Maybe I'd sponsor a softball team or some of the local
women's or gay events."

Taylor stifled her surprise at the last comment, deciding not to broach the subject at that moment. Melanie was
on a roll. "See? It sounds to me like you've got this all
mapped out."

Melanie blinked once. "I do, don't I?"

"I think so."

"And you know what? If it doesn't work out, it doesn't
work out. At least I will have tried, and I won't ever be sitting around regretting the fact that I was too chicken to
give it a shot."

They sat in companionable silence for a long moment,
Melanie's eyes sparkling with confidence, Taylor enjoying

the view. "Feel better?" she asked.

"Much." She favored Taylor with a beaming grin of thanks. "You are the best. That is exactly what I needed. Where'd you learn to pep talk like that?"

"Hey, you did all the talking. I just got you started."

"You did. Thank you."

"My pleasure."

Taylor unwillingly glanced at her watch, rolling her eyes, then slipped her stocking-clad feet back into their shoes of torture and stood. "I've got to run." She didn't miss the flash of disappointment that flickered across Melanie's face, and it warmed her insides. Suddenly, she blurted out, "Hey, what are you doing on Friday?"

"Um...Friday, I'll be here, and then back at Sam's, I guess."

"They're calling for rain and I've got those Xena tapes you wanted to see. What do you say? We can order a pizza or something."

"Or you can cook for me." *Good God, who said that?*

Taylor poked the inside of her cheek with her tongue. "Or I could cook for you. Okay. Anything you don't like?"

"Sausage, veal, and I'm not crazy about onions."

"Sausage, veal, onions. Got it. I'll be over about six-thirty, okay?"

"See you Friday."

The little bell jingled as Taylor left. Melanie stood looking at the closed door for a long time, smiling like a teenage girl who'd just been asked to the prom.

Okay, I'm getting signals. I am definitely getting signals. If those aren't signals she's sending me, then I haven't the foggiest idea what a signal is.

Taylor took off her suit coat and hung it across the back of the passenger seat, noting the sweat rolling down her side. She'd never felt like such a love struck kid before. How the hell did Melanie do that to her?

Taylor Rhodes prided herself on being a sensible, in-control young woman. She had a sense of humor, yes. She liked to have fun, yes, but giddy schoolgirl was not a phrase she wanted to be used to describe her. She flopped into the driver's seat of the Honda and scrubbed a hand across her face. She sighed from deep down in her bones.

She was falling for Melanie Larson.

She was falling fast.

She was falling hard.

Slowly, she pounded her head against the steering wheel.

Chapter
13

TJ's had been a small, quiet bar and restaurant at one time in its history, before new managers came along and made it into a dark, loud, dance club. The weather was gray and rainy, so the patrons were all inside, rather than out on the deck, where the majority of them would hang during the summer evenings. The place wasn't packed, but it held quite a crowd for the early evening hour. The DJ hadn't started yet, but there was a throbbing dance beat coming from somewhere anyway. The overhead fans and invisible ventilation system did nothing to subdue the thick blanket of cigarette smoke that floated conspicuously in the air.

Melanie had to blink several times, then stand still and allow her eyes to adjust to the sudden darkness. Lynda had her by the wrist; Julie trailed behind her. When they could see, the café owner led them to the far corner of the bar where two other women waited.

Melanie had been unexpectedly nervous about this evening out. She didn't know why, except that she'd never been to a gay bar before and wasn't sure what to expect. Picking out the right outfit had been a more difficult task than usual. Lynda had said to dress casually. Actually, her

exact words were, "Christ, Melanie. It's a bar." That came
with plenty of eye rolling and teasing pokes. She hadn't
packed much that was suitable for a night out, but after
much deliberation and a quick trip through Samantha's
closet, Melanie had finally decided on a comfortable pair
of jeans and a sleeveless button-down top in a deep green.
Brown sandals, a leather belt, simple gold hoops in her
ears, and a touch of perfume, and she had been ready. Scrutinizing herself in the mirror, she had been pleasantly surprised by what she saw. She wasn't used to having a tan.
She'd spent so much of her time in her office, she barely
noticed the changing seasons. She'd smiled at the unfamiliar bronze tint to her normally fair complexion, as well as
the shining blonde highlights the sun had coaxed from her
auburn hair. She'd felt a nervous, yet exciting pang in her
gut, heading to the bookshop to meet Lynda with an
uncharacteristic spring in her step.

Lynda was introducing her to the two women at the
bar. "Mel, this is Dina and Steph. Guys, this is Melanie
Larson. She just bought the bookshop next door to my
place."

Dina and Steph each shook Melanie's hand. They were
closer to Lynda's age than Melanie's, and were dressed
similarly, in jeans, polo shirts, and work boots like
Lynda's. Melanie tried not to notice the not-quite-as-sub-
tle-as-intended appraisal she was getting from two sets of
eyes. She swallowed nervously and turned to Julie, who
was asking her what she'd like to drink.

"Um, beer is fine. Anything light."

Julie was a small, mousy young woman in her late
twenties. She was very soft-spoken, but Melanie noticed
almost immediately that she had a biting wit, which
seemed to come out of nowhere. She handed the bottle to
Melanie, who sipped gratefully, scanning the crowd around
her, trying to take it all in.

There were only two couples on the dance floor, a pair
of men and a pair of women. Melanie found their presence
interesting, since the DJ didn't start for another three

hours, so they were essentially dancing to the radio. At the other end of the bar, a group of men were laughing loudly. All were painfully good-looking, two of them holding hands. Melanie smiled at the stereotype that said gay men were gorgeous, and how, sometimes, stereotypes were more on the money than people cared to admit. Two women were standing across the room, a blonde with her back to the wall, a black woman facing her, resting one forearm against the wall near the blonde's head. Judging from the looks on their faces, their discussion was heated, although Melanie couldn't hear them over the music. The blonde was frantically talking with her hands, and the black woman suddenly looked guilty, dropping her eyes to the floor. The blonde looked away, and Melanie could see unshed tears shimmering in her eyes. Feeling suddenly intrusive, she pulled her gaze away.

The majority of the patrons were men, which surprised her since Lynda had said it was Ladies' Night. She turned to ask Julie about it and found the younger woman observing her with a smirk. "What?" she asked self-consciously.

"First time in a gay bar?"

Melanie was grateful for the darkness that covered her furious blushing. She cleared her throat. "That obvious, huh?"

"You're watching things much too intently to have ever seen them before."

Not sure how to respond, she smiled and took a somewhat nervous sip of her beer.

Julie chuckled, excusing herself to the ladies' room, which was on the other side of the room, very near the spatting couple. As Melanie watched her go, she noticed the couple was now into a heavy make-out session, complete with quite a bit of tongue and much groping.

Suddenly finding herself very warm, Melanie turned to Lynda and her friends.

"How we doing?" Lynda asked, a twinkle in her eye.

"Great," Melanie answered with a smile. "Hey, I thought you said this was Ladies' Night. There seem to be an awful lot of men here."

Lynda exchanged glances with Dina and Steph. "It's a men's bar. Nobody in Rochester can seem to keep a women's bar open for longer than six months," she explained, the disgust clear in her voice. "They open something new, expect it to turn a profit in a week. When it doesn't, they give it a complete face-lift. Nobody knows where the hell they are the next time they walk in. I keep telling these people, 'Don't change it. Leave it alone for a while. Let people get used to the place. Customers like familiarity, especially in their bars.' Nobody listens to me. They change it anyway. Not long after that, they close it."

"The guys who own this place are nice enough to offer us a Ladies' Night here and there," Dina told her. "They understand our frustrations."

"It must be nice to have someplace to go," Melanie offered.

"So, you're from Chicago?"

Melanie nodded. "I didn't grow up there, but that's where I've been for several years now."

"Must be a wild gay scene there, huh?"

Melanie blinked several times, trying to formulate the right answer. What the hell did she say to that? *Oh, I'm not gay. I wouldn't know...?* Or, how about, *Yeah, baby. You better believe it. It's wild in the windy city...?* She glanced at Lynda, hoping for help, but her café-owning friend was leaving her hung out to dry. That's when Melanie realized that Lynda herself was probably wondering exactly where Melanie was coming from.

She was saved from embarrassing herself any more than she already had with her hesitation by the bartender, who brought a shot glass turned upside down and set it in front of Melanie. "The lady at the end of the bar would like to buy you a drink," he said, smiling.

Melanie's eyebrows raised in surprise, and she met the eyes of a tomboyish blonde who raised her glass in salute. Melanie panicked.

"What do I do?" she whispered to Lynda.

"Go talk to her. Apparently she likes what she sees."

"I don't want to talk to her," the redhead hissed. "You said you'd protect me."

Lynda was finding this all very amusing. "Oh, all right. Say thanks."

Melanie smiled, mouthing *thank you* in the direction of the blonde. Lynda was talking to Dina and Steph again, but Melanie suddenly felt a heavy arm around her shoulders, gentle fingers twirling a lock of her hair. She smiled in quiet appreciation. Lynda had quickly put up a *No Vacancy* sign without even looking at the offender. When Melanie found the courage to steal another glance at the blonde, she was gone.

As time passed, Melanie loosened up and enjoyed herself. The crowd increased in size the later it got. More women arrived and the DJ started up. Melanie was on her fourth beer, feeling much more relaxed. She chatted with Julie and Lynda's friends on and off, but mostly, she stood with her back against the bar, just watching.

The rain was falling harder and the increase in bodies was making the temperature in the little bar climb steadily. Hot and sweaty figures were writhing against one another on the dance floor. Melanie watched them with amusement and a little bit of envy. She was awed by the moves some of the people displayed, and she tapped her foot to the pounding rhythm.

She was jarred—literally—out of her surveillance when the woman at the bar next to her attempted to lean her elbow on the edge and missed completely. Whatever liquid was in the rock glass she held ended up splashing over Melanie's hip, absorbing warmly into the leg of her jeans.

"Oh my God, I'm sorry," the woman exclaimed, grabbing a handful of napkins from the holder on the bar and clumsily attempting to clean Melanie up. She had chestnut-colored hair cut in a bob and stood an inch or two shorter than Melanie. She swiped uselessly at the stain with fumbling hands.

"It's okay," Melanie assured her, trying to politely avoid the help.

"I'm such a klutz," she said. "I can't do anything right."

"Hey, it's no big deal," Melanie laughed, attempting to lighten the mood. "They're just jeans. Don't worry about it."

When the woman looked up, Melanie was surprised to see her startlingly green eyes bloodshot and rimmed with tears. She grabbed the woman's trembling hands to stop her from cleaning, and ducked to look her directly in the eye. "Really. It's okay." She smiled her warmest smile. "Really."

The woman shut her eyes tightly and tossed the napkins onto the bar with a grimace. She took a second to compose herself, swiping angrily at her eyes. Then she cleared her throat and held her now-empty glass up for the bartender to see. He slid another one her way in a matter of seconds. The woman took a sip, visibly relaxing as the liquid entered her system. Melanie watched in awe as a calm, cool, in-control façade settled over the frazzled, upset one that had been there a minute ago. The transformation was incredible and instantaneous. She looked like a totally different person. Slowly, Melanie came to the realization that this was a woman who probably spent a lot of time here, or someplace just like it...that the liquid in her glass was like air to her.

Glancing at her recently drained bottle of beer, Melanie quickly ordered herself a Coke.

It was strangely comforting, not to mention somewhat arousing to watch the couples around her, especially the women. Many were holding hands or locked together at the lips, but it was the couples that were very subtly—but at the same time very obviously—together, that fascinated her. It was the casual touch on the hip, the gentle stroking of a cheek, the affectionate brushing aside of a stray lock of hair, that entranced Melanie. She watched them with a mix of emotions...pleased that they were in a place where they could feel comfortable enough to be themselves, envious because she wasn't part of it.

She thought about her life, up to that point. She really had nobody special...hadn't ever. Only John, her boyfriend in college, the first man she'd slept with...clumsy and inept as the two of them had been together. Although she hadn't been in love with John, she had loved him very much, and she knew the feelings were reciprocated. When they had finally gotten around to going their separate ways, it had been hard, but necessary. John had admitted, at long last, what Melanie had suspected for some time: he preferred the company of men. They'd said a tearful, but not bitter goodbye, and his parting words had echoed in her head for years. *Maybe you should take a good long look inside yourself, Mel. Don't let life pass you by because you're too blind or too stubborn to see things for what they are.* He'd winked at her, kissed her on the top of her head, and disappeared out of her life. What the hell had that meant? To this day, it was still a mystery to her. The only way for her to avoid thinking too deeply about his warning had been to throw herself into her career, so that's what she had done. Wholeheartedly and headfirst. As long as she had filled her life with something that took most of her time and all of her concentration, she hadn't had to dwell on other things. It had worked, too. She hadn't thought of John in several years. Funny that he would snake his way into her brain now.

"You seem to be having a pretty good time." Lynda was at her side.

"Actually, I am." Melanie smiled over the edge of her glass.

"Sorry I haven't been very entertaining. Dina and Steph tend to monopolize the conversation, and it gets harder and harder to break away."

"Oh, don't worry. I'm a big girl."

Lynda narrowed her eyes at her friend, a small battle playing itself out in her mind. She'd had enough to drink, was sufficiently loose-lipped. She decided to broach the subject she'd been tiptoeing around for nearly a week. "So, what's the deal with you anyway, Ms. Larson?" She kept the tone playful enough not to be intimidating, but serious enough so Melanie would know exactly what she was asking.

Melanie held Lynda's curious but friendly gaze for a long moment, before turning away and taking another sip of her Coke. "When I find out, I'll let you know," she said softly.

Chapter
14

Friday had been a blur for Taylor. Work was incredibly busy, but she had managed a quick trip to the grocery store at lunchtime to pick up what she needed for dinner. She'd even managed to escape her office an hour and a half sooner than usual, not an easy task with the phone ringing off the hook as it had been.

Pleased with herself for leaving when she did, she stood in the kitchen in simple nylon shorts and a T-shirt, chopping zucchini, yellow squash, eggplant, and green peppers for the vegetable lasagna she was going to cook for Melanie. She had taken a bowl of homemade tomato sauce out of the freezer that morning to thaw, and all the remaining ingredients were bagged up and sitting on the kitchen table, complete with a bottle of Riesling from Glenora, Taylor's favorite local winery. A distant rumble of thunder rolled softly across the gray sky as Taylor scooped the diced veggies into a Tupperware bowl and added it to the pile going next door.

She took the cooked strips of pasta out of the strainer where they were cooling in the sink, and deposited them into a Tupperware container as well, adding a little bit of water to keep them from drying out too much. She smiled as she remembered how she used to tease her mom about her plastic bowl collection. She looked up as Ben came in the back door.

"Hi, Dad."

"Hiya, T. How was your day?" Ben was pleased to see his daughter in a good mood.

"Not bad. Not bad at all."

He peered over her shoulder. "Mmm. When do we eat?"

Taylor chuckled. "You can eat whenever you want. There's a little pan in the fridge for you. Pop it in the oven on 375 for about forty-five minutes."

Ben pouted. "What about all this?" He gestured at the bowls and bags, his eyebrows raising at the sight of the wine.

"All this," Taylor mimicked the sweep of his arm, "is for Melanie and me. I'm cooking her dinner at her place...er, Sam's."

"Oh." A flicker of something crossed his handsome features, and Taylor suddenly wished she hadn't just blurted it out like that. The flicker was gone in an instant, and he smiled a smile that didn't reach his dark eyes. "Sounds like fun. Tell her I said hello, would you?"

"Sure, Dad."

She watched him depart the kitchen to change out of his suit, and couldn't keep the guilt from creeping up on her, settling on her shoulders like a boa constrictor.

Ben sighed as he loosened his tie and kicked off his wingtips. He was disappointed. He had hoped to take Melanie up on her dinner invitation from the previous weekend, but he'd gotten sidetracked by an overly demanding client. He should have just called her when he'd thought about it. Maybe he would have beaten Taylor to the punch.

Beaten Taylor? *Listen to yourself, man,* he scolded his

reflection. *You're acting like this is some sort of competition.*

Well, it certainly feels like one, the reflection snapped back. Was it? He'd known his daughter was a lesbian, but he had never spoken to her about it. Not once. Not even a mention. He'd always left that subject for Anna. She was so much better at sensitive things. He wondered now if Taylor resented the fact that he'd never talked to her. Maybe he should have. But, what would he say? "Honey, I know you're gay. Way to go"? No. It was easier for a man like Benjamin Rhodes to let things be. He was not an emotional guy. Taylor knew that. He would always be there for his daughter, no matter what. She knew that, too.

Didn't she?

Now, what to do about Melanie...Maybe she'd be free tomorrow night. He'd give her a call in the morning. He had thought about her quite a lot over the past few days, and was surprised to find that he was anxious for her company once again.

But, did she want his?

He wasn't sure where that thought had come from. He furrowed his graying brows as he pulled on his shorts. She certainly seemed to enjoy his company. And when he'd kissed her, she hadn't pulled away or acted offended.

Still, the thought worried him.

Melanie checked her appearance one more time in the bathroom mirror, straightening her T-shirt and running her hands through her hair before hurrying to answer the knock at the front door. The butterflies in her stomach had morphed into flying saucers, and she was annoyed at her own nervousness. It was just dinner, for Christ's sake. It was just Taylor. What was the big deal? She opened the front door.

"Hey." Taylor smiled, her arms full of plastic grocery bags. Melanie laughed at the sight.

"Hey, yourself." She took two of the bags, stepping aside to allow Taylor to enter.

"Did you bring the entire store?" She tried to see what the bags contained. "What's for dinner, dear?"

"Vegetable lasagna. Okay with you?"

"Sounds wonderful."

They lugged their parcels to the small kitchen. Melanie began to snoop in each of them. She yelped in surprise when her hand was slapped playfully.

"Get out of there," Taylor scolded.

"I was just peeking." Melanie pouted.

If she uses that boo-boo face on me, she'll get anything she wants, Taylor thought with amusement. "No peeking."

"Can't I help?"

"You can pour the wine."

"Okay." She jumped at the task, searching Sam's kitchen drawers until she found the corkscrew. She scrutinized the label carefully. "Glenora. Hmm."

"It's one of our local wineries...well, I say local. It's about forty-five minutes from here on Seneca Lake. There's a whole slew of them around here. Glenora happens to be one of my favorites."

Melanie uncorked the bottle, nodding with appreciation at the aroma that wafted up from the opening. "I don't think I've ever seen a winery."

"Well, we'll have to take care of that then, won't we? My friends and I go on a wine tour every year in the fall. We get a van and one of us is the designated driver. Then, we drive down by the lakes, and hit all the wineries we come across, tasting any samples they'll give us. There are dozens of places, and there's really some good stuff around here."

"That sounds like fun."

"It is. Maybe you could come with us on our next tour."

"Maybe I could."

Melanie smiled up at Taylor, who was smiling back,

and handed her a glass of wine. The redhead lifted hers in a toast. "Here's to new friendships."

"To new friendships." They clinked glasses and sipped.

"Oh, that's good," Melanie commented.

"Told you." Taylor turned back to the counter to work on dinner.

Melanie stood on her tiptoes, and peered over Taylor's shoulder at the pan, which Taylor had coated with a thin layer of sauce and the first level of pasta. She wasn't using any utensils - other than a spoon for the sauce - just her hands.

"Teach me," Melanie requested softly.

Taylor swallowed hard as Melanie's voice tickled her neck, sending an exciting chill down her spine. Then she nodded. "Okay. Come here. Stand here." She grasped the older woman's shoulders, stepping aside to position Melanie in front of her.

"This is a lot of stuff," Melanie noted, taking in the array of bowls, each containing a different ingredient.

"Yeah, but it's no big deal. Lasagna is very easy, just construction. You just have to put it together. It's a layering process. Okay, we've got the first layer of pasta down. Now, grab that bowl and put a little sauce on the strips."

Melanie spooned some sauce onto the pasta. She felt undeniably safe and warm with Taylor pressed against her back. "Like this?"

"Yup. Spread it around a bit." After Melanie did as she was told, Taylor moved on. "Next, some veggies."

"Which ones?" Each vegetable was in a different one of the four bowls.

"You're the cook. Your choice."

"Zucchini," she stated confidently, reaching for a fork. Taylor caught her hand.

"No, no. Use your hands. A real cook doesn't need utensils. My mom never did. 'That's why God gave you hands,' she used to say. Use 'em."

Melanie grinned. "Okay, but you have to let go."

"Oh. Right." Taylor snatched her hand away as if Melanie's skin had burned her. "Sorry."

Melanie sprinkled diced zucchini, then peppers, then squash, then eggplant over the pasta. Next came some parmesan cheese, along with a touch of shredded mozzarella. Taylor held her position directly behind Melanie, far too happy there to even think about moving. Every now and then she'd help her sprinkle or straighten or spread, her arms around either side, her lips very close to Melanie's ear.

If I had any idea cooking was this much fun, I'd have taken it up long ago, Melanie thought.

Both women found themselves mildly disappointed when they finished their task.

There was one more sealed bowl on the table that hadn't been opened. "Uh oh," Melanie said, when she noticed it. "Did we forget something?"

Taylor snatched the bowl away before Melanie could look inside. "Nope. That's a surprise."

"Dessert?" Melanie's eyes lit up.

"Maybe," Taylor teased as she put the bowl in the refrigerator, and refilled their glasses. "You'll just have to wait and see."

An hour and a half later, they sat on the sofa, slumped and groaning.

"I'm stuffed," Melanie whined. "God, that was *so* good."

"I'll say. You're a terrific cook." She winked. "Think you're too stuffed for dessert? It's okay if you are," she taunted. "I can just take it home. It's no problem."

"Did I say stuffed?" Melanie asked, sitting up straight. "I meant *almost* stuffed. Not quite stuffed yet."

"Stay here. And no peeking."

Melanie smiled as she watched Taylor's departing form disappear into the kitchen. She couldn't remember when she'd had such a relaxing, comfortable, fun evening. And they hadn't even started watching Xena yet. Taylor wasn't leaving any time soon. The thought warmed her insides.

"Okay, close your eyes," Taylor ordered from the kitchen.

"What?"

"You heard me. Close 'em."

Melanie did as she was instructed, listening for, then feeling Taylor's presence as she came closer.

"Okay. Open your mouth."

Melanie cocked her head. "Yeah, right. So you can feed me a jalapeno or something? How stupid do I look?"

Taylor chuckled at the hesitation. "I would never do that. Come on. Open up."

Melanie still hesitated, unsure.

Taylor's voice became softer, almost sexy. Their faces were barely inches apart. "Do you trust me, Melanie?" She smiled as she saw Melanie's throat move when she swallowed. The older woman nodded and opened her mouth. Taylor gently deposited the spoon on her tongue and watched her lips close around it. Her eyes popped open, then closed again she moaned sensuously.

"Oh my God. Chocolate mousse. I love chocolate mousse. And this is *real* whipped cream, isn't it? Do you know how long it's been since I've had *real* whipped cream and not that Cool Whip crap?" She pried the spoon from Taylor's hand, stealing the bowl as well. "How did you know I love this?"

Taylor shrugged, incredibly pleased with the reaction. "Lucky guess."

Melanie moaned again at the second spoonful. "God, this is good. Where did you get it?"

"I made it."

Melanie blinked at her. "You did not."

"Did, too." She went to the kitchen and returned with her own bowl and spoon, thoroughly proud of herself.

Melanie looked like a little kid, her legs curled up under her body, completely content with her dessert, licking the spoon clean each time. She smiled at Taylor as she sat on the couch next to her. "Thank you."

"My pleasure."

Melanie laughed. "Not this time. This time, the pleasure is *mine.*"

Not entirely, Taylor thought.

Taylor woke to the distant rumbling of thunder. It took her several moments to orient herself to her surroundings, finally remembering she was in Melanie's house. Funny how she thought of it as such. After all, Melanie didn't even live here. She was a guest. It was Sam's house. Or was it? It felt so right having Melanie here, like she'd been around all along. Taylor felt an uncomfortable anxiety when she thought of Melanie leaving to go back home.

Taylor could smell the nighttime summer rain through the open screen door, clean and natural, and she knew the world would be sparkling when the sun finally rose. The television was still on, its eerie blue glow bathing the tiny living room in a milky light, not unlike the moon. Miniscule dots of snow danced on the screen and Taylor figured they must have fallen asleep during the last episode, the VCR automatically stopping at the end of the tape. They'd been watching while stretched out on the open sofa bed after Melanie caught Taylor shifting uncomfortably and suggested they pull it out. When they had managed to get as close together as they currently were, Taylor couldn't recall. She swallowed hard, her heart fluttering in her chest as she realized that Melanie was sleeping soundly in her arms.

The older woman was half on top of Taylor, her head tucked snugly under Taylor's chin, pillowed comfortably on her chest, the sweet, peachy fragrance of her hair filling Taylor's nostrils teasingly. Her left arm was draped loosely across Taylor's ribcage, just below—and dangerously close to—her breasts, and her left leg was resting comfortably between Taylor's thighs, as if that was where it belonged. Her breathing was deep and even, the cadence of a soundly sleeping body that effectively pinned Taylor to the bed.

Taylor noticed, although not really to her surprise, that she was as much to blame for their position, as her left arm seemed to have wrapped itself around Melanie's shoulders possessively, ensuring their closeness. Had all this been done during the innocence of slumber? Had they gravitated to each other like this as they slept? Taylor found herself smiling at the notion of their two bodies moving toward one another on some subconscious plane. *Well, if you won't be together while you're awake...*

She gazed at the arm lying across her body. The unblemished, creamy skin downed very lightly with reddish-blonde hair. She studied the hand, its neatly filed nails, finished with a coat of clear polish. The delicate fingers relaxed against the sheet. She had a flash of that hand on her own body, in her hair, tugging gently. She swallowed hard, moving her eyes to gaze upon the beautiful face that rested on her chest. The glow from the television cast soft shadows, intensifying the angles and planes of Melanie's cheeks, the fullness of her lips. Taylor wet her own with her tongue as she tried not to think about how sweet that mouth must taste, how incredible it would be to devour those lips with hers, how intoxicating it would feel to slip her own tongue between them and explore what lay beyond. She tried not to look at the intricate folds of the ear, a diamond stud peeking out from under gold-tinted scarlet strands; tried not to imagine herself whispering into it, telling its owner how amazing Taylor was going to make her feel, flicking it teasingly with her tongue.

Okay, cut it out, her inner voice scolded her. *Where is this train of thought getting you?* Before she could defend herself against her own mind, Melanie shifted in her sleep, pressing her knee firmly into Taylor's groin. Taylor stifled a gasp, shocked by her own wetness, praying Melanie was sleeping deeply enough that she didn't notice the dampness on her knee that must surely have soaked through the thin fabric of Taylor's shorts. She couldn't remember ever having been so aroused just by being near someone. And Melanie wasn't even trying.

With massive effort, Taylor managed to get herself to relax, and eventually, she drifted back into a light sleep, knowing the sun would be rising in a short period of time.

The next time she opened her eyes, the sun was streaking through the picture window, a rectangle of yellow light caressing Melanie's bare calf, still draped over Taylor's leg. Taylor was both nervous and delighted that neither of them had abandoned the positions she had discovered them in a few short hours before. They hadn't even shifted slightly.

For some unknown reason, she couldn't bring herself to move. Her mind screamed at her to remedy the situation before Melanie woke up, but her body wouldn't obey her. It was simply way too comfortable, and did its best to shut out the shrieks of her always-smarter-when-it-comes-to-these-things brain. Instead, she listened to her own heartbeat, and felt the other beating so close to hers, with the hand she had rested on the redhead's back. She slowly released a deep sigh of contentment, wishing to the heavens that this didn't feel as good as it did.

Several long minutes passed, and Melanie stirred. Taylor took the opportunity to inhale one last lung full of her sweet-smelling hair, closing her eyes as she did so.

Melanie opened her blue eyes slowly, blinking against the daylight. She took a deep, awakening breath, feeling better than she had since...she couldn't remember. She'd slept so well. She examined the soft cotton T-shirt her head was pillowed on, finding it amusing that she couldn't remember falling asleep. She and Taylor had watched about a zillion episodes of Xena, laughing and discussing each episode, its pros and cons. Melanie remembered finding the tape with the episode titled "The Quill is Mightier." She knew immediately that it was the perfect name for the bookstore. She'd decided not to mention it to Taylor, to surprise her, and...

Her eyes widened as she suddenly became conscious of her body's position. She mentally cataloged all her body parts, as well as what each of them seemed to be atop. She was mortified to realize she had fallen asleep half-on and half-off of Taylor.

She swallowed hard, and slowly raised her head. She felt a mixture of dread, overshadowed by something she didn't want to deal with, but both melted away when she met those gorgeous dark eyes smiling back at her.

"Morning, sleepyhead," Taylor said.

"Hi." Melanie could immediately feel the blush creeping up her neck, feel her ears turn red. She extricated herself from the tangle of limbs. "I'm sorry about this..." she began, unsure how to finish.

"Oh, no problem." Taylor brushed the comment aside as if shooing a fly. "Did you sleep okay?"

"As a matter of fact, I slept great." She was surprised by the honest admission. Then, she lowered her eyes sheepishly. "I hope you weren't too uncomfortable."

"Actually, I slept like a baby. I don't even remember drifting off."

Melanie smiled at that. "Me neither."

"Hey, listen," Taylor said a few minutes later, as they worked together to fold up the sofa bed, and straighten the living room, each avoiding further discussion about their bodies' betrayals. "Work has box seats to the Red Wings games, and I've got them for Sunday night. Remember, we drove by Frontier Field?" When Melanie nodded, she continued. "Would you be interested in going with me?" She kept her eyes on the bed she was tidying and babbled on, afraid to look Melanie in the eye. "It's a blast. The seats are great. We can eat hot dogs and cotton candy until we explode."

"Well, how can I possibly refuse an offer like that?" Melanie chuckled.

Taylor's smile lit up her face, and she felt a mix of relief and anxiety. "Game's at seven, so I'll pick you up around six thirty?"

"It's a date." Melanie had to make a conscious effort to keep from wincing at her own choice of words.

Saturday morning's sun didn't last long, and Melanie was treated to some typical, temperamental Rochester weather, complete with gray skies and distantly rumbling thunder that continued on for much of the day.

She was seated at the small kitchen table, legal papers spread out everywhere. She was busy going over the details her uncle had FedEx'd to the bookstore earlier in the week. Though she considered herself relatively savvy in the ways of business proceedings, she was baffled by much of the legalese that lay before her. She was sure everything was as it should be, knowing Uncle Phil, but she didn't like to decorate anything with her signature unless she knew exactly what it was she was signing.

After studying the paperwork for several days, refusing to show this particular weakness by phoning her uncle and simply asking him what certain things meant, she gave in and decided she did, indeed, need some help.

The phone rang just as she was reaching for it, scaring the hell out of her. She sat with her hand over her racing heart for three rings before snatching it up.

"Hello?"

"Melanie?"

"Uh huh."

"It's Ben."

She took a deep breath, her heart rate finally decreasing. "Hi, Ben. Well, this is weird. I was just about to call you."

"You were?" The pleasant surprise in his voice was obvious.

"Yeah. I was wondering if I could pick your brain for a few minutes. I've got the papers for the bookstore from my uncle and there are a couple parts that I'm stuck on. I thought maybe you'd have a better handle on this sort of thing."

"Under one condition."

"What's that?"

"Since I was phoning you to call in my debt, how about we do it over dinner?"

"You're sure? I don't want to bother you with this stuff if you'd rather not deal with it." Melanie hated that she couldn't grasp some of the phrases, didn't like to admit to a lack of understanding. It made her feel dependent, something she despised.

"Not at all," he assured her in an easy tone. "Why don't you meet me by my car in an hour and bring your papers with you?"

"That would be great." She tried not to let her relief appear in her voice. "Thank you, Ben."

"Certainly. See you soon."

Melanie hung up the phone feeling much more at ease. She gathered up the papers into a neat pile and put them in her briefcase. In doing so, she noticed she still had the Katherine Forrest novel she'd borrowed from the book-store. She took it out, skimming the synopsis on the back. She held it for several minutes more before setting it care-fully on the kitchen table and heading into the bedroom to change her clothes.

Across the yard, Ben was smiling smugly to himself. *She'd been about to call, eh?* A wave of relief had swept over him at that statement from her. He'd been less than pleased when Taylor had strolled in this morning, whis-tling as she fixed herself a bowl of disgustingly colorful cereal.

"Glad you could make it home," he'd remarked sternly, eyes glued to the paper he was reading.

"I was only next door, Dad," she'd replied, brushing it off as if he were being unreasonable.

"The phone doesn't work over there?"

"Dad, I'm twenty-seven years old. Do I really need to check in with you if I'm having too much fun to come home?"

He'd peered over the newspaper at her, and she'd smiled innocently. Her eyes were twinkling mischievously, masking some secret from him. Having too much fun to

come home? He'd had to bite his tongue to keep from asking exactly what she and Melanie had been doing over
there.

"No, I suppose not," he'd replied grudgingly, deciding
he didn't really want to know anyway.

When he had decided to ask Melanie to dinner
tonight—her own promise to buy him a meal last week
offered up the perfect excuse—he was afraid Taylor may
have already nabbed her for the evening. He winced at the
verb, erasing it from his head with a shake. But, lo and
behold, she had been just about to call him. Ha!

Choosing not to analyze the part of him that was still
treating Melanie as the prize in a contest between father
and daughter, he skipped up the stairs two at a time, trying
to decide what he would wear to dinner, feeling like an
eighteen-year-old kid. Tonight, he was going to impress
the hell out of Melanie Larson.

Chapter
15

Melanie felt infinitely better about the legal aspects of purchasing the bookstore after she'd gone over them with Ben. Asking for his help had been a smart move. He seemed to be well versed in such things, and Melanie was happy to find out that she hadn't been that far off in her interpretations. According to Ben, everything looked to be in order, but he gave her the business card of his own attorney and suggested she double-check with him, just to be safe.

They'd spent almost three hours in a comfortable booth at a little Italian restaurant called Rizzi's, which was nestled just outside of the city proper. The food had been superb, especially the appetizer of greens and beans, which she'd suggested they share. Ben had warned against it, claiming that once she tasted them, she wouldn't want to give him even the smallest of nibbles. He was right. She'd had to make a conscious effort to keep from bringing the bowl to her lips and actually drinking the buttery garlic broth that was left when she'd eaten the last leafy bite.

They'd talked almost exclusively about business, a little about the bookstore and a lot about Rucker and Steele. Melanie tried not to notice that Taylor was avoided as a topic of conversation, no matter how often she tried to bring up the woman's name. It was also rather obvious how quickly the subject changed when she'd mentioned the theme of the bookstore. He'd found a tangent somehow, and segued into an in-depth story about one of his clients.

In the two weeks she'd known him, Melanie had found Ben to be nothing but charming. Tonight, she'd found his behavior...odd. That was the only word she could think of to describe it. Maybe she'd ask Taylor about it tomorrow.

For his part, Ben had seemed not to notice that Melanie had grown uncharacteristically quieter as the evening wore on. He'd been generally pleased at the way the evening had turned out. He'd patted himself on the back for sticking to general subject matter, avoiding his daughter like the plague. He'd known his shying away from the "feminist bookstore" topic was less than discreet, but she'd caught him off guard on that one and besides, he wasn't sure how he'd felt about it. Feminist bookstore? He didn't like the sound of that. The little voice in his brain giggled quietly.

Melanie was embarrassed now at the wave of relief that washed over her as they pulled into the driveway of Ben's picturesque home. Ben spoke as she reached for the door handle to let herself out.

"It's still fairly early. Care to join me for a nightcap?"

"Oh," Melanie stumbled, flipping frantically through the Excuses File in her mind. "You know, I really have a lot of work to do if I want to get this bookstore in working order."

"But, tomorrow's Sunday," he pointed out, his disappointment clearly written on his face.

She smiled, trying to make light of the situation. "Retail knows no weekends."

Realizing he wasn't going to change her mind, he relented. The last thing he wanted to do was push too hard. "All right, then. At least let me see you to the door like a proper gentleman."

Melanie was touched by the chivalrous gesture. "I'd

like that." They began a leisurely stroll across the property. "Ben, thank you so much for looking over my papers. I really thought I'd be able to figure them out, but...God. I think lawyers must make up words as they go along, just to make the rest of us feel stupid."

Ben chuckled. "If you understood every word in a legal document, you wouldn't need a lawyer. Think of it as self-preservation on their part."

They reached the front door of the carriage house, Melanie bending her head to unlock it. Ben became suddenly uncomfortable. "Melanie..."

"Mmm hmm?" When she looked up, he had trouble meeting her eyes. "What's the matter, Ben? What's wrong?"

He blew out a determined breath. "That's just it. Nothing's wrong." He fidgeted, searching for the right words.

Melanie felt the red flags popping up all over the place.

"I keep waiting for something to be out of whack," he explained, "but it hasn't happened. I know there's quite a bit of difference in our ages, but..." He took hold of her hand. If only she knew how hard it was for him to open up this way. "I'm just really enjoying spending time with you."

There. He would leave it at that. If she didn't know what it was he was trying to convey, she must be thick.

Melanie stood blinking at him, not sure how to respond, trying to force a smile that didn't look forced. She must have succeeded because he smiled back and squeezed her hand.

"I'll let you get some rest." He needed to get out of there, fast. He always felt so vulnerable when he let somebody see what he was feeling. He wanted to run. "Thanks for dinner. I had a...magnificent evening." He kissed her softly on the cheek, absently rubbing his thumb over the spot. Then, he turned away, heading back to his house, leaving Melanie standing on the stoop, wondering how the hell she hadn't seen this coming.

She let herself into the house, leaning heavily against the door once she was inside.

"Shit."

She closed her eyes and shook her head, disgusted with herself for allowing things to go this far, for not politely shutting Ben down from the start. Isn't that what she should have done? What she'd wanted to do?

No, she admitted to herself. That's not what she had wanted. She had enjoyed his company very much. He was intelligent, as well as respectful. He talked to her like she was on his level, not like he was several steps above her and she should look up to him, wishing to be as large as he was someday, like so many of the men in Chicago. Ben was different. Ben was what her mother would refer to as "a good catch." Yes, he was nearly two decades older than she was, but so what? Such couplings were more and more common these days. She should be flattered and consider herself lucky to have somebody like Benjamin Rhodes interested in her. Shouldn't she?

So why did she want to hide under the nearest piece of furniture and never come out?

Her mind reeled the entire time she undressed, pulling on flannel boxers and a long-sleeved T-shirt. It was spinning as she cleaned up the breakfast and lunch dishes she had left earlier, and it continued to spin while she scrubbed the bathroom until she could see her own reflection in the tub. She was just about ready to pull her own hair out when she noticed the book she'd left on the kitchen table.

That's it, she told herself. *I'll just put all this crap away and lose myself in a good book for a while. Things will be much clearer later.*

She made herself a cup of tea, carrying it to the over-stuffed chair she had been drawn to that very first day she arrived. She curled up with the book and her tea, an afghan thrown over her feet, much as she had envisioned herself then. With a contented sigh, she opened to the first page of *Curious Wine.*

Chapter
16

The Red Wings were having an awful season. Their record was hardly impressive, and by the seventh inning, it was clear that Taylor and Melanie were about to witness their ninth loss in a row. However, neither woman seemed to mind. They were having too good a time.

The seats Taylor had commandeered from her office were wonderful. They were on the third base side of home plate, but up one level, affording them a perfect view of the entire field. They were in the front row of their section, which meant there was nobody sitting in front of them. They put their feet up on the railing, stuffing themselves full of hot dogs, beer, French fries and for Melanie, cotton candy.

Melanie was impressed with Frontier Field. It was quite large, smartly organized, and very clean. The seats were surprisingly comfortable, and the choice of foods was so wide, it flustered her momentarily. Taylor explained to her how the stadium had only been constructed three years prior, and was now a source of pride for the people of Rochester. The previous field had been in a not-so-pleasant section of the city and was about half the size, with very little parking. The development of this new stadium had been part of Mayor Johnson's overall plan to rebuild downtown Rochester, to give it a facelift of sorts, bringing people into the heart of the city without fear of crime. It was working remarkably well. With the addition of the stadium came many new restaurants and bars, catering to the pregame and post-game crowds, filling up storefronts and warehouses that had been previously vacant or falling apart. With the improved appearance came confident patrons. Plus, Taylor informed her, the Red Wings were the farm team for the Baltimore Orioles and Rochesterians took their baseball very seriously. Despite their lackluster record, the stadium was nearly filled to capacity with screaming Red Wings fans.

Taylor sat down, handing Melanie another beer, and smiled, sipping her own Coke. "You having a good time?"

"I'm having a *great* time. This is wonderful. Can we do it again sometime?" She sipped her beer, her blue eyes watching Taylor over the rim of the plastic souvenir cup the brunette had gotten for her. The joy on Taylor's face was unmistakable as she turned back to the game, unable to keep the smile from spreading widely, making her sparkling brown eyes crinkle around the corners.

"Absolutely. I'm enjoying myself, too." She left it at that, afraid to venture too far into how much she truly was enjoying herself, for fear of ruining the moment by scaring her companion. She decided to change the subject. "Do you want something else to eat?"

Melanie widened her eyes, clamping a hand over her stomach. "Ugh...Not unless you want to be carrying me home in a garbage bag."

"Well, maybe you shouldn't have eaten *all* the cotton candy. Ever heard of moderation?" Taylor teased.

"Hey," Melanie defended herself with a mock-frown, "I haven't had cotton candy since I was a kid. I lost control. It happens."

"Apparently."

Melanie beamed, turning back to the game in time to

see a double play by the Wings. She and Taylor both cheered and whistled, along with the rest of the crowd. Melanie couldn't remember when she'd had such a good time. Things were so different when she was with Taylor. She shook her head in amazement. There was no pressure to impress when she was with the brunette. She felt like herself, like she could be herself and not have to make any excuses for it. She felt like she could be silly or goofy or serious or passionate, and it would be okay. Taylor would be okay with her, no matter what. How she was so sure of this, she had no idea. She just was.

When she'd dated in the past—what few instances there had been—she'd always felt like her date expected a certain behavior from her, like they had some preconceived notion of whom she was and how she should act. Even Ben seemed to expect her to fall right into his business-centered conversation, no matter what she felt like talking about or what kind of mood she was in. It wasn't like that with Taylor. Being with her was pressure-free, simple, and fun. She realized with surprise that she could easily spend all her free time with this woman and never be bored or uncomfortable. She wasn't exactly sure how that made her feel. Nervous seemed to be the best description. She grimaced at the fact that she could go from incredibly happy to totally neurotic in a matter of seconds.

The Red Wings dropped the game, 4-1, of course, but Taylor and Melanie had laughed a lot and completely enjoyed themselves. Each was sorry to see the evening end. More than once, Taylor had wished she could turn the clock back, just an hour or two, so she'd have more time to spend with Melanie. She had stopped fighting it...this feeling she had around the older woman. She knew nothing good could come of it, but she found it impossible to stay away. At first it was no big deal, because Melanie would eventually go back to Chicago, and Taylor would get on with her life. The purchase of the bookstore had changed all that drastically, and Taylor found herself in much deeper than she had planned. It was as though she had two little angels, but they didn't sit on each shoulder, as one would expect. Instead, one of them floated in front of Taylor, constantly reaching out for Melanie. The other followed behind Taylor, constantly kicking her in the butt, muttering about how stupid she was and how she should know better than to let herself fall for somebody she couldn't have. Taylor, sandwiched between the two halves of her conscience, had no idea what the next step should be.

As they pulled into the driveway, Melanie turned to Taylor and asked, "Can you stay a bit? I've had such a good time, I don't want the evening to end. I've got Pepsi, unless you want a beer." She had noticed that Taylor only had one beer early on in the game, and Melanie admired the fact that she took a responsible approach, since she had driven.

Despite the bickering of the two "angels," Taylor tried not to act too excited by the invite. "I'd love a beer, if you think you can put up with me a bit longer."

Melanie bit back the teasing remark that fought to shoot off her tongue, and exited the car without comment, heading for the carriage house, Taylor close behind. As they reached the door and Melanie stepped up onto the front stoop to unlock it, she turned to ask Taylor when she thought they could go to another game. She was unaware that Taylor was only inches behind her and when she turned, they ran right into one another. Their faces were barely two inches apart, their eyes level since Melanie was standing on a step.

They stood frozen.

Taylor dropped her gaze to Melanie's full lips, and when the older woman wet the bottom one nervously with the tip of her tongue, it was all over. Taylor lost all sense of control, and found herself leaning forward, covering the distance between them and pressing her lips to Melanie's, kissing her softly, the "angel" behind her screaming at the top of its lungs, kicking as hard as it could.

To Taylor's surprise, Melanie did not pull away, nor

did she slap Taylor, which was the response the brunette was expecting. Instead, she pressed into Taylor, and the kiss became deeper. Melanie's lips parted under Taylor's and her heart pounded thunderously in her chest as their tongues touched, flitting uncertainly around one another.

Several minutes later, when they finally pulled themselves away from each other, they were both heaving breathlessly.

Melanie swallowed hard. "Oh, boy."

"Yeah," was all Taylor could manage.

Melanie's eyes darted around the yard nervously, finally settling on Taylor's as she swallowed again. "I've...um...I never...I..." she stammered. Taking a deep, steadying breath, she closed her eyes and whispered softly, "I've never done that before. Kissed a woman, I mean."

Taylor cupped Melanie's chin so she could look into her eyes again, and smiled reassuringly. "I've never been anybody's first kiss before." That earned her a small grin from the redhead. "Are you okay?" Taylor asked, trying to cautiously get a feel for exactly where they stood.

Melanie touched her fingertips to her own lips, still tingling from the contact with Taylor's. She then reached across the small space between the two of them and touched Taylor's lips, absolutely astounded by the softness of them. Before she could think twice, she pressed her mouth to Taylor's once again, bolder this time, probing and exploring, allowing Taylor to do the same.

Endless moments later, Melanie wrenched her lips away for air. "God," she gasped as she did so. "Where on earth did you learn to kiss like that?"

Taylor felt herself blushing under the compliment. "I used to practice on my teddy bear." She shrugged with a grin.

"Lucky bear," Melanie stated seriously.

Taylor gathered Melanie in her arms and hugged her tightly. They stood silently on the stoop for long moments, wrapped around one another, each lost in the feelings that were pummeling them. Finally, Taylor made the decision for both of them.

"Maybe I should take a rain check on that beer, huh?" She phrased it as a question on purpose, giving Melanie the chance to agree or disagree. She didn't want Melanie to think she was bailing on her, but she also didn't think she could keep her hands to herself once they were inside. She'd never wanted anybody so much in her life, but the last thing Melanie needed at this point was pressure.

Melanie looked relieved at the suggestion, smiling sheepishly. "That's probably a good idea." She paused, taking Taylor's hand and examining it as she sorted her thoughts. "I really had a good time tonight."

"Yeah?"

"Yeah."

"You're not just saying that?"

"I'm not just saying that."

"Think we can do it again? Um...I mean the game. Well, the kissing part too, but I meant the game..." She sighed and pointed to her own mouth. "There's probably room in here for your foot, too."

Melanie laughed, feeling the tension ease away. "I'd love to do it again. And I think I mean the kissing part, too." She squeezed Taylor's hand and kissed her softly on the cheek. "Good night. Sleep well, okay?"

Taylor waited until Melanie was in and closing the door before she turned to head home. She wasn't sure if she should be elated—which she was—or terrified—which she was. This could be either really, really good or really, really bad. She knew already that sleep would be far from her reach that night. She could practically hear the cold shower calling her all the way across the yard

It was as though some unseen force had surgically planted a grin onto Taylor's face as she slept. She felt it the minute the alarm went off and she opened her eyes. There it was on her reflection in the mirror, and try as she

might, she couldn't even wash it off in the shower.

She tried to be considerate as she fixed herself breakfast. Smiling like the proverbial cat that ate the canary certainly wasn't going to sit well with Ben. He knew with whom she had spent the evening. Nevertheless, he had noticed his daughter's cheerful demeanor, and lines of concern creased his forehead almost immediately. He tried unsuccessfully to focus on the stocks page of his morning paper.

As her Fruit Loops pinged musically into the bowl from the box, Taylor glanced out the window, noting with a bit of apprehension that Melanie's Jeep was gone.

She had toyed with the idea of bringing her breakfast, but had decided against it. Melanie had said she'd never kissed a woman before. Then, logically, it was safe to assume she'd never *been with* a woman before either. In turn, that could only mean that the whole lesbian thing was new to her. Or news to her, as the case may be. *Hell, it was news to all of us at one time or another*, Taylor thought. She herself had been a fairly late bloomer, so she could understand, to a certain extent, the confusion Melanie was probably feeling over what had happened last night.

The hard part for Taylor was trying to decide what she should do for the older woman. She wanted nothing more than to be there for her, answer her questions if she could, hug her when it was needed. On the other hand, Taylor was actually part of the problem. A big part. Maybe it would be best for her to just stay away. Maybe she should just leave the ball in Melanie's court and sit tight until Melanie decided it was okay to play.

Much as she hated the second option—she was not a patient woman and waiting was not something she did well—she knew it was the right decision for Melanie. It wasn't going to be easy for the redhead. There would be mountains of questions and Taylor had the sneaking suspicion that Lynda would be up to the role of Answer Queen. Anger, confusion, and denial...all emotions Taylor had experienced during her own realization.

Then, of course, there was also the possibility that
Taylor didn't even want to think about, the one that would
squash her the flattest. There was the possibility that last
night's kiss was simply a fluke, a by-product of the fun
they'd had and the beer Melanie had consumed. The poten-
tiality that she may have been a daring little experiment
managed to tone the blinding smile down a few watts, and
Taylor tried not to let herself dwell on it.

"I was thinking," Ben said suddenly, snapping Taylor
out of her analyses. When her eyes cleared and met his, he
continued. "It's been nearly two years, T. I am so grateful
to you for moving back here and looking out for me."

"It was no big deal, Dad, really." Taylor brushed off
the gratitude, having an idea where this was going.

"You need your own space. I know that."

"You're throwing me out?" she deadpanned.

"Wha—? No. Absolutely not. You can live here until
you're ninety-five. You know that." His voice softened
when he figured out she was teasing him. "I just want you
to know that it's okay with me when you're ready to go."

"Okay," she replied simply. "Thanks, Dad."

He winked at her as he gathered his briefcase, donning
his suit jacket and heading to work. Giving Taylor his per-
mission to leave was a big step for him. Taylor was aware
of that. Her father was by no means an open or emotional
man. How her mother had put up with the constant mind-
reading, she'd never figure out. In BenSpeak—as she had
affectionately and sometimes not so affectionately dubbed
his way of expressing himself—he had just told her that he
was ready to move on, to finally let go of Anna and get on
with his life. The realization brought tears to her eyes. As
she blinked them away, another thought hit her.

Was it just a coincidence that Ben had made such a
monumental decision only weeks after meeting Melanie?

*God, she's having quite an effect on this family, isn't
she?* she thought wryly. *I hope Frankie doesn't decide to
come for a visit any time soon.*

Melanie hadn't been able to even see sleep in the distance, let alone grab some for herself. At five in the morning, she had gotten up, dressed in some gym shorts and a sweatshirt, snatched up the classifieds from Sunday's paper, and headed off in the Jeep, no particular destination in mind, just unable to sit still any longer. She wasn't one to have trouble sleeping. As a matter of fact, she couldn't now, as she coasted slowly up and down the streets of Rochester, even come up with another instance when she'd tossed and turned as much as she had the previous night.

She wasn't sure what to make of that little tidbit. This whole thing was effecting her more than anything else in her life...more than her parents' divorce, more than her choosing a college, even more than taking the job with Rucker and Steele, relocating to a large, unfamiliar city. No, this was big. Way big. A woman had kissed her.

A woman had kissed her.

She let the phrase roll around in her head, then said it aloud.

"A woman kissed me."

She listened to the way it sounded, then edited it.

"Taylor kissed me."

An entirely different meaning, and almost the whole truth.

"I kissed her back."

Closer. She cocked her head, as if listening, then reworded.

"*I* kissed Taylor."

The words sounded odd, but not uncomfortable. She pressed her luck.

"I kissed Taylor and enjoyed every second of it."

She pulled the Jeep to a stop in the small parking area behind her bookstore. Leaning her forehead against the steering wheel, she exhaled a long, slow, breath.

"And I want to do it again."

There it was. The truth, the whole truth and nothing

but the truth.

After several minutes of silence, she lifted her head. According to the clock on the dash, it was nearly seven. She'd meandered aimlessly for almost two hours. Grabbing the newspaper section she had brought with her and the Rochester map she had purchased during her first week in town, she locked the Jeep and wandered down Monroe Avenue.

Chapter
17

The lunch rush wouldn't start for another hour and a half. Lynda had noticed Melanie's Jeep in the back lot and decided to pop into the bookstore and say hi.

She found her friend slumped into one of the over-stuffed chairs, her legs thrown over one arm, the copy of *Curious Wine* on the floor, her blue eyes gazing off into space.

"Hey," Lynda called cheerfully. "You got a damn name for this joint yet?"

"Sorry, what?" Melanie looked as though she'd been jarred awake.

"A name. Have you found a name for this place?"

"Oh. Yeah."

Silence.

"Mel?"

"Hmm?"

"Name? For the shop?" Lynda studied her closely. She looked confused, a little scared, and just generally disheveled. "What is going on with you? Are you okay? Did something happen? Paperwork fall through? Sam go through the roof? What is it?"

Without meeting the café owner's eyes, Melanie

asked, "Lynda, when did you know? I mean, when did the realization that you were gay actually hit you?"

Here we go, Lynda thought. She took a seat in the other chair and scrutinized Melanie carefully. "Well, let's see. I was twenty-two and a senior in college. Looking back now, I know I always had 'crushes' on women, but I was raised out in the country by conservative, old-fashioned parents. I didn't even know what a lesbian was. Anyway, during the summer of my senior year, I joined a recreational softball team. A high school friend of mine played, and they were looking for a second baseman. I found out later that the entire team was gay and I had no idea. How 'bout that?" She chuckled at Melanie, who smiled in return. "Anyway, there was a woman named Sarah on the team. Short stop. She was a couple years older than me, but we hit it off. We were inseparable for the whole season.

"During the end of the season party, Sarah and I bailed out of the house and went for a walk. We got to talking about things...parents, school, and life in general. She told me she was gay, along with the rest of the team—boy was I embarrassed—and..." She stopped, still amused by a story she'd told hundreds of times. "I still don't know exactly how she did it, but she managed to get me to realize and admit that I was, in fact, a lesbian. She talked about her past, about growing up, about girls and teachers she'd had crushes on and it was like she was talking about me. I couldn't believe it. I'd finally found somebody who understood me. All this time I had thought there was something weird about me, but come to find out, I was just gay."

"Were you surprised to find out?" Melanie asked softly.

"Stunned. It seemed so simple. Why none of my relationships with men had ever worked. Why all my friends in high school were worried if they didn't have a boyfriend and not only did I not have one, I didn't want one." Her eyes fell to the book on the floor and she gestured to it. "You read it?"

Melanie followed her glance. "Yup."

"Liked it?"

"It was beautiful. I loved it." She looked like she wanted to say something more, so Lynda waited her out. "I found it interesting that the two main characters fell for each other so quickly," she finally said.

Lynda chuckled. "Occupational hazard of being a lesbian."

"Really?"

"What does a lesbian bring on her second date?"

Melanie furrowed her brow at the riddle, then shrugged. "I give. What?"

"A U-Haul."

Lynda was relieved to see Melanie's face split into a genuine smile. She even laughed out loud. After a couple of minutes, Lynda leaned forward, her elbows on her knees, her chin in her hands. "What's going on, Mel?"

The smile slid slowly off the redhead's face and Lynda was surprised to see her eyes brimming with unshed tears. "I kissed Taylor," she whispered.

Lynda's eyebrows raised in surprise. "Really. Wow. Okay. And?"

"And?"

"And, you wish you hadn't? And, you're glad you did? And, she punched you in the face?"

"And, it was the best kiss I've ever experienced." Her voice was barely audible.

"And, this is a new thing for you, isn't it?" she said, the comprehension lighting up her face. *Now, we're at the heart of the matter.*

"Yes." The tears flowed silently. She looked up at her friend, and Lynda thought she seemed much younger than she was. "I'm gay, aren't I?" she asked in a small voice.

Lynda smiled gently. "The signs are kind of pointing in that general direction, yeah. But that's something only you can decide."

"I'm not sure what happens now." She hated being this lost, this unstructured.

"Have you talked to Taylor about it?"

She hesitated. "No. I...I don't know if I can. I'm not sure what I'd say."

Lynda chose her next words carefully. "You just kissed, right?"

"What? Oh." Melanie blushed an attractive shade of pink. "Yeah. Just kissed."

"You really should talk to her, you know."

"I know. I will. Just...later." She sat up and wiped her eyes. "Okay. I can't deal with this any more right now." She snatched up the newspaper and handed it to Lynda. "I walked by most of the circled ones this morning. I was up early," she added at Lynda's surprised look. "What do you think?"

I think you have some heavy-duty feelings for Taylor, she wanted to say. *And she's got 'em for you.* Lynda had seen the way Taylor had looked at Melanie, how they had interacted with one another during Taylor's visit to the bookstore recently. Anybody could have picked up on it. *You'd better get things sorted out and talk to the poor girl before you break her heart.* Aloud, she said, "Ooo. Dartmouth is a nice street."

Much to Melanie's surprise—and against her better judgement—she put a deposit down on the first apartment she looked at. It was on Dartmouth Street, only a few blocks from the bookstore and easily within walking distance, at least during nice weather. It was perfect...beautiful hardwood floors, connected living room and kitchen, one generous bedroom, an average-size bathroom, there was plenty of closet space and she liked the quiet, tree-lined street. She'd pulled out her checkbook on the spot. She'd never done anything quite so spontaneous before, and she wondered why Rochester was having such an effect on her personality.

"I buy a business, I rent the first apartment I see, I

make out with a girl," she mumbled out loud as she sat down in the office to eat her lunch of a Quarter Pounder with cheese and fries. "Rochester's certainly done wonderful things for me."

The bell over the door jingled and Melanie scowled at herself for again not remembering to lock it behind her. She still had work to do and was not yet ready to deal with customers. "Lynda?" she called as she left the office. Rather than her next door neighbor, she was faced with a giant bouquet of flowers.

"Melanie Larson?" came a voice from the delivery person, whose face she couldn't see.

"That's me."

"Sign here, please." A clipboard held in a hand, attached to an arm appeared from out of nowhere.

Lynda chose that very instant to pop in, carrying a small bowl and spoon. "Mel. I'm trying a new soup and I want you to taste...wow. Now *that's* what I call a bouquet." She winked as the delivery person, who turned out to be a gentleman old enough to be Melanie's grandfather, headed for the door. "Think they're from the Kissing Bandit?"

Melanie shot her a warning look.

Lynda shrugged. "Hey. Small joke. Sorry."

Melanie opened the envelope and pulled the card out.

Looking forward to many more dinners...Ben

"Shit," she said softly, closing her eyes. "Can this possibly get any worse?"

"I think it's sweet that she sent you flowers," Lynda offered.

"They're not from her. They're from him."

Lynda looked confused. "Him? Him who?"

"Him Ben."

"Who the hell is Ben?"

"Taylor's father."

"Oh, shit."

Chapter
18

Taylor tried hard to keep her chin up, knowing that leaving the ball in Melanie's court was the only reasonable way to handle the situation. She thought Monday had been the longest day of her life until she got to Tuesday without a call or visit from Melanie. Several times, she'd picked up the phone, prepared to dial the redhead's number, only to have the little voice inside tell her not to push, let her come to you.

By Wednesday, she was miserable.

She split all her energy between two emotions: depression and anger. When she wasn't on the verge of tears, she was snapping the heads off people who were stupid enough to simply ask her a question. Before long, not only was she being avoided by Melanie, her coworkers were steering clear, too.

She was alone in her cubicle Wednesday evening. It was after five and most of the staff had gone home for the night. When the phone shrilled loudly, Taylor snatched it up immediately, annoyed at the startling sound it made.

"Taylor Rhodes," she said curtly.

"Hi, Tay. I can't believe I finally got you."

Fuck. Taylor shut her eyes, praying for a lightning bolt to strike her dead and put her out of her misery. "Hello,

Maggie," she said carefully, keeping her tone noncommittal.

"I've been trying to call you for over a week."

"Really."

"Doesn't your voicemail work? If I didn't know better, I'd think you were avoiding me."

Taylor could picture her ex-lover, twisting the phone cord around her finger, waiting for the answer she wanted...the answer she expected, truthful or not. Taylor had learned the hard way that playing Maggie's game, telling her what she wanted to hear, was often worse than telling her the truth. Besides that, Taylor was hardly in the mood to play.

She sighed, saying simply, "I've been busy, Maggie."

"Busy?" Maggie's voice could be sweet. Sexy, even. Now, it held a combination of hurt and anger. "Too busy to return a friend's phone calls?"

I am NOT in the mood for this, Taylor thought, her irritation mounting. "Look, Maggie, I'm buried here. I've got to go, okay?"

"Why won't you at least talk to me?" Taylor could hear the tears beginning, an inevitable occurrence during their last few months together.

"Mags, please, just let it go." She rubbed slowly at the throbbing ache that had set in behind her eyes. "I really don't want to get into this again with you."

"I don't understand why you gave up on us, Tay. I really don't. I told you I could change. You bailed on me."

"I *bailed* on you?" Taylor repeated incredulously. "Trust me, Maggie, you don't want to go down this path with me right now."

Instead of a warning, Maggie took that as a challenge. "Oh, really. And why not? Because you can't face the fact that you couldn't handle the normal pressures of a grown-up relationship?"

"Normal pressures?" Taylor had been through this very discussion with Maggie dozens of times, and had always been able to sugar-coat her comments to keep from cutting too deeply. She'd always felt protective of Maggie, even during their break-up. This time, however, Taylor could feel her control sifting rapidly through her fingers like so many grains of sand. "Normal pressures?" she repeated. "One half of the relationship being a falling-down drunk is not considered a normal pressure, Maggie."

"You left when I needed you the most," Maggie whispered pathetically.

"*Jesus Christ.* I don't believe you're still pulling this shit. I will not let you make me feel guilty. Not any more. I'm done."

"There's somebody else, isn't there?" The whisper was gone, replaced by a hard edge.

Taylor rolled her eyes. It was just like the last time they'd had this conversation. *What, does she have a script?* she thought to herself.

She heaved a deep breath, tired beyond words. "Yup. Yup, there is. You're right, Maggie. There's somebody else. Happy now? Is that what you wanted to hear? That I'm fucking somebody else? Well, I am. You're right. My leaving had nothing to do with your alcohol problem. I left you because I had myself a babe on the side. Satisfied? Now, will you get yourself some help and *leave me the hell alone*?" She slammed down the receiver, immediately shocked at her own brutal words. She'd never purposely tried to hurt somebody like that before, but her own pain was so close to the surface, she felt no alternative but to strike out at anybody trying to hurt her further.

The phone rang again and she watched it until her voicemail picked it up.

She had been inexcusably cruel to somebody she had once adored.

Melanie hadn't called. Again.

She covered her face with her hands as silent tears slid from beneath her closed eyelids.

Chapter
19

By late Thursday afternoon, Lynda couldn't take the distant look in Melanie's friendly blue eyes any longer. She finished her chores in the café, preparing for the next day and cleaning up the earlier messes, and untied the apron from around her waist. She turned to Julie, who was jotting down a note for the produce supplier, who would come on Monday.

"You guys going to Happy Hour?"

"Hmm?" The assistant turned her attention to her boss. "Oh. Yeah. You?"

"I think I'm going to drag our little bookshop owner there. I just wanted to make sure there'd be some friendly faces."

Julie furrowed her brows. "Yeah, I noticed that she's been pretty quiet this week. Even for her."

Lynda locked the front door from the inside. "She's got some issues to deal with. I'm not sure how to help, but a night out might do her some good. Get her to meet some new people."

"She seemed to enjoy herself last time. Maybe it's just what she needs."

"I hope so," Lynda said as she held the back door for

her assistant. "I'm afraid I may have to drag her kicking and screaming. I don't get the impression Melanie likes to share her sorrows."

"Good luck. See you there." Julie headed to her Cavalier, while Lynda scooted to the back door of the bookshop, a few yards down the building from her own.

She could tell immediately that Melanie had decided to deal with her turmoil by focusing on something other than her turmoil. There were boxes strewn all over the floor of the shop. Some spilt over with the older books Melanie had pulled off the shelves, books that were headed for local libraries or other bookstores. The others were freshly opened, smelling of newly printed paper, their colorful spines lining the shelves Melanie was currently scrubbing with Pine Sol.

"You scrub those shelves any more, they're gonna be too thin to hold the books."

Melanie jumped, closing her eyes when she realized the identity of her surprise visitor. "Jesus, Lynda," she snapped. "What did I tell you about sneaking up on me?"

Lynda smiled, knowing the snipe wasn't aimed at her. "You told me it serves you right for becoming so absorbed in your work. Or something like that."

"Touché." The redhead grinned. "Sorry." She waved her hands in circles on either side of her head. "Spinning, spinning, spinning. You know?"

"I know. Come on. Get your stuff and shut the place down."

"Why?"

"We're going to Happy Hour for a drink."

"Oh, Lynda. I don't think so. I..."

Lynda held up a hand, stopping the flow of excuses. "Nope. None of that. Let's go. There's a DJ early tonight. We can dance, drink, meet some people, and forget our troubles for a while."

"You don't have any troubles."

"That's 'cuz I go to Happy Hour."

Melanie chuckled, knowing there would be no arguing

with Lynda. Hell, she wouldn't put it past her friend to toss Melanie over her shoulder and bodily carry her to the bar. She reminded Melanie of Angela, her secretary back in Chicago, and was grateful for the way Lynda watched over her. Angela would be pleased.

She sighed, defeated. "Oh, all right. One drink."

Lynda held out her hand, a glimmer in her eye. "That's all I ask."

At least Lynda had allowed her to go home and change out of her dusty clothes. Her hands had been blackened by the book print; that in turn had made some very artistic streaks on her face. A quick shower, a new pair of navy blue chino shorts she'd purchased the day before, and one of Samantha's sleeveless button downs in an off-white and she felt like a new woman. She could feel the bass of the dance music in the pit of her stomach, even as she stood in the parking lot of *TJ's*. She swallowed hard, suddenly nervous about going inside by herself. She kicked herself for insisting Lynda not wait outside for her.

She'd made her bed. Time to lie in it.

She tucked her hair behind her ear and strode to the front door, puffed up with false bravado. She cleared her throat and pushed it open, the music washing over her in a loud wave.

Much to her surprise and secret delight, she was stopped by the bouncer and asked for ID. She handed over her Illinois driver's license with a grateful smile. The bouncer was a large, intimidating woman, balanced precariously on a stool that seemed ready to collapse any minute under her weight. Her face softened dramatically when she smiled, however, and Melanie smiled back, accepting her license, as well as the gentle stamp the woman placed on the back of her hand.

The bar was unexpectedly full for this early in the evening. Melanie pretended not to notice when several pairs of female eyes wandered up and down her body appreciatively. She shifted slightly under the gaze, half uncomfortable and half flattered. She spotted Lynda waving frantically from the end of the bar and heaved a sigh of relief, now that she had a destination.

Lynda pressed a beer into her hand the second she could reach Melanie. "I was afraid you might not show," she said, leaning close to Melanie's ear so she could be heard over the music.

"I knew I'd never hear the end of it," the redhead replied with a grin.

Early evening slid slowly into night as Melanie felt herself loosen up considerably. Lynda was very attentive, introducing her to as many people as she possibly could. Her anxiety dissipating, she jumped with delight when the DJ launched into a medley of eighties tunes. She turned to Lynda and shouted over the strains of *Express Yourself*, "I *love* this song. Can we dance?"

Lynda's eyes lit up, ecstatic to see this new friend that she'd grown so fond of in such a short time looking happier than she had in days. "Absolutely." She seized Melanie by the hand and led her to the crowded dance floor.

Melanie had never danced with a woman before, and an inkling of panic crept into her conscience, as she tried to decide how close was appropriate. Lynda seemed to sense it. Sliding her hand around Melanie's waist, she pulled her in a little closer, bringing her lips to Melanie's ear. "Relax," she coaxed. "It's okay. It's just me."

The soothing voice so close to her ear sent an unfamiliar and not entirely unpleasant shiver down Melanie's spine. She wet her lips self-consciously and concentrated on following Lynda's moves. *Express Yourself* segued into Frankie Goes to Hollywood's *Relax*, and soon Melanie and Lynda were moving like they'd been dancing together for years.

The evening progressed. The dance floor was crowded with sweaty bodies and the air was close and humid, but Melanie felt like she was in her own little world. Lynda was a great dancer, something Melanie hadn't expected from her friend, and she felt her anxiety slipping away, leaving her free to enjoy the evening.

With each passing song and each disappearing beer, Melanie felt more and more comfortable in her surroundings. Every time she tried to buy a drink, a full bottle appeared miraculously in front of her before she was able to pull out her money. She sent a mock-glare Lynda's way. The café owner—conveniently—never seemed to be looking.

Melanie turned to lean her back against the bar, taking a swig from her beer. She'd lost track of how many she'd had, and although she wasn't drunk, she was definitely feeling tipsy. The throbbing bass stopped and a slow groove began. The bodies that had been bumping and grinding a minute ago closed into pairs and swayed slowly. Melanie watched in fascination as couples of men and women alike entwined with one another, some more familiarly than others.

She felt the breath in her ear before she actually heard the voice, and it made the hair on the back of her neck prickle with excitement. "Could I have this dance?"

She turned to meet the sparkling dark eyes that had been invading her dreams for the past four nights, the same eyes she couldn't get out of her head no matter how hard she tried to push them away. Words failed her, as she became lost in the depths of those eyes; she could only nod. She felt Taylor's fingers slide down her bare arm and clasp her hand softly, leading her into the sea of swaying bodies. She was unaware of the observing pair of blue eyes at the bar, filled with equal parts approval and worry.

They found an open corner of the dance floor and only then did they face one another. Taylor slid her arm around Melanie's waist, finding she didn't need to do much else to move the older woman closer. Melanie reached her left arm up, resting it on Taylor's shoulder. Her fingers seemed to move of their own accord as they tangled themselves in the ponytail of brunette waves they found at the nape of Taylor's neck. Taylor brought their clasped hands in, resting them against her own collarbone. They fit together like two connecting pieces of a puzzle, a fact not lost on either of them.

Melanie's nose reached Taylor's chin and she looked up into the dark eyes. "Hey."

"Hey, yourself."

She pulled the dark head down slightly so she could be heard over the music. "It's good to see you."

Taylor pulled her head back so she could see Melanie's face. "Yeah?"

"Yeah." Melanie nodded.

Taylor moved back to Melanie's ear, barely able to keep from tasting it. "You didn't call," she said quietly. "I wasn't sure." She felt Melanie nod.

"I know. I'm sorry. I've got some...things...to deal with, you know?"

It was Taylor's turn to nod.

"Just bear with me, all right? Please?" The redhead's voice was small and barely audible over the music and Taylor wanted nothing more than to make everything all right. She pulled Melanie closer, the length of their bodies touching. Melanie caught her breath at the contact, an erotic gasp that didn't escape Taylor's notice.

"Okay," Taylor promised, feeling Melanie relax with relief in her arms. When she looked up and blue met brown, the connection was electric and at the same time, comforting. Melanie had never felt so safe with anyone before and she wanted nothing more than to curl up in the deep, gentle gaze and stay there. Without realizing she was doing it, she raised her chin, pulling Taylor's head down to meet her lips softly.

The charge that ran through her was even stronger than she remembered, despite the gentle, undemanding nature of the kiss. She brushed Taylor's lips a second time, feeling the younger woman applying slightly more pressure, seemingly unsure of exactly how far to go, letting Melanie set the pace. Melanie freed her other hand from Taylor's grasp, bringing it up to join the first, pulling Taylor's head down to meet hers with authority, pressing her lips firmly and imploringly against the brunette's. Taylor slid her hands up to capture Melanie's face, kissing her deeply, her heart skipping a beat when she felt Melanie's tongue demanding entry, allowing it without a second thought. They could hardly qualify as "dancers," barely swaying to the music, standing in a corner of the dance floor, kissing with abandon, seemingly oblivious to the rest of the world.

They remained that way, that close, swaying slowly to the fast song that had replaced the slow one for several minutes before they were jostled by other dancers.

"Hey, get a room," somebody shouted playfully.

Melanie flushed a rosy shade of pink and, untangling herself from Taylor's grasp, buried her face in Taylor's chest, hoping the room would just disappear. Both of them were heaving breathlessly, suddenly aware of the various eyes watching them, many with envy. Taylor blushed almost as deeply as Melanie, shocked at her own behavior. In a public place, no less. She put her arm protectively around Melanie and led her off the dance floor and into a somewhat private corner. Slipping her fingers beneath Melanie's chin, she brought her face up and looked into the blue eyes, clouded with a mixture of fear, embarrassment and desire.

"You okay?"

Melanie swallowed, not trusting herself to speak, and nodded.

"I'm sorry about that," Taylor said. "I...I shouldn't have done that. But..." She looked off into space, searching for a logical explanation.

Melanie brought her back by capturing the hand on her chin with her own. "Hey. Let's get one thing straight, okay? *I* did that. You just wanted to dance. I just...I can't seem to..." She blew out a frustrated breath. "Since Sunday, I can't be that close to you and not touch you. I don't know why. I just can't. I'm sorry."

Taylor smiled. "Don't you dare apologize for complimenting me like that, okay? There are people who would give their eyesight to have somebody say that about them."

Melanie could feel herself relax. "What is it about you, Taylor?" she asked softly.

"I could ask you the same thing, Ms. Larson."

Melanie touched Taylor's lips with her fingertips, still amazed at their softness. "Are you free for dinner tomorrow night?"

Taylor tried not to let her ecstasy show. She scrunched up her face, pretending to think. "Hmm. Tomorrow? Lemme think. That's Friday, right?" Melanie slapped her playfully. "Now that you mention it, I think I'm having dinner with a beautiful woman."

"You think so?"

"I think so."

"Beautiful, huh?"

"Beyond beautiful. Breathtaking. And she kisses like nobody's business."

Melanie couldn't stop the blush, hard as she tried. She checked her watch instead, trying to busy herself with something. "Oh my God. Is it really that late?"

"It is."

"I need to go. I've got so much to do at the store tomorrow."

Taylor studied the redhead's face closely. "Did you drive?"

Catching the hidden question, Melanie frowned. "Yeah."

Taylor scanned the bar, her eyes meeting the watchful pair that was closely observing them. "Stay here for a sec."

Lynda tried to keep her face neutral as Taylor approached her. She had been paying very close attention to the couple since their dance, and she had mixed emotions about what she saw. Melanie was obviously crazy about Taylor, whether or not she was ready to admit it to herself or anybody else. To anybody looking in from the outside, it would seem that Taylor felt the same way. But, there was no way to be sure and Lynda felt slightly uneasy.

Maybe it was her unused maternal instincts. She felt an inexplicable need to protect the redhead.

"Hi, Lynda."

"Taylor." The café owner nodded.

"Um...Melanie's had a bit too much to drink, I think."

"I think you're right."

"If I drive her home, can you follow us in her Jeep?"

Lynda weighed the options. The maternal side of her said she could follow the couple home and make sure that Taylor didn't overstep her bounds. On the other hand, the part of her that was Melanie's friend suggested she should just accept the fact that Melanie was a big girl who could take care of herself, and Lynda could take the Jeep to the bookstore in the morning.

"That was some dance you had out there."

Taylor swallowed. "Yeah."

"How drunk is she?" The question was loaded, and Taylor knew it.

"She's not trashed, but she can't drive. I won't let her." She looked deeply into the blue eyes boring into her and saw nothing there but concern. She understood at that moment that Lynda didn't view her as competition for herself. She viewed her as a potential heartbreak for Melanie. New respect for the café owner welled up inside her. She was grateful Melanie had somebody else keeping an eye on her. "Lynda, look. If this is meant to happen, there won't be any alcohol involved," she said sincerely, surprised to feel her eyes misting. "Tonight is not the night."

Lynda was visibly relieved, feeling a sudden admiration for the tall brunette before her. She exhaled, making a decision. "Can you get her to the shop in the morning?"

"Sure."

"Gimme her keys. I'll take the Jeep home tonight and drive it in tomorrow morning. Julie can follow me in my car."

They held one another's gaze. "Thank you."

"I'm not doing this for you. I'm doing it for her." Lynda poked her playfully in the ribs. "You're on your own."

They drove home in relative silence, each simply enjoying the presence of the other. Melanie was grateful for the ride. She realized as trees and houses whizzed by that she was, in fact, a little too drunk to drive. Taylor had taken care of her without a second thought. The idea warmed her heart. She was disappointed when they pulled into the driveway all too soon. Ben's Saab sat quietly in the dark, and Melanie felt a prickle of anxiety. She was going to have to talk with him soon.

What the hell do I say? she thought. *Gee, Ben, you're a great guy, but I'd rather be with your daughter.* She rolled her eyes, willing the subject away. She'd deal with it later. Much later, if she could help it.

"We still on for tomorrow?" Taylor's voice cut into her thoughts, bringing her back to the present situation.

"I haven't had so much beer that I forgot the invitation, you know," she chuckled.

"Oh, I know." Taylor backpedaled. "I just thought it might have been...I don't know..." She swallowed nervously. "The heat of the moment or something."

Melanie was touched by Taylor's attempt to give her an out if she needed one. "Walk me to my door?"

"Sure."

They strolled the short distance to the carriage house in the dark. At the door, they turned to regard one another. Melanie smiled and stepped up onto the stoop, putting her eye to eye with Taylor.

Silently thanking whatever gods had caused Melanie to forget to turn on the outside light before she left, the brunette reached out a hand to caress the creamy skin of Melanie's cheek with her thumb.

Melanie's eyes closed, absorbing the touch, just as soft lips met hers. Taylor's mouth was so soft, so sweet. She could taste the tang of lime that was left lingering from her drink. Despite the gentleness of the kiss, she felt a wave of want course through her blood, astounding her yet again with its intensity. She briefly wondered if the alcohol haze she'd been in was causing her senses to go haywire. How was it possible to desire somebody so much?

Taylor had meant to give Melanie a simple, chaste peck, but her body had betrayed her. Now, she had to fight to keep it calm and without ardor. It was harder than she imagined, especially when Melanie sighed softly and pressed into her. She had to use every ounce of strength she possessed, but she managed to pry herself away from the sweetest lips she'd ever tasted.

Melanie whimpered with disappointment, endearing her to Taylor even more. They stood in each other's arms, cloaked by darkness, Taylor trying hard to catch her breath. Melanie was finding herself surprisingly brave due to the alcohol still in her system, and softly pressed her lips against Taylor's bare neck, utterly shocked by the softness she found there. Taylor felt her eyes drifting shut at the tentative assault on her overly-sensitive skin. She caught herself, snapping them open and catching Melanie's face in her hands, forcing her eyes up to meet her own.

"Melanie..."

"I want to be with you, Taylor."

Taylor smiled. "I know. I want to be with you, too, but..." The sentence slid from the grasp of her brain momentarily as her mouth was covered with another. This kiss was much bolder, and Taylor allowed the exploration of lips, teeth and tongue for several minutes longer than she intended. Forcefully pulling herself from the cloud of desire hanging over the two of them, she tightened her hold on Melanie's face and kissed her way to the redhead's ear.

"Believe me," she whispered as her lips brushed the swirls of skin, sending a delicious shiver down Melanie's spine, "we *will* be together. I *will* make love to you. But when I do, I want you perfectly, one hundred percent sober. I want you to know everything I'm doing to you and exactly how it feels."

Melanie held onto Taylor's shoulders. It was the only way she could remain standing, as her knees had grown so weak they could no longer hold her. She swallowed hard, eyes wide, breath ragged. Taylor softly kissed her ear, then looked her in the eye.

"Thanks for the dance. I'll see you tomorrow?"

All Melanie could do was nod.

"Seven all right?"

Another nod.

After assuring herself of Melanie's balance, Taylor took a couple steps backward. "'Night, Melanie. Sleep well."

Melanie stood on the stoop several minutes after Taylor was in her own house, waiting for the blood to redistribute itself throughout the rest of her body. Only then was she able to turn and enter the carriage house. "Sleep," she mumbled to herself. "Yeah. Right."

Chapter 20

This is quite possibly the longest Friday in the history of mankind, Taylor thought with disgust as she glanced at the clock on her desk for the fifth time in a half-hour.

She was nervous and excited and apprehensive and aroused all at once about her date that evening. Her entire body was humming with anticipation of such intensity, she was surprised the people in the cubicles around her didn't hear it.

Tonight was the night. She could feel it in her core. She would be with Melanie tonight. The physical possibilities of the evening had been playing out in her head all day long. God, she'd *never* wanted something so raw and primal in her life. She could almost hear Melanie's voice, teetering on the edge of ecstasy, a pitch or two higher than usual, quietly begging Taylor for release. She could imagine the beauty of Melanie's naked form under her own, glistening with sweat and passion...could hear her breath coming in ragged pants. The thought of the older woman's creamy soft skin beneath her fingers made her woozy, and she closed her eyes, gripping the edge of her desk to steady her nerves.

The emotional possibilities of the evening were what

scared her. She'd tried to avoid thinking about them, but it was difficult. She felt so much already for this kind-hearted, gentle woman who had simply appeared out of nowhere barely three weeks ago. It wasn't supposed to happen this fast, was it? They were supposed to be friends first. Isn't that how it worked? A person didn't just show up one day and make you fall in love with them, did they? Taylor had always scoffed at those people...the ones who got together in a matter of days. What was the matter with them, anyway? Didn't they know it was impossible to fall in love that quickly?

She hadn't fallen nearly as fast with Maggie. It had taken a lot of coaxing, a ton of reassuring, and a fair amount of good, old fashioned seduction before the smaller woman had won Taylor over. Taylor had been too practical, too organized, to throw caution to the wind and just let herself go. Maggie'd had her work cut out for her, trying to make Taylor fall for her...and Taylor had gone over that edge kicking and screaming. It had been months before she would even admit that love was, indeed, what she'd felt for Maggie.

So what was this two and a half weeks bullshit? Taylor cursed herself for not paying enough attention to what was going on. She'd simply fallen while she wasn't looking. And there was no turning back now.

Taylor rested her head in her hands, leaning her elbows on the desk. Deep down inside, she knew she had to accept the truth. In a scant two and a half weeks, she'd fallen head over heels, madly, irretrievably in love with Melanie Larson. Melanie Larson, a woman who, up until five days ago, had never even kissed a woman before.

Did she feel the same way about Taylor? Could she? Was it even possible? That was the scariest part for Taylor, the part that would make her blood run cold and her stomach churn if she dwelled on it too much. What if Melanie decided this wasn't right for her? What if she chalked Taylor up to a little bit of experimentation? What if she just wanted to see what it was like? What if she laughed at the depth of Taylor's own feelings, thinking she was silly and childish?

What if Melanie broke her heart?

The thought made bile rise in her throat, and she choked it back with effort, her fingers digging viciously into the foam stress ball on her desk. *That's why I can't think about this,* she told herself. *Think positive. Think positive. Think positive.*

She closed her eyes and a vision of Melanie came unbidden into her mind, causing her mouth to curl into a lopsided grin. The redhead was smiling sweetly at Taylor, her blue eyes sparkling in the sunlight, streaks of gold and red combining together perfectly to make just the right shade of hair...a color she'd only ever seen on Melanie.

This is the woman I love.

The sentence warmed her heart and she tried mightily to concentrate on her work, willing the hours to pass as quickly as possible.

Melanie had done her best to throw herself into her work. Most of the books from Jeff's inventory were gone now, most donated to libraries...not the most economical solution, but the quickest. The rest had been purchased by various stores around the state, and she'd shipped the last box out that morning. New books were arriving every day. She really needed a computer. There was no way she was going to use the paper route Jeff had taken. She knew she'd be much more organized and be able to keep infinitely better track of her inventory if she had it all on a database. She'd have to make a trip back to Chicago very soon. Maybe Taylor would want to tag along...

She'd received the new sign for the front of the shop a couple of hours ago. She wanted to surprise Taylor, so she kept it a secret from her. When she'd shown it to Lynda that morning, however, the café owner whooped with delight.

"*The Quill is Mightier*? That's a terrific name," she'd stated, scrutinizing the color, which matched the new exterior of the shop perfectly. "And if you ask me, the majority of your feminists, as well as the lesbians, are Xena fans, so they'll know right away that this is a store for them. Not one of the better episodes, in my not-so-humble opinion, but a great name. Brilliant choice, Mel. I commend you."

That was first thing in the morning, when Melanie had thanked her friend for taking care of the Jeep, which sat parked neatly in the back parking lot. She'd brushed off any attempt by Lynda to discuss the previous night, not quite finished analyzing it herself and not quite ready to verbalize any of it.

There was a timid knock on the glass of the front door and Melanie couldn't help but giggle at the café owner, whose nose was pressed tightly against it. She stood with her hands on her hips, a mock-scowl on her face, before unlocking the door and letting Lynda in.

"I hope you brought your Windex, young lady," she scolded.

Lynda waved her off with a flick of her hand and looked around. "Hey. Lookin' good. Got an opening date yet?"

"Week from Monday."

Lynda nodded her approval. "You're really moving right along on things. I'm impressed."

"Be impressed when I actually get customers in here."

The older woman could sense the tension in the air, and she knew it didn't come only from the impending grand opening of the shop. She was beginning to know Melanie quite well, and she could tell when the woman was about to open up, when she needed to talk. This morning, she'd been nearly unapproachable. Now, she was different. Lynda plopped herself into one of the reading chairs and waited.

"Do you remember the details in *Curious Wine*?" the redhead asked after several minutes of stocking shelves in silence.

"Burned into my memory forever."

Melanie opened her mouth, shut it, opened it again, shut it again. She took a deep breath. "In the book, Lane and Diana...um...fall in love...in, like, a matter of days."

"Uh huh."

She turned to Lynda, the chaos in her mind clearly visible in her eyes. "Has that ever happened to you? To somebody you know? Or is it just fiction?"

Lynda smiled gently and studied Melanie for several minutes. Finally, she asked the question she'd been wanting to ask ever since Taylor came in the bookstore nearly two weeks ago, the question she already knew the answer to. "Are you in love with Taylor?"

Melanie's hand stopped in mid-air, the book she was about to shelve floating just inches from its destination. Finally, she set it down, staring at it as she turned the question over and over in her mind. It was a pretty simple one, really. Just yes or no, right? The problem was, she'd been avoiding asking herself the very same question, scared to death of what the answer might be.

Lynda watched her carefully, watched the various emotions as they marched across her expressively beautiful face. She was surprised to find herself thinking what a lucky woman Taylor Rhodes was and hoping that the young brunette knew it. "Melanie?" she prodded softly.

Melanie nodded almost imperceptibly before answering. "I think I am," she whispered at last. "My God, I think I am." She laughed, a sound which held very little humor. "What the hell happened? I'm thirty-three years old, for crying out loud, I just now realize I'm a lesbian?"

"Consider yourself lucky," Lynda chuckled. "I know some women who didn't come out until they were in their fifties."

Melanie turned a stricken face to her friend. "No."

Lynda laughed out loud. "True."

Melanie dropped into the other chair. "Oh, Lynda. What do I do?"

"First thing I suggest you do is chill. Stressing yourself out is going to get you nowhere fast."

Melanie nodded. She never got this worked up. Never. Not even when an account was in danger of deserting Rucker & Steele. Nothing had ever made her stomach churn and her head ache like the current situation. "You've got a point."

"Have you slept with her?"

"No." She said it almost sadly, which Lynda found amusing. Not that Melanie hadn't thought about sleeping with Taylor, dreamed about it, obsessed over it. Images of the two of them together, Taylor moving above her, Taylor touching her with those beautiful hands, Taylor's fingers, lips, tongue on her, in her, stroking, coaxing, driving her higher, making her gasp for breath...she swallowed hard, feeling her face flush.

"Have you talked to Taylor? About how you feel?"

"What? No. Absolutely not."

"Why?"

"What the hell would I say?"

"Have you stopped to think that maybe she feels the same way?"

Melanie fell silent. Yes, she had thought of that. Several times. Several hundred times. Hundreds of thousands of times, probably. She knew it was a possibility. She also knew there was the possibility that Taylor *didn't* feel the same...that Melanie was just fun. A fling. That was the part with which she had all kinds of trouble dealing. So she just didn't.

"Are you seeing her again?"

"Tonight."

"Melanie, you need to talk to her."

The redhead sighed. Lynda was right, whether or not she wanted to admit it. "I know."

"Look, Taylor seems like a really approachable person. It'll be okay. Look at you. You're a mess over this. At least if you talk to Taylor, you'll know. One way or the other, you'll know."

"What if I don't want to know?" *What if I just want*

things to go back the way they were, with me and my job and nothing else? a little voice inquired. A second, louder voice added, *No friends, no hobbies, no love...Yeah, that was great. Is that really what you want to go back to?*

Lynda's voice softened as she took Melanie's hands in her own. She cared so much for this new found friend, and she hated seeing her in such emotional turmoil. "Honey, we're all afraid to get hurt. It's a fact of life. It sucks to have your heart thrown on the floor, and we all know it. But, if it's bound to happen, maybe it's better just to get it over with so you can deal with the pain and move on."

"Maybe you're right." Melanie forced a smile, praying to any god that would listen, to please let it not be her heart that was thrown on the floor tonight.

Chapter 21

Taylor took a deep, shaky breath as she stood on the front stoop of the carriage house. She lifted her hand to knock, then withdrew it before doing so. She looked down and surveyed herself one last time.

She'd tried not to get too dressed up, finally settling on a soft pair of khaki colored shorts and a deep green scoop-neck T-shirt. She'd pulled some of her dark waves back and fastened them behind her head in a gold clip that matched her earrings, leaving the rest of the locks to flow freely around her shoulders. A spritz of musk and a touch of clear lip gloss, and she'd headed across the yard, glad that Ben was working late so she didn't have to explain where she was going.

She brushed her wispy bangs off her forehead, taking one more deep breath, and forced herself to actually make contact with the door. She finally steadied her breath, then felt it leave her completely as the door was opened.

Never had a woman dressed so simply looked so stunning to Taylor. Melanie was dressed in a pair of cargo shorts the color of charcoal and a pale blue tank top that almost exactly matched the color of her eyes. Unable to keep her own eyes under control, Taylor's gaze followed

the curve of Melanie's body down past the swell of hips,
over the sexy, now-tanned legs, and settled on her bare
feet. Melanie was fully aware of the scrutiny and let it happen, watching Taylor with amusement, equally taken with
what she saw standing outside her door.

"Hey." Taylor forced her eyes back up to meet Melanie's.

"Hey yourself," she replied, tucking a strand of hair
behind her ear.

"Can I come in?"

Melanie grinned sheepishly and stepped aside. "Sure.
Sorry."

"No problem." Taylor moved through the doorway,
stopping to kiss Melanie softly on the cheek, quietly inhaling the sweet, citrus scent of her. She stepped further into
the room as Melanie closed the door, noting with pleasure
how she thought of the carriage house as Melanie's, like
she was just supposed to be there. Taylor plopped herself
down on the couch and smirked at the older woman. "How
was your day, dear?"

Melanie smiled, liking the easy banter, and sat down
next to her. "Great. I really got a lot done at the shop, but I
wish I had my computer. The inventory's pouring in, and
I'm trying really hard to keep track of it."

"Jeff wasn't real keen on modern electronics, that's for
sure."

"I'm going to have to make a trip back to Chicago
fairly soon, I think. I can't use paper much longer before I
lose something important."

"Is it a long drive?"

"Brutal. Ten hours on a good day." She studied her
hands for a long moment. "Um...maybe, if you...if you
don't have anything else going on...maybe you could, you
know, keep me company?"

Taylor's smile lit up her entire face. "I'd love that.
When do we leave?"

"I don't know. Sometime this weekend, I think."

"Count me in. I'm a great co-pilot."

"I bet you are." Melanie stood. "Want something to drink?"

"Sure. What's for dinner?"

Melanie stopped in her tracks. "Oh my God." She turned a stricken face to her houseguest. "I invited you for dinner, didn't I?"

Taylor tried to stifle a giggle.

"Oh my God. What an idiot I am." Melanie covered her mouth with her hand in disbelief.

Unable to maintain control any longer, Taylor laughed out loud, which only succeeded in making Melanie feel worse.

Seeing her sinking face, Taylor abruptly stopped laughing, guilt settling over her like a cloud. She went to her hostess and quickly turned the redhead to face her. "Melanie." She forced Melanie's head up to look her in the eye and smiled warmly at her. "Hey. Relax. It's me. It's just me."

"I know." The two words spoke volumes, and Taylor felt a flood of warmth at the prospect that maybe...just maybe...Melanie had been dealing with some of the same turmoil Taylor herself had been going through.

Taylor put a comforting arm around Melanie and led her to the kitchen. "Okay. Apparently, you don't know who you're dealing with here," she said, grinning. "I can make dinner out of anything. Let's see what we've got."

Melanie was amazed at how quickly Taylor could make everything all right, just by putting an arm around her. She felt so safe and protected, like nothing in the world mattered beyond her little circle within Taylor's arms. Her anxiety faded away like a dying ember, and she watched with amusement as Taylor bent to stick her head in the refrigerator. She shocked herself when she realized she was actually enjoying the very pleasant view of the brunette's backside, and tore her gaze away with embarrassment, deciding to study the ceiling instead.

"Hmm," Taylor mused. "I see this will be a challenge. Jesus, don't you or Sam ever shop?"

"I did when I first got here, but I was afraid if I went back to *Wegmans*, I'd never be able to get out. The place is huge and just sucks you in,"

Taylor's shoulders moved as a low chuckle erupted from the refrigerator. "That's true. There are several documented cases of tourists who have disappeared and were never heard from again. It's a dangerous place."

"Ha ha."

Taylor stood, arms full of various items. "Cheese omelet? I'd put mushrooms in it, too, but I'm not sure how good these are." She held up a soggy carton.

"Omelet sounds great," Melanie replied, taking the eggs from Taylor's grasp. They deposited the ingredients on the counter to the right of the sink, Taylor removing the necessary dishes from the cupboard.

Melanie watched her work, admiring the grace of movement, the flexing of thigh muscles as she squatted to retrieve the frying pan from a lower cupboard, the casual toss of hair over her shoulder. She felt the now-familiar warmth seeping into her blood and welcomed it. "I'm glad you're here," she said softly.

Taylor stopped what she was doing, an egg held in one hand, and turned loving eyes to her companion. "So am I."

Their gaze held for a deliciously long moment.

"Here," Taylor finally said, handing a Ziploc bag containing a brick of white cheese to Melanie. "Cut this?"

"Yes, ma'am." Melanie set it on the cutting board. "What kind is it?" she asked, retrieving a knife from a drawer and setting to work.

"It looks like some kind of cheddar. Didn't you buy it?"

"Well, yeah, but there were nine hundred twenty seven kinds of cheese at *Wegmans*. I just grabbed what was closest." She cut herself a small piece, popping it into her mouth and chewing thoughtfully. "Hmm. I'm not sure."

"Let me taste."

Melanie cut another tidbit and held it up to Taylor's lips. The younger woman took it from her, her tongue lightly brushing the redhead's fingertips. Melanie tried to ignore the jolt that shot through her body like lightning. She swallowed hard as she watched Taylor chew.

"I don't know...I don't think it's cheddar after all...hmm...give me another bite."

Melanie complied, again holding the morsel up for Taylor to accept with her lips. She did so, but this time closed them around Melanie's forefinger as well. Melanie caught her breath as a pang hit low in her body, her heart skipping a beat. She watched, transfixed, as her entire finger disappeared into Taylor's mouth, being thoroughly and gently bathed by her tongue.

Taylor reached up to grasp Melanie's wrist as she slowly withdrew the finger. "You, um, had some cheese on it," she said softly, chewing and swallowing what was left in her mouth.

"Uh huh." Melanie nodded, the formation of actual words proving to be a nearly impossible task.

A gentle tug on her wrist and Melanie found herself in Taylor's arms. She wrapped her own arms around the taller woman's waist, felt Taylor's hands slide up her back, nestling in her hair. Slowly, so slowly, Taylor lowered her lips until they were a fraction of an inch from Melanie's. Shallow breathing was the only sound to be heard. Only when Melanie thought she'd scream from the torture of anticipation, did Taylor close the distance and softly brush Melanie's lips with her own. The touch was feather-light, teasing. She pulled back slightly, flicking the tip of her tongue across Melanie's upper lip. Melanie was startled to hear herself whimper.

The corner of Taylor's mouth crooked up in a tiny half-grin, and she repeated the same maneuver, even slower this time, with the same result. She felt Melanie's fingers digging into her back; she was torn between frustration and arousal. The third time, Melanie surprised them both by growling, grabbing the back of Taylor's head, and pulling her down into a searing kiss. Both women moaned at the contact, as their mouths crashed together, lips bruis-

ing, tongues warring for space. Melanie's head was spinning, and she was sure if she let go of Taylor, she'd be cast
off into oblivion.

Taylor took two steps, using her hands to feel behind
Melanie—never breaking the contact of their mouths—
until she had the redhead's back against the kitchen
counter. Slipping her hands down Melanie's back, she cradled her rear for several minutes, simply enjoying the feel
of it under her fingers, before she gripped it and lifted,
depositing Melanie in a sitting position on the counter. She
stood between the redhead's knees, her hands caressing
creamy smooth thighs, her mind awash in the disbelief of
what was actually happening.

The sensation of Taylor's hands on her backside was
positively delicious, and Melanie felt a wave course
through her body. When Taylor actually picked her up to
set her gently on the counter, Melanie had to consciously
fight to keep herself under control. Something about the
quiet physical strength Taylor possessed was proving to be
a hell of a turn-on for the redhead, and she kneaded the
back muscles that were subtly rippling under her fingers in
pure ecstasy. She wrapped her own legs around Taylor's
waist, pulling herself as close to the brunette as she could
get, stifling a gasp as the hard button on Taylor's shorts hit
directly at her center. She wondered if a person could die
of sensory overload. Unintentionally, her hips ground
against the woman assaulting her mouth.

Taylor sighed with pleasure as she felt Melanie's legs
wrap around her, pushing against her in a primal rhythm,
heels digging into her back. She grasped Melanie's shirt
and tugged it out of the waistband of her shorts. Both
women moaned when Taylor's hands rested on Melanie's
bare sides, skin on skin.

Slow down, Taylor's inner voice screamed at her. *Slow
down.* She couldn't manage to pry her own lips from Melanie's, and she was unable to obey the orders from her
brain, as her hands seemed to have minds of their own. In a
matter of seconds, they had slipped around behind Melanie

and unclasped her bra, then quickly slid around to the front, reveling in the heat radiating from her skin.

Her thumbs brushed lightly over the sensitive nipples simultaneously. Melanie inhaled sharply, arching into the touch.

Crack!

Taylor opened her eyes in surprise at the sound, realizing with amusement as well as empathy, that Melanie had whacked her head into the cupboard behind her. There was a beat of silence as Melanie turned several shades of red. She was still breathing heavily, turning her shaded blue gaze up to meet Taylor's eyes.

"Ow."

Taylor burst out laughing, trying to look somewhat sympathetic, as she cupped the back of Melanie's head, pulling it forward so the redhead could rest her forehead on the brunette's shoulder. She stroked it softly, kissing her temple. "You okay?" she asked in Melanie's ear.

The breath sent tingles down her spine. "Yeah. I'm fine."

Taylor's left hand was still under Melanie's tank top, and she slowly caressed the small but firm breast beneath it. "Oh, I think you're more than fine," she whispered. She inhaled through her teeth, the sound resembling a hiss, as she felt the nipple harden in her palm and Melanie's hips resume their undulation.

Melanie had never felt so much at once. "God, Taylor," she whispered, her forehead still on Taylor's shoulder, her fingertips digging into Taylor's back. "What are you doing to me?" Another whimper escaped her as Taylor caught, then gently rolled the nipple between her thumb and finger. Melanie tightened her legs around Taylor's waist, another rush hitting her as Taylor's hand left her head and slid down to the small of her back, helping her push herself against the front of Taylor's shorts. They moved together, rocking on the kitchen counter, Taylor very precisely fondling the nipple in her grip, paying close attention to the incredibly sexy sounds emanating from the lips near her chin.

In a very short few minutes, she felt Melanie's fingers grasping handfuls of the back of her shirt and felt the thighs tense around her waist. Melanie managed to stutter a barely audible, "Oh, God," before her breathing stopped altogether and she clenched her teeth, every muscle in her body stiffening. Taylor held on tightly, wearing a big grin and enjoying the ride immensely. She pulled Melanie's hips against her and stopped all movement, allowing Melanie's orgasm to take its course. There was plenty of time to learn what would prolong the redhead's pleasure later. For now, she let her have the release she'd sought when she'd wrapped her gorgeous legs around Taylor in the first place.

Not until her breathing had almost returned to normal did Melanie lift her head, finding it difficult to meet Taylor's gaze. Taylor smiled, ducking her head to catch the eyes trying so valiantly to avoid hers.

"Wow," she stated simply, her dark eyes sparkling.

"Understatement of the year," Melanie commented, her beautiful face flushed both from arousal and embarrassment. "I'm sorry...I don't know what...I don't usually..." She stumbled over her own words in an attempt to make her point. Taylor silenced her with a kiss, soft, gentle, probing.

"Hey," she reassured, after finally managing to regain possession of her own lips. "Don't apologize. You were amazing." She gently tucked a strand of Melanie's hair behind her ear.

"I think that title belongs to you."

It was Taylor's turn to blush. She shrugged. "I was inspired."

"I guess so. That's never happened to me...that fast...before."

"I'll take that as a compliment." She wrapped the redhead in a loving hug. They sank into one another, and Melanie wrapped her legs around Taylor's waist again, allowing her to hug the taller woman with her entire body. Taylor's lips were at Melanie's ear. "You were beautiful, you know. All passionate, with your muscles tensing and your breath coming in gasps." She felt the familiar warmth returning. "You were gorgeous."

Melanie lightly slapped her shoulder. "Stop it. You're embarrassing me."

Taylor pulled up to look at Melanie's smiling face. "It's true," she said, pouring as much sincerity as she could into the statement. "I have never, ever, been so attracted to somebody in my life. You are beautiful inside and out. I can't believe you're here with me...that you're letting me touch you...that you just came on your cousin's kitchen counter."

Melanie gasped in horror, slapping at Taylor again as the brunette laughed at her own joke. In a short few seconds, she was laughing, too. Taylor leaned into Melanie's shoulder as their laughter subsided, Melanie's gentle fingers working through the long dark hair, deftly unclasping the clip that held some of it back. Taylor sighed in total contentment, wondering if it would be possible to just stay that way forever.

It was when Melanie began absently massaging the scalp beneath her fingers that Taylor decided there were better options than staying in the kitchen. She raised her head, her lips unerringly finding Melanie's. Melanie noticed with amusement that their kisses always seemed to start softly and gently and within a matter of minutes, ended up deep and searching and breathless.

Taylor managed to extricate her own lips from Melanie's long enough to mutter, "Bedroom."

Melanie nodded, sliding off the counter to the floor. Her face was immediately captured by strong hands, her mouth covered by Taylor's once again. They stumbled together from the kitchen down the short hallway to the small bedroom, their lips never parting.

Melanie's knees buckled as they made contact with the side of the bed, and she fell back onto the soft down comforter.

"No," Taylor protested, her voice thick with passion as

she grasped Melanie's hand and pulled her back to her feet. "I want to see you first."

She gently tugged the tank over Melanie's head, taking the unclasped bra with it, and tossed it onto the floor. Melanie expected a wave of discomfort, but was surprised to find herself enjoying the hungry look Taylor raked over her bare torso. Taylor kissed each shoulder softly and nibbled up the side of Melanie's neck, her long fingers unfastening the button on the cargo shorts. They slid down her legs to land quietly around her ankles. The only thing obstructing Taylor's view was the pink pair of panties. Feeling emboldened by the simple, carnal desire in Taylor's eyes, Melanie slipped the panties off and stood before the taller woman, completely naked, silently offering herself.

"My God," the brunette whispered in awe. "You're beautiful."

She reached for the smaller woman, only to have her hand stopped halfway to its destination. "Ah, ah, ah." Melanie waggled a finger at her. "Your turn."

Her voice was husky, her blue eyes hooded, and Taylor nodded with a grin. "Yes, ma'am." She held her arms to the sides as Melanie took a step forward.

She'd never undressed a woman before, and her mind fought to stay clear in the midst of the myriad of emotions with which she was being bombarded. Nervousness, desire, fear, passion, want, need, self-consciousness, and raw hunger all warred for space in her head. With trembling fingers, she grasped Taylor's shirt and pulled it up and off, tossing it into the pile with her own clothing. Taylor stood quietly before her, watching her face, wearing only a white sports bra and her shorts. She unfastened the shorts, dropping them down Taylor's legs, stepping back to take in the body in front of her. Melanie's mouth went dry at the sight. Taylor was strong and athletic, things that were obvious whether or not she had clothes on. What shocked Melanie was the sheer femininity of her body. Her shoulders were incredibly sexy—round and tan. Her breasts were larger than Melanie expected, held in check by the strong fabric of the sports bra. Her hips curved sensuously and Melanie swallowed hard. She lightly ran her fingertips over Taylor's taut abdomen, causing the taller woman to flinch involuntarily, but when Melanie looked up, the brunette's eyes were smiling, inviting.

Melanie laid her palm flat against Taylor's stomach, the combination of heat and softness making her dizzy. She slipped a finger beneath the lower band of the sports bra and looked questioningly at Taylor. The taller woman obliged by removing the offending garment.

Melanie caught her breath as the bra hit the floor. Taylor's breasts were beautiful...full and round, with dark nipples standing at attention. She reached out a tentative hand, almost imperceptibly caressing the side of one, causing goose bumps to erupt across Taylor's flesh.

"You're so soft," Melanie said, almost to herself. "Everything is so soft. Do I feel like this to you?"

"No," Taylor responded. "Softer."

Melanie slid her hand down Taylor's side and turned clouded eyes to her partner. Her voice almost inaudible, she said, "You know I'm new at this, right?"

Taylor silenced her with a finger. "Shh. I know. I don't want you to worry." She bent to Melanie's neck, running the tip of her tongue up to an inviting ear. "There's no pressure here, and I would never expect you to do anything you're not comfortable with." She flicked the ear with her tongue, delighting in the shiver she felt run through Melanie. "All I want is to be with you."

She caught Melanie's lips with her own and soon tongues were dueling, blood was rushing, skin was burning, lungs were heaving. Taylor pulled the covers back, guiding Melanie down onto the bed and pulling off her own panties. She slid into the bed next to the redhead who opened her arms, allowing Taylor to roll half-onto her. Both women groaned at the delicious full-body contact.

If Taylor didn't have an entire body to explore, she was sure she could have kissed Melanie all night long.

Their lips just seemed to fit together. She'd never enjoyed simply kissing somebody so much. Her lips left a blazing trail down Melanie's neck to dance across her collarbone. Melanie gasped as Taylor circled her nipple with her tongue, purposely avoiding it until Melanie thought she'd burst. After what seemed like forever, Taylor raked her tongue across the swollen pebble of flesh, causing Melanie to arch into her.

"Oh my God, Taylor," she exclaimed through clenched teeth.

Taylor continued to assault the nipple, claiming the other with her free hand after separating Melanie's legs enough to allow her to slip her own thigh between the red-head's. She caught her breath when she felt the slick liquid silk immediately coating her leg. God, she was wet. Taylor set a rhythm, her mouth, fingers and thigh all working together to drive Melanie higher. An unexpected bonus came when Melanie pressed her own thigh into Taylor's center, causing the brunette's hips to spasm. Taylor continued rocking against the gorgeous woman beneath her, feeling the smaller hands in her hair, listening to the change in her breathing. It was only another minute before she felt the fingers in her hair clutch a desperate handful, and heard the soft, pleading voice—a pitch higher than usual, as predicted in her fantasy. "Taylor...Taylor...Taylor..."

Jesus Christ, how does she do this to me? Melanie held onto Taylor with a death grip, the weight of Taylor's body serving only to excite her further. She heard herself chanting Taylor's name...never had she called out somebody's name in bed...and she felt Taylor smile against the breast still held possessively in her mouth. *She's enjoying herself*, Melanie realized, and found that she was pleasantly surprised by the thought.

And then it was upon her. Her second orgasm crashed down around her before Melanie had time to prepare...again. She arched into the body above hers as colors exploded behind her eyelids. A small cry tore itself from her throat, much to her surprise, as she was traditionally rather quiet during lovemaking. She was sure she heard some sort of humming coming from Taylor...she could feel it in her chest where Taylor was still suckling gently, sending tiny aftershocks through Melanie's body as her hips slowly returned to the bed. She threw an arm over her eyes and concentrated on steadying her breathing.

After several minutes, Melanie's heart finally beat at a somewhat normal rate. When she removed her arm, she saw smiling, dark eyes looking up at her. Taylor was still lying half on her, her chin propped on the arm that was resting across Melanie's chest. Melanie managed a shaky smile.

"Again, wow," Taylor commented.

Melanie took a deep, shuddering breath. "Wow is right."

"Wonder what will happen when I actually touch you."

The thought sent an erotic chill through Melanie's entire body and her hips twitched involuntarily.

Taylor cocked an eyebrow at her and smiled wickedly. "Oh, you like that idea, do you?"

She inched up so their lips were even and kissed Melanie slowly, softly. Melanie felt herself drowning in Taylor's touch. Her lips seemed to drive all thought from the redhead's mind, and she lost herself in the silken mouth that was softly, yet insistently devouring hers. Despite her recent exertion, she was astounded to feel the passion quickly building within her yet again.

Taylor moved her lips from Melanie's, down her throat to fasten onto the nipple she'd neglected earlier. She smiled as she heard Melanie inhale sharply, her fingers re-twining in Taylor's dark hair. Melanie's body was subtly undulating beneath her, and she couldn't believe the response she evoked from her. Taylor liked to think of herself as a good lover...she always made the effort to be very attentive and sensitive to her partner, but this was different. It was like she had some sort of inside information on where to touch Melanie and how, like they had a kind of psychological connection to one another, allowing Taylor to take Melanie as high as possible. The thought served to heighten her own excitement with the gorgeous woman under her, and she shifted her position, gently spreading Melanie's thighs to accommodate her hips between them.

Letting go of the nipple she'd thoroughly bathed, she raised herself up on her hands, firmly pushing herself against Melanie's soaked center. The action caused the redhead to moan erotically, arching her own pelvis up into Taylor's and grabbing the brunette's forearms, hoping they would keep her anchored and prevent her from drifting away on the waves rolling through her.

Taylor lowered herself down again, capturing Melanie's lips in a fierce kiss before moving slowly down her body. She stopped to pay homage to each beautifully firm breast, before continuing down and running her tongue from one side of the redhead's stomach to the other and back again. As she did so, and without warning of any kind, she swiped one finger slowly through the glistening folds of skin between Melanie's thighs...just once. Melanie's hips jerked as she gasped.

"Oh my God," she whispered.

Taylor smiled at the exclamation and pushed Melanie's thighs farther apart, settling her shoulders between them, kissing and licking each creamy smooth leg, taking her time and enjoying the squirming and tremoring of their owner.

Melanie was nearly delirious. She was overwhelmed by the sensations coursing through her from so many different directions. Nobody had ever made her feel this way, and part of her was frightened by that fact. At the same time, she'd never felt so safe or so loved in her entire life. Her heart was hammering in her chest when she felt Taylor's tongue leave her legs. She could feel the brunette's breath on her center, which, by this point, was absolutely aching for attention. Part of her wanted to grab Taylor's head and push her into the wetness with savage authority. Another part was so terrified, it wanted to cry.

"Taylor...?"

Taylor's voice came back to her husky and sweet. "Are you scared?"

"A little."

"Trust me. Okay?"

There really was no question. Somehow, some way, for some inexplicable reason, she trusted Taylor implicitly, no doubts, no second thoughts. It only took her a heartbeat to answer.

"Okay."

The word was barely out of Melanie's mouth before Taylor's tongue descended upon her, slicking across her once, from bottom to top. Another cry was ripped from her throat, regardless of the effort she'd put forth to keep it inside. A second stroke of Taylor's tongue got the same response, and the good little girl Melanie had always been was mortified to find herself clutching at Taylor's head and making every attempt to open her legs as wide as possible...anything to keep this incredible feeling from leaving her. She felt Taylor's hands on her thighs, stroking them, sliding under to cup her rear and pull Melanie further into her mouth. Melanie heard the gentle humming again, something she now knew was a sign of Taylor's own pleasure. The sound sent another surge through her.

Melanie felt herself cresting, the orgasm so close she could almost see it behind her closed eyes. One of Taylor's hands left her, and Melanie arched dramatically when she felt a finger, then a second, slip deliciously into her. Taylor moved in a gentle rhythm, fingers and tongue working together, and that was all it took. Melanie went plummeting over the edge, shouting Taylor's name loudly all the way down. Taylor held tightly to Melanie's hips with one hand, feeling the muscles contracting around the fingers of the other, and pressed the flat of her tongue against Melanie, holding it there while she watched the redhead climax.

It was the most beautiful thing she'd ever seen.

When Melanie's shudders had subsided, Taylor gathered her up in her arms and hugged her tightly.

"Oh my God, Taylor," Melanie whispered over and

over. "Oh my God."

Taylor smiled against Melanie's hair, then rolled them over so Melanie rested against Taylor's side.

Melanie's entire body felt as though it was made of Jello. Her arms were weak, and she couldn't feel her legs at all. She allowed Taylor to shift them around, pleased with the result when she found her head tucked snugly under Taylor's chin, her own leg thrown possessively over Taylor's.

"I can't even get my eyes to open," she complained. She felt Taylor's body move as she chuckled beneath her.

"Shh." Melanie felt warm lips pressed softly against her forehead. "Go to sleep."

She needed no more coaxing and she drifted off in a scant few seconds, her last thought being amazement at how incredibly well their two bodies fit together, like two pieces of a puzzle.

Chapter
22

Melanie opened her eyes to the cheerful sound of birds outside the window and the sun streaming across the bed in a dazzling display. She was lying on her left side, facing the window. She'd never noticed the small birdfeeder attached just outside it, and she smiled as she watched the sparrows chatter busily over their breakfast.

She let her eyes drift shut again, and snuggled into the warmth pressed against her back. Taylor was spooned behind her, one arm draped over Melanie's stomach, one knee firmly ensconced between Melanie's thighs. A flush crept through the smaller woman as she flashed back to the previous night, and she felt her face redden. She sighed, amazed at how good it felt to be held by this woman. Her eyes flicked to the bedside clock, then flew open wide.

Ten-thirty?

God, that's the longest I've slept since I was in college, she thought. *Not to mention the soundest.*

She extricated herself from Taylor, and stood next to the bed looking down at her as she continued to snore softly. A pang of guilt crept into her mind as she realized she hadn't done anything to alleviate the pressure that must have been building in Taylor's body the night before.

Taylor had been so gentle, so passionate... *God, she knew how to touch me.* She knew Taylor had been excited...she had felt the proof coating her own thigh as she'd pushed against the taller woman. But, Melanie had been very nervous about touching Taylor any more intimately than that. After all, she'd never been with a woman. What if she didn't know what to do? She immediately shook her head in self-deprecation. That wasn't it. She was rationalizing. She had been scared, plain and simple. She vowed to talk to Taylor about it when the brunette finally woke up. *Well, she worked hard last night. She deserves a rest.*

She smiled as she memorized each and every line on the brunette's face, noticed the tiny brown mole on the side of her neck, and catalogued four strands of gray hair, filing their locations away for use as ammo later on. She bent and placed a light kiss on Taylor's shoulder, hearing Lynda's snickering laughter in her head.

"I think I love you," she whispered. Standing, she found an old, oversized T-shirt in a drawer and slipped it over her head.

She felt reborn. That was the only word she could come up with as she padded to the bathroom. Even her reflection looked oddly different. She studied it intensely for several moments, before giving up on finding the change. Her stomach rumbled loudly, reminding her that she'd had no dinner the night before and she padded into the kitchen, wondering if it would be possible to salvage any of the food they'd left out over twelve hours ago.

The kitchen was a mess. Dishes and a large frying pan were strewn about. The eggs had been left out all night...Melanie wondered if they were still usable and decided to wait until Taylor was up. The white brick of cheese had darkened slightly and was covered with a greasy film, causing Melanie to wrinkle her nose at the sight. "Yuck," she murmured.

She hummed a tune as she returned dishes to the proper cupboards, thinking maybe they'd just go out for breakfast. She was so lost in her thoughts and the din of clattering plates, that she didn't hear the front door open, nor did she realize she had company until the voice from behind her nearly gave her a heart attack.

"Hey, Mellie."

Melanie dropped the plate she was holding and it shattered on the floor at her bare feet. "Jesus Christ." She turned to meet the smiling eyes of her cousin. "Are you trying to scare me to death?"

"Sorry, baby cousin," Sam apologized with a chuckle, squatting to help Melanie pick up the pieces. She wore skin-tight jeans and a bright yellow tank top, her blonde hair pulled back off her tanned face. "I forget how lost in your own little world you can get." She did a double take at her younger cousin, a smirk forming on her pretty face. "Um, Mellie? Did you forget something?"

Melanie looked up. "What?"

"Your pants, maybe?"

Melanie's head snapped down and she realized her cousin was right. Before she could say a word, Taylor came skidding into the kitchen, clad in only a sheet.

"What the hell was that noise? Are you okay...oh. Hi, Sam."

Samantha stood up slowly, the smirk sliding right off her face. Her eyes moved from her cousin to her friend and back, taking in their various states of undress, comprehension lighting her face.

"What exactly is going on here?" she asked in an unnervingly quiet voice.

"Um...well," Taylor began, searching for the right words. She turned to Melanie for help. The redhead's eyes were darting from Sam's feet to her own. She looked very much like a cornered animal.

"We had dinner together," Melanie offered feebly, feeling like she had magically reverted to her awkward, shy, teenage years when she fought as hard as she could to please Samantha so her cousin would look out for her socially.

"Looks like you had dessert, too," Sam added sarcastically. The disappointment in her voice cut through Melanie like a knife.

"Sam," Taylor began gently. "Melanie's a big girl."

"She's also straight," Sam snapped. Taylor flinched as though she'd been slapped. "What did you do, get her drunk? Get her drunk so you could seduce her?"

"No, I didn't get her drunk," Taylor responded, trying unsuccessfully to keep the anger out of her voice. "And I didn't seduce her."

Melanie squeezed her eyes shut as the animosity level in the room increased.

"Well, then, tell me. How else does a dyke get a straight girl into bed?"

Refusing to begin a debate about Melanie's sexuality, Taylor decided to channel her anger in a different direction. She focused instead on the pain of these insults that were being hurled at her by somebody she considered a friend. Her only defense was to hurt back.

"What the hell is your problem, Sam? Rob dump you off somewhere?"

"Shut up, Taylor." Samantha's voice was a low, warning growl.

"Don't you dare tell me to shut up. You come in here spouting off about what a wretched seductress I am, tempting innocent straight women to their doom with my lesbian charms, and you have the audacity to tell *me* to shut up? No, Sam, I think *you* should shut up."

"What on earth is going on in here?"

Ben's voice was as unexpected as his presence filling the front doorway.

"Oh, God," Melanie whimpered upon seeing him, self-consciously pulling down on the hem of her T-shirt.

"I came over to see Melanie and I heard shouting. What is going on?" His eyes took in the sight before him slowly. Several emotions visibly crossed his handsome face: realization, shock, disappointment, anger, hurt.

"What's going on? I'll tell you what's going on," Sam spat. "Your daughter's fucking my cousin."

"*Sam*! That's enough," Melanie cried. "Please." Her eyes shimmered with tears. This was too much. Too much, too soon. She turned and walked to the bedroom, snapping the door shut behind her.

Taylor watched her go, torn between running to hold her, to comfort her, and staying put to defend them against this unexpected onslaught of hostility.

"Dad..." she began.

Ben held up a hand to silence her. "No, no, T. You don't have to explain anything to me. You're a big girl." The pain in his voice was so apparent, it made Taylor wince. He looked like he wanted to say more. Instead, he turned and made a quiet exit, feeling ten years older than he actually was.

Taylor and Samantha stood alone in the kitchen for several awkward minutes, neither able to meet the other's eyes.

God, how did this become such a mess? Taylor asked silently. She swallowed back the lump in her throat, gathering up the sheet around her ankles and approaching the closed bedroom door. She hesitated for a minute, then knocked softly.

"Melanie?" *Please.*

Several minutes went by with no answer.

"Melanie?" she repeated, unable to disguise the crack in her voice. "Are you okay?"

"I just need to think, Taylor," came the soft voice. "Okay? Just...give me some time to think?"

There was such confusion and uncertainty in the tone, and it filled Taylor with dread. She leaned her forehead against the door, willing the tears not to fall until she was alone. She cleared her throat. "Okay, sweetheart. Whatever you need. You got it. I...um...I need my clothes, though."

There was a rustling behind the door, then it opened and Melanie handed a pile of clothing to Taylor, her head down. She knew if she looked into those dark, loving eyes, she'd be lost forever. She had a hard time ignoring the searing fire that shot through her at the simple touch of Taylor's hand as she took the clothes from Melanie's grasp.

"It'll be okay," the brunette whispered softly.

The door shut again quietly. Taylor closed her eyes for a minute, then went into the bathroom to rid herself of the sheet. She put on the clothes from the previous night, stopping when she noticed that Melanie had mistakenly—or purposely—put her own pale blue tank top in the pile. Taylor lifted the soft fabric to her nose and inhaled deeply, drawing the scent of the woman she'd fallen head over heels for into her lungs. The action caused her eyes to brim with tears. She shook herself, tucked the tank under her own shirt and exited the bathroom.

Samantha was still standing quietly in the kitchen, not sure what to do next. Taylor stopped in front of her, keeping her eyes downcast, her voice low and calm.

"I would *never* force *anybody* to do something they didn't want to. Especially not Melanie. I was under the impression that you, as my friend, would know that."

With that, she left the carriage house. Halfway to her own house, she stopped. She looked from one building to the other. She didn't want to face her father, though she knew she owed him some sort of explanation. She couldn't go back to the carriage house. She wasn't exactly welcome right now. Completely at a loss, she fished her keys out of her pocket, unable to believe she actually had them—not having them would have been icing on the cake of such a disastrous morning—and headed for her car. Right now, she needed to get the hell away from everybody.

Chapter
23

"Mellie?"

The soft voice was perfectly partnered with the soft tapping at the door. Melanie shut her eyes and buried her face in the pillow she had wrapped in her arms. She realized the scent she detected was a mixture of Taylor's perfume and the passion of the previous night. She was unable to stop the flow of tears she'd been suppressing for over an hour now.

"Mellie, come on," Sam's voice pleaded. "I'm sorry. I know I was out of line."

"Way," Melanie answered angrily.

Sam felt a blend of relief at finally being acknowledged and guilt over knowing Melanie was right. "Okay. Way out of line. You just...I was surprised. That's all. You caught me off-guard."

The blonde jumped as the door flew open unexpectedly. Melanie faced her, dressed in the same T-shirt and a pair of paint-stained gym shorts, her blue eyes flashing with anger.

"That's a cop-out, Samantha, and you know it," she snapped as she breezed past her cousin to clean the chaotic kitchen.

"What do you mean?" Sam followed her.

"I mean, because you were surprised, that's excuse enough for you to insult somebody who's supposed to be your friend?"

Sam shifted uncomfortably. "Oh, I did not. Taylor knows I didn't mean it."

"You called her a dyke, Sam. Hell, you might as well have called her a perverted predator the way you were talking. You don't think she might have been hurt by those remarks?"

"Hey, you shouldn't be talking about hurt. I'm not the one playing both sides of the fence."

"What the hell is that supposed to mean?"

"Oh, come on, Mellie. It was pretty obvious that Ben was hurt by what he saw. Since he knows Taylor's into girls, I can only assume he had an interest in you, too. My, my, baby cousin. You're a regular heartbreaker."

Melanie stopped what she was doing and looked at her cousin for a long moment, digesting the words Samantha had carelessly tossed her way. She felt the guilt slowly seeping into her body, like water through a sieve. What if she had seriously damaged Taylor's relationship with Ben? What if her own inability to control herself had put a permanent strain on their father-daughter existence? Her shoulders drooped slightly with the added weight and she sighed heavily. Wiping her hands on a dishtowel, she gestured to the kitchen table.

"Sit down, Sam."

Sam did as she was told, unfamiliar with the steely look on her little cousin's face.

"First of all, yes, Taylor is my friend, regardless of this fiasco with Ben. Insulting my friend insults me, plain and simple. Second, your comments lead me to believe that you actually think I'm stupid enough to let somebody get me drunk and take advantage of me. That just pisses me off. And third, it isn't any of your fucking business who I sleep with. You got that?"

Sam looked stunned for a split second and struggled to compose herself. "So, you did sleep with her? You're...a lesbian?"

Melanie sighed with great weariness. "I don't know, Sam. Yes, I slept with Taylor. Because I wanted to, not because she tricked me, not because I was trying to play some perverted game with her and her father. Because I wanted to."

"Is this...what you want? How can you choose that kind of lifestyle?" Sam was honestly baffled. "I mean, why would you want to be in a minority like that, with what you'll have to put up with?"

Melanie laughed harshly. "Allow me to enlighten you, my dear cousin. The whole 'it's their choice' thing? It's a big crock of shit. There is no choice." Her voice cracked, much to her dismay, putting a chink in her calm demeanor. "And now I need to deal with all of this, and I'm not sure exactly how." She squeezed her eyes shut against the sudden vision of Taylor's concerned face. God, how she wanted to be with her right now. But, not like this. Not when she was so messed up in her own head.

She'd never expected the hostility they'd received from Samantha, not in a million years. And Ben. Poor Ben. Finding out like that. She could kick herself for letting things go as far as they had with him. That was just cruel. And now, she'd put a wedge between him and Taylor— even Sam saw it. That only made her feel infinitely worse.

"I need to get out of here for a while," she said suddenly. She'd just get away...out of everybody's hair. It was the only solution. Ben and Taylor could work things out. Samantha could go back to her life...whatever that was. And Melanie would have the thinking space she so desperately needed. She strode with purpose to the bedroom, dragging out her suitcase and throwing things in without folding them.

Samantha followed her into the small room and watched silently for several minutes without speaking. This was so much for her to absorb. She felt guilty now that she had left Melanie on her own in a strange city for so long. She still stung from Rob's brush-off and was infinitely embarrassed that Taylor had struck the nail directly on the head in her assumptions.

"You know, Mellie, you can come back any time you want." Samantha tried to keep her voice light as her eyes traveled around the room, anything to avoid looking directly at her cousin. "I know this hasn't been the greatest vacation for you, and I'm sorry. Can we try it again?"

Melanie hardly seemed to hear her and kept right on packing. Going back to Chicago immediately was something of which she was sure, the only thing of which she was sure, and she clung to it with both hands. "Oh, I'm coming back. Some time next week. I've got the bookstore to contend with."

Sam blew out a relieved breath, much more relaxed to be talking about familiar things again. She waved a hand nonchalantly. "Oh, that. Don't worry about it."

Melanie stopped what she was doing and met her cousin's eyes.

"Really, Mellie," Sam continued. "I've been thinking. I'm gonna take a second look at it and see if maybe I can give it one more try, ya know?"

Shit. This was all she needed. *When it rains, it pours, isn't that what they say?* She finished tossing items into the suitcase, fastened it shut, and sat on the bed with yet another heavy sigh, patting the space next to her with her hand.

"Sit down, Sam."

Taylor watched as the fourth plane took off from the runway. The day was clear. The sky was blue. The planes were moving right on schedule. Part of her wished she were on one of them.

She sighed and leaned her head back against the headrest of the driver's seat. This was a place she frequented when she needed to get away. It was a small clearing about a hundred and fifty yards from the main runway of the Rochester International Airport, tucked away between an abandoned field and a small wooded area. She'd pull her car right up to the fence and watch the airplanes come and go, forgetting about her life for a while. Not many people knew how to get to it...back roads that were tough to find...and she usually had it to herself. Occasionally, some other car would make its way to the chain link fence, but today, the little red Honda sat alone like a drop of blood on a plain piece of cloth, facing the runway.

How had such a beautiful thing gotten so terribly messed up so fast? Taylor had hoped to come here to clear her head for a bit, but the same question kept popping up. How could she fix this before it became irrevocably damaged?

Melanie needed some space. She understood that. She didn't like it, but she understood it. Coming to terms with your alternative sexuality was never an easy thing. Melanie's being over thirty wasn't going to make it any easier for her. Taylor had never been somebody's first, and she'd avoided it for this very reason. Too much turmoil, too much insecurity, too much fear on the part of the first-timer. People rarely stayed with their firsts. More likely, they grew apart from them and eventually moved on. That thought terrified Taylor almost as much as never having Melanie in the first place.

This morning hadn't been exactly the way Taylor pictured it. She hadn't put a lot of thought into how they would reveal their relationship to the people close to them, but her father walking in on them when they were both half-naked had not been on her list of ideal situations. The pain on his face was still crystal clear in Taylor's mind, the pain and the look of betrayal. It was only a brief flash, but it was there, making Taylor feel as if she'd stolen something right out from under his nose. And the anger Sam had radiated...Taylor shook her head, still in shock over that one. Something must have definitely happened between her

and Rob. Samantha was flighty and self-centered, but prej-
udiced was not a word commonly used to describe her.

Her thoughts returned to the gorgeous auburn-haired
woman she'd made love to less than twenty-four hours ago.
Taylor could still smell Melanie's scent on her fingers,
could still taste the salty tang on the back of her tongue.
They had made music together last night, there was no
denying it. She had known exactly where to touch Melanie,
when, and how. In Taylor's eyes, that was simply further
testament to the fact that they were supposed to be
together. She was never one to subscribe to the beliefs of
destiny and fate and people being meant for each other.
She was actually something of a cynic when it came to
such things. That is, until Melanie had entered her life.
Taylor knew, without a shadow of a doubt, that the two of
them were supposed to be together. She didn't know how
she knew. She just knew.

She swallowed hard and got out of the car. Moving
around to the front, she slid herself onto the hood, tilted
her head back and looked up at the clear, blue sky. Taylor
did not consider herself a religious person by any means,
but at this point, she was ready to appeal to whoever was
willing to listen.

"Okay, look," she said aloud, feeling infinitely silly. "I
know I don't talk to you all that much, but I'm at a loss
here. I need a little guidance. See, I'm in love with this
person...of course, I suppose if you actually do exist, you
already know the details." She studied her hands for several minutes. "I have never felt so close to somebody, so
connected to another person. I've never fallen so hard or
so fast for anybody in my life. I'm not proud of that, mind
you. I just...I really, really don't want to lose her, but I
feel like it's out of my hands. I don't know what to do
now."

She sat unmoving, and part of her actually expected to
hear some sort of answer. Her eyes brimmed with tears as
she listened to nothing but the deafening roar of a departing plane.

Chapter 24

Samantha grimaced as she took another sip from her fourth glass of wine. She hated red wine. Especially dry varieties like the one she was drinking now. Unfortunately, it was the only bottle left in her wine rack...obviously a gift from somebody, as she would never buy Merlot for herself...and she desperately needed a drink after the day she'd had.

The sun streaked through the picture window in the living room, but she had no desire to be out in it. The bottle of wine was on the floor, more than half empty. Sam lay sprawled on the couch, the hand holding the wineglass dangling precariously over the carpet, allowing her depression to completely surround her, cradling her in its cold and lonely arms. Today, Samantha Richter had been forced to take a good, honest look at herself.

She had not been impressed.

Rob, the bastard. He'd actually expected that they'd stay with his ex-girlfriend once they arrived in Vancouver and Sam wouldn't have a problem with it. Truth was, she didn't have a problem until she came back from a quick trip to the drugstore to pick up tampons and found them in bed together. Just like old times.

She'd used the credit card her father had given her to get a bus ticket so she could come home. To her advantage, the long, tedious ride had given her ample time to collect herself and put her unshakable façade back into place. She couldn't have her adoring baby cousin thinking she'd been humiliated by yet another one of her scoundrel boyfriends.

Truth be told, she didn't know why she'd been surprised at Rob's betrayal. He was no different than any of the other men she'd dated. He certainly wasn't that far removed from the loser she'd actually married. Screwing around was just part of his character. They were all the same. She had known that going in. For some reason, though, this one hurt more than the others. She wasn't sure why.

"I'm getting too old for this shit," she muttered at the ceiling.

And what the hell was going on with Melanie? She rolled her eyes and drained her glass when the thought popped into her head. *God, I really fucked that one up.* Even Samantha had the good sense to feel remorse for her behavior that morning. She had completely lost it. She had been trying so hard to put on a happy face after the Rob fiasco. Then she'd walked in to find her half-naked cousin in the kitchen and her equally-as-naked new female lover in Samantha's own bed. The blonde hadn't known how to handle it, so she'd snapped, plain and simple—something of which she was not proud.

Apparently, she didn't really know Melanie at all. Had Samantha really spent her life so self-absorbed that she failed to notice something as important as her closest cousin's penchant for women? Nah, she decided. That was definitely new. And she had to admit that if Melanie was going to pick a woman to fall for, Taylor was an excellent choice. Samantha herself had entertained the thought more than once of taking her harmless flirting with the brunette a step further, just to see what it would be like.

And fall for Taylor was exactly what Melanie had done. That much was glaringly obvious. Much as her little cousin had tried to keep her emotions in check, Samantha had seen her as if she had been an open book. It was right there in her eyes, as apparent as if she had written it in black marker on her forehead. Melanie was in love with Taylor. She also seemed to be pretty aware of the fact, which only caused her more anxiety. Samantha may have been considered selfish by a lot of people, but she did pay attention to how Melanie acted when they were growing up, and she was surprised when the redhead ran. Her cousin had never been one to avoid anything.

Sam pressed the heels of her hands tightly to her eyes. Four glasses of wine on an empty stomach worked quickly with her. Unfortunately, all the messes of the day still stared her in the face. Who was it that came up with the brilliant idea to drink away your problems? They just seemed bigger now that she was inebriated.

She had wanted to stop Melanie from leaving, but she had still been smarting from the news of the bookstore. She knew, deep down inside, that Melanie would have much better luck than she would have, but still. Yes, she had flippantly told Melanie to tell her father to sell it, but Melanie actually buying it felt like a betrayal of sorts. The reasonable adult in Sam's mind understood that it was strictly business, that Melanie would be a terrific owner, but the little girl inside was stomping her feet and scowling, mad that she'd lost something to her younger cousin.

A shadow passed by the window—she noticed it because it blocked the sunlight shining warmly on her closed eyelids for a brief second. She furrowed her brow, sitting up and blinking at the window.

She stood abruptly—too abruptly and had to reach out to the arm of the couch for support—when she heard the distinct sound of the scraping of shoes against the cement stoop at the front door. She surprised herself, as well as the person standing there, when she pulled it open.

Samantha and Taylor blinked at each other for several seconds. The brunette spoke first.

"I...um. I was just...uh, looking for Melanie," she stammered, feeling incredibly uncomfortable in the present company. "But her Jeep's not here, so I wasn't going to knock."

"She's gone." Sam waved her hand as if batting away a fly and turned back into the house.

Taylor followed her, well aware of the poorly disguised weaving in Samantha's step. "Gone? What do you mean, gone?"

Sam plopped back down to the couch and poured herself another glass of wine. "Gone. Outta here. Bye-bye. Back to Chicago."

"Back to—" Taylor felt her stomach lurch, panic seizing her. Melanie had gone back to Chicago? Just like that? Without so much as a goodbye? "I was going to go with her," she murmured, the softness of the voice doing nothing to hide the pain it held. She glanced about the room, noting Sam's indifference, as well as the nearly empty bottle of wine. "Sorry to have bothered you," she whispered. Swallowing audibly, she turned on her heel and left the carriage house without another word.

Sam watched all this with rapt attention, feeling mildly disappointed to see Taylor go. Part of her knew she needed to talk to her friend, to apologize, but she just couldn't bring herself to do it.

"Ah, maybe tomorrow then," she said aloud, bringing the glass to her lips. For the moment, she was content to consume her wine and wallow in her own self-pity.

Ben was seated at the kitchen table eating a late lunch when Taylor entered the house. He glanced up at her, immediately concerned by the expression on her face, his earlier anger and humiliation automatically kicked aside by his fatherly instincts.

"T.? You okay?" he asked softly.

"Fine," she replied, not looking at him, crossing through the kitchen to the doorway leading to the rest of the house.

At the doorway, she stopped, her hands resting on the moulding on either side of her. Both father and daughter were quiet for several minutes. He watched her. She stood in the doorway, her back to him, her head hanging forward. She spoke without turning around.

"I'm sorry, Dad." Her voice was barely audible, but Ben heard it and was surprised by the pain it held.

"It's okay, T."

"No." She turned to face him, and he saw the tears brimming in her dark eyes. She looked so much like Anna, and he felt his heart constrict in his chest...he could never stand to see Anna cry either. "No, it's not okay. I need to explain."

Ben wasn't sure he wanted to hear what she had to say, but he remained quiet as she pulled out the chair across from him and sat down, her arms on the table, her eyes studying her hands.

"I should have talked to you about Melanie." She took a deep breath. "I knew you were interested in her, but by that time, so was I, even if I didn't want to admit it."

Ben nodded, said nothing.

"I wasn't even sure...which...whom she...preferred," she stammered. "Men or women."

"You didn't ask her?"

"Did you?"

Ben shook his head, taking his daughter's point in stride.

Taylor met his eyes, softening her gaze, speaking as sincerely as she could. "I'm not sorry for what happened between her and I, but I am sorry for not talking to you when things got complicated. We've been through too much together. You deserved more respect than that, and I apologize. I didn't mean to hurt you. Neither did she."

Ben was quiet for a long time, thoughts swirling around in his head so rapidly, he had trouble grasping hold of just one. Finally, he addressed his daughter.

"So, can I assume then that she's...that she prefers women?"

Taylor fought hard to keep the smirk from her face at the childlike quality of the question. "I think we'd have to ask her that," she responded carefully, uncomfortable with the fact that she herself didn't quite know the answer to that one.

"Mm." he nodded. He was struggling. Taylor could see it on his face. "What happens now? Are you two...um...an item?"

Taylor's face fell slightly, but it was enough for her father to catch. She turned her eyes to gaze out the window at the late afternoon sunlight. "I don't know. Sam says Melanie's gone back to Chicago. I think this morning may have been a bit too much for her to handle."

It still amazed Ben how quickly parental instincts took over. His immediate concern was to smooth away the worry lines on the face of his beloved child...to say something to make her feel better. She'd been there for him during the lowest point in his life, and she'd done everything she could to ease his pain. It was time to return the favor.

"Don't you worry about Melanie," he ordered, patting her hand. "You know as well as I do how tough she is. Don't underestimate what she can and cannot handle."

A tear finally spilled over and tracked down Taylor's cheek as she looked at her big, strong daddy, trying so hard to take away her pain, despite his own. She felt like she was eight years old again and wanted nothing more than to crawl up in his lap and let him protect her from all the hurt in the world.

"What if she doesn't come back?" she whispered.

"She owns the bookstore now," he reasoned. "She has to come back."

"Maybe she doesn't own it yet. What if she puts a halt to it?"

"She owns it. Trust me. I've seen the paperwork." He wiped the tear off her cheek. "She'll be back, and then you two can sort things out, okay? Just give her a little time. Maybe she's...struggling with this." He couldn't believe the words coming out of his own mouth. He was not the heart-to-heart type, he never had been. But, it seemed to be working, he noticed, as Taylor's face brightened just the slightest bit.

"I love her," she said softly, swallowing the lump in her throat, a little embarrassed about the vulnerability she was suddenly showing her father.

"I know you do," he replied, and it was the truth. "And that makes Melanie Larson one very lucky lady." She looked at him in surprise. "Now come here and give your old man a hug, then go wash your face."

She didn't hesitate as she went around the table to wrap her arms around him, squeezing as tightly as she could. It was a game they had played when she was little. Ben wasn't a big talker, but hugs had been his specialty. He would always tease her, instructing her to hug him as tightly as she could. "Are you squeezing yet?" he'd rib her, knowing full well she was squeezing as hard as her little arms would allow.

"T.," he wheezed now, chuckling at the same time. "I'm an old man now, remember? Go easy. You're gonna break my ribcage."

She laughed, loosening her hold slightly but not letting him go. "Thanks, Dad." She kissed him lightly on his cheek, remnants of his Old Spice after shave tingling on her lips. She left the kitchen and headed upstairs. Although she didn't feel great, she felt a lot better than she had twenty minutes ago. Melanie would come back eventually, right?

Chapter
25

Melanie knew as soon as she set foot in her apartment that she didn't really want to be there. It looked exactly as it had when she left it, only covered with more dust. She dropped her suitcase on the hardwood floor and sifted through three weeks worth of mail. She tried valiantly to pretend she was actually paying attention to the return addresses for a good two and a half minutes before throwing the envelopes angrily to the floor. She'd managed to make the entire ride from Rochester to Chicago without shedding a tear, but now that she was so far away from the one person she wanted to be near most in the world, she was unable to stop the flow of emotion and it washed over her like an ocean wave, forcing her down against the couch with its intensity.

How had this happened? How had something that felt so right suddenly become so wrong? Why was it so hard for her to accept that she loved another woman? She didn't understand, a fact that was making her crazy, because understanding was something she normally did very well. She plodded to the bathroom to grab the box of Kleenex, then returned to the couch, blowing her nose loudly.

She was furious with Samantha. After all they'd been through together, Melanie couldn't believe the reaction her cousin had had. Melanie had always been able to overlook Sam's selfish motives and conceited statements, because they had never extended to her. As Sam's flesh and blood, she'd always been safe from the biting comments and self-serving actions. This morning had hurt her more than she cared to admit, and Melanie had actually found a tiny bit of perverse pleasure in telling Sam about the bookshop.

She had to go back. It was that simple. She had the bookshop, her new apartment, and the movers already lined up. Bailing out like a coward was not an option she had ever entertained, and she certainly wasn't about to start now. No, she would return to Rochester, move into her new place and open *The Quill is Mightier*, just as she had originally planned. It was that other matter that she couldn't seem to sort out...the one about falling in love with a woman named Taylor, then proceeding to destroy the relationship Taylor had with her father in a matter of minutes.

Melanie was definitely having trouble with that one.

She was so angry with herself. If she had just kept to herself, not led Taylor on the way she had, stayed away from Ben from minute one, none of this would have happened. The father and daughter would have ended up casual acquaintances of Melanie, and their relationship would still be intact.

Melanie wondered about the validity of that statement. Would it have been that way? Could it have? The pull she felt drawing her to Taylor was undeniable and virtually unavoidable. She wasn't sure she could have stayed away from the gorgeous, younger woman even if she'd wanted to. Which she hadn't.

As if she wasn't feeling enough guilt over the mess she'd made between Taylor and Ben, she started to wonder how Taylor was feeling. It was quite clear how the brunette felt about her. Nobody had ever made love to Melanie the way Taylor had. Nobody had ever worshipped her body that way, concerned with nothing more than Melanie's pleasure. She'd never been in bed with somebody that loving and that giving. Taylor loved her; that much was obvious. And how had Melanie reciprocated? By running like a scared child, leaving poor Taylor to wonder what was going on in Melanie's head and exactly where she stood.

Melanie dropped her head into her hands as fresh tears leaked from sad, blue eyes. Escape had seemed like a good idea that morning. Now, she wondered what kind of person she had become. She had never run from anything in her life, but she'd abandoned Taylor without a second thought.

"God, she must hate me," she muttered aloud, raking her fingers through her hair in frustration, disgusted with her own behavior. This whole mess was driving her nuts. She wanted things to slow down...wanted the myriad of thoughts swirling through her head like debris in the eye of a twister to stop, just for a minute, so she could catch her breath. She needed a touchstone, something, someone who knew her. She needed to be grounded. She needed familiarity. She craved it.

Without giving herself time to think twice, she picked up the cordless phone on the end table next to her and dialed a number.

"Hello?" The phone was answered on the first ring by a husky, male voice.

"Is Angela in?"

"Sure. Hang on."

There were muffled voices in the background, a child squealing happily, as if being tickled.

"Hello?" came the beloved voice. Melanie was amazed to feel herself immediately relax.

"Hi, Angela," she said, unable to keep the smile out of her voice. *God, it's good to hear her.*

"Melanie. Oh my God," Angela gushed. "Were your ears ringing? I was just talking about you today."

"As a matter of fact, they were." Melanie played along, letting the familiarity of Angela's voice drip over her like honey, soothing her anxieties immediately. "How are you?" She heard the child again, erupting into toddler-size giggles. "Is this a bad time?"

"For you? Nonsense. It's good to hear from you. I've been worried. I tried to call you last week, but there was no answer and I couldn't get your machine."

Melanie glanced at the phone, seeing the blinking red light that indicated the tape had run out. "I've been out of town. So, how are you? Everything okay? The kids? Grandkids?"

"Everybody's great. I found myself a terrific part-time job in a little flower shop near my house."

"Good for you." Melanie was glad to hear that Angela had found something that didn't force her to work ten-hour days, as she often had at Rucker and Steele. "You like it?"

"Love it. I practically run the joint, and I'm still home with plenty of time for dinner..." Angela stopped herself, stumbled a bit on her words. "Not that working for you—"

"Oh, please, Angela," Melanie interrupted her. "You worked like a dog when you worked for me. I know that. I'm glad you found something better for you. Really."

"So, you went out of town, eh?" she asked slyly.

"Yes, I did. I took that break you suggested."

"Tell me all about it."

An outsider didn't need to hear one shred of the conversation to know how it affected Melanie. Her body visibly relaxed, sinking into the cushions of the couch, her feet making their way to the coffee table and propping themselves upon it comfortably. Melanie tucked her hair behind her ear, laughing often, eyes sparkling as she told the story of her incredible disappearing cousin and the bookstore that just fell into her lap. Talking to Angela, truthfully the one person in the world who knew her best, stabilized her instantly.

"You've mentioned this Taylor person an awful lot," Angela commented after Melanie finished her recitation. Angela and Melanie had never gotten into such personal issues as one another's love lives, but the former secretary had never heard her ex-boss speak of anyone with such warmth and high regard. Melanie was like one of Angela's children, and Angela paid attention to her as such, monitoring the young woman's happiness as any mother would. She worked hard to keep the knowing smile from appearing in her voice. "She sounds like a nice girl."

"She's wonderful," Melanie replied simply, the smile in *her* voice glaringly apparent.

They talked for another fifteen minutes about Angela's family, Melanie's move and what they missed and did not miss about their previous jobs. The conversation was like a magic elixir for Melanie. Suddenly, things didn't seem quite so bad...at least not anything she couldn't handle.

"Well, I'll let you get back to your family," Melanie finally said, reluctant to end the connection. "It was great to talk to you. I've missed you."

"I've missed you, too, Melanie," Angela said sincerely. "I think this bookstore is going to be good for you."

"You think so?"

"Everything will be fine. I'm sure of it."

Melanie heaved a sigh of relief, surprised by the calming effect of those simple words. She wished the bookstore was closer so she could steal Angela from the florist. "Thanks."

"You take care of yourself, Melanie. And call me once in a while."

"I promise."

Melanie stared at the phone in her hand for several long minutes after hanging up. *Everything will be fine...*

She crossed to the television and plugged it in, content to put the packing off for a few more hours. She flopped back onto the couch, unable to stop the growing smile that spread across her face when the mesmerizing, blue eyes of the Warrior Princess appeared on the television screen.

Chapter
26

The next few days were a blur for Melanie. Between
the packing, situating things with the movers, the drive
back to Rochester, the bookstore, and her new apartment,
she barely had time to breathe, let alone think too deeply
about the events of the previous weeks.

She was in the bookshop on Wednesday morning, waiting for the sign guy to come and hang the new sign out
front, when Lynda popped her head in the unlocked front
door. Melanie smiled, peeking around the doorjamb of the
office and recognizing her visitor.

"Hey, there, stranger," Lynda called in greeting. "I was
getting worried. Haven't seen you in a couple days."

"I went home," Melanie stated, dusting her hands on
the legs of her gym shorts. "Had some loose ends to tie
up."

Lynda looked around in appreciation. All the shelves
were fully stocked. Melanie had pushed the overstuffed
chairs into a corner, where she had a display of periodicals,
including the area gay newspapers, creating a cozy and
inviting spot to take a load off. The windows had been
washed. There were small, unobtrusive bowls of potpourri

set out to give the place a warm, charming aroma.

Lynda nodded. "This place looks terrific. Are you just about ready for Monday?"

"Almost," Melanie answered, leading the café owner to the chairs and taking a seat herself. "I'm trying to get my computer hooked up in the office. I want to get the inventory on it...of course, most of it's here already. The sign guy is coming this morning to take care of that. I'm only waiting for a couple more shipments of books, and I think we're there."

She sounded excited, Lynda was glad to note, although there was a glimmer of something in the younger woman's eye that the café owner couldn't quite define.

"I saw your ad in *The Empty Closet*," Lynda commented, referring to Rochester's gay newspaper. "Looks great."

"Yeah, I was happy with that."

"You nervous?"

"About the opening?" Melanie took a deep breath. "Yeah. Yeah, I am. I mean, I don't expect that I'll get swamped with customers or anything. I'm not *Barnes & Noble*. I know that. Hell, I may not get one customer. But..." She searched the air for the right words. "This really means something to me, and I want to do it right. I want to make it work. You know?"

Lynda smiled and nodded, completely understanding the anxiety of her companion. "Absolutely. I felt exactly the same way when the day came to open the café for the first time. I had so many butterflies in my stomach, I thought for sure I'd be sick. I was so excited, it was terrifying."

"That's exactly it," Melanie cried, pointing to her friend. "That's how I feel. I'm so excited about this that I'm contemplating hiding under my desk for the duration. How silly is that?"

They laughed together like childhood friends, thinking how ridiculous human nature sometimes was.

"How are things with Taylor?" Lynda asked.   .

Melanie's chuckles died away quickly and she swallowed.

"Uh oh." Lynda was concerned about her friend's sudden change in demeanor. "What happened?"

"Long story," Melanie said simply, leaving her chair to brush a nonexistent spec of dust off a shelf.

"I've got plenty of time," Lynda said simply, sitting back in her chair, resting one ankle on the opposite knee.

After several minutes of silence, Melanie resigned herself to the fact that Lynda wasn't going to change the subject, and she sighed in frustration. Suddenly, there was a rapping on the glass of the front door. Melanie was relieved to see a smiling young man in ratty jeans and work boots...Glen from the sign shop. *Saved,* she thought and let him in.

She spent a good twenty minutes with Glen, going over the details of where and how to put up the large, wooden sign, before leaving him to his duty. When she returned to the corner, she was dismayed to note that Lynda had not even shifted her position and was watching her expectantly.

"God. You're relentless," Melanie complained.

"My middle name. Now spill it. I can tell it's bothering you."

"All right, all right. You win." She sighed in defeat and plopped into the opposite chair. She debated with herself for several minutes, before deciding to just be blunt and honest about the situation. "I slept with Taylor."

Lynda clapped her hands in delight. "That's great." Seeing the look on Melanie's face, she furrowed her brow. "That's not great?"

"Oh, it was great," Melanie assured her, a blush creeping up her neck. "It was really, really great, as a matter of fact. The next morning's what wasn't so great. Sam showed up out of the blue. She put two and two together pretty quickly."

"Now there's a surprise," Lynda joked. "Okay. So Sam found out. So what?"

"Well, that on top of the whole bookstore thing left her in somewhat of a foul mood."

"I repeat: so what?"

Melanie sighed. "Not five minutes after Sam came home, Ben decided to drop by."

"Ben..." Lynda wrinkled her nose, trying to place the name. "Ben. You mean the flower dude Ben? As in Taylor's father? That Ben?"

"That Ben."

"Oh, shit."

"Yeah. Taylor and I were half-dressed."

"I bet that wasn't the least bit awkward."

"Oh, no. Not at all."

"A fun time was had by all, huh?"

"Uh huh. You bet. I somehow managed to have the best sex of my life, seriously piss off my closest relative, and completely destroy a father-daughter relationship all in the course of a twelve-hour period. That's got to be some sort of record, don't you think?"

The sarcasm was a weak attempt to lighten the mood, but Lynda could plainly see the pain in her friend's eyes.

"So, what does Taylor have to say about all this?"

Melanie studied the floor carefully. "I don't know. I haven't seen her since."

"You what?"

The redhead winced. "I kind of...well...left for Chicago right after the shit hit the fan."

"You *what?*"

"I didn't know what else to do." Melanie sounded very much like a twelve-year-old defending herself against a grounding she knew she deserved. She looked at her hands as she tried to explain the turmoil she'd felt that morning. "It was such a mess. Sam was so mad and Ben just looked...God, he looked so hurt. And Taylor...she just wanted to make everything okay. It was too much. I couldn't take it."

"So you ran like a coward."

Melanie's head snapped up, eyes suddenly angry.

"That's not how it was."

Lynda wasn't cutting her any slack at all. "That's what it looks like from here."

"You weren't there, Lynda. You don't know." Sam's words echoed in her head. *I'm not the one playing both sides of the fence...* "All I've been able to think about is how I've turned Taylor and Ben against each other. Taylor's mom is dead. They need one another. What they don't need is me driving a nice, fat wedge between them."

"You know, it's funny." Lynda sat forward with her elbows on her knees and looked Melanie squarely in the eye. "I would have never pegged you as somebody who wouldn't stand tall to face down a problem. I thought you were one of the strongest people I've ever met." She shrugged. "My mistake."

Melanie didn't know what to say. Deep down, she knew Lynda was right. That didn't make admitting it any easier. She returned her gaze to her hands, feeling foolish and embarrassed. It was true, she had been busy since her return to Rochester the day before, but it would not have been that difficult for her to take five minutes out and pick up the phone to call Taylor.

The problem was, she didn't know where Taylor stood. Melanie missed the younger woman terribly, but she was mortified that she had come between her and her father, and she was discomfited by the situation in general. Most of all, she was terrified that Taylor would never want to see her again. Rather than face that reality head-on, Melanie chose to simply stay away and hope everything would just blow over on its own.

Lynda was right. She was a coward.

Lynda could practically see the train of thought as it chugged through Melanie's head and across her smooth face, and she knew she had struck home with the harsh comment. Before she could utter another word, the bell over the door jingled and a handsome, middle-aged man stepped into the store. By the expression of sheer panic that suddenly appeared on the redhead's face, Lynda guessed it to be Benjamin Rhodes, the flower dude.

"I gotta go help Julie," she said, standing, patting Melanie's knee as she did so. "Come see me later."

With that, she was gone. Melanie stood awkwardly facing Ben, shifting her weight from one foot to the other, the only sound being the pounding of Glen's hammer outside.

Ben seemed equally uncomfortable, but managed to speak first.

"Hi, Melanie."

"Hi, Ben." He looked dashing in his black, double-breasted suit and black and cream-striped tie, black leather briefcase dangling from one hand. He made a show of looking around, nodding his approval.

"It looks wonderful in here. And the exterior...nice color choice."

Somehow, the pretense of small talk was more unbearable than the silence. Melanie barreled ahead with the inevitable.

"Ben, I'm sorry about the other day...I..." She had trouble with her words, unable to find the right ones to express what she wanted to say...not really sure what she wanted to say, anyway.

Ben silenced her stumbling with an upheld hand and a small grin. "You and I have a lot in common, Melanie." At her puzzled expression, he ticked them off on his fingers. "We're both intelligent, we both like and dislike the same things about Corporate America, we both love my daughter..."

Melanie was annoyed to feel her eyes fill with tears, and she looked away. She was more annoyed that she couldn't think of any response.

"I won't say this has been easy," Ben continued. "You're the first woman since my wife died that I had serious thoughts about. The first one I thought maybe I could have something meaningful with. I'm not telling you this to make you feel bad. It's just a fact."

"I *do* feel bad," Melanie said, unable to keep a tear

from slipping down her cheek.

Ben smiled warmly. "I know you do. You're too kind not to. But, there's no reason. Taylor and I are adults. We've talked. We'll get through this. We're okay."

Melanie blinked. "You are?"

Ben shrugged. "Well, I'm okay. I've dealt with things, and I understand them. Taylor, on the other hand..." He let the sentence dangle.

Panic gripped Melanie's heart in its fist, and her stomach threatened to rebel against her at the thought of Taylor being anything but happy. "Taylor what? Is she all right?"

Ben smiled at the undisguised concern. "No, I don't think she's all right. I think she's miserable, Melanie. She's miserable without you. She'd never admit it, but she misses you so much it's tearing her up. And if she knew I was here talking to you, she'd kill me."

Melanie snorted a laugh through her tears. "It'll be our secret."

"You haven't called her."

"No, I haven't." Melanie sighed. "This is a lot to deal with, you know?"

"She deserves to know what's going on in that pretty little head of yours, don't you think?"

Melanie nodded silently.

"Maggie wore her out, Melanie." Ben's voice hardened. "She wore her out and I watched, helpless. She put my daughter through the emotional wringer, and I don't want to see that happen again. Taylor's like her mother—she pours her heart and soul into things she loves, without restriction. Anna used to say Taylor was the most passionate person she'd ever known. If you can't handle that, you need to tell her. *Now.* Before it's too late to save her from another disaster."

He was amazed with himself. He was actually talking on a strictly emotional level, although he did have to admit that it was much easier when he wasn't referring to his own emotions.

Melanie was amazed, too, not only by the wisdom of

Ben's words, but by the fact that she'd acted so blatantly selfish by not contacting Taylor even in some small way. She'd never considered herself a selfish person. Now, she was faced with the fact that maybe there was more of Samantha in her than she cared to admit. The thought only made her feel worse.

Chapter
27

"You don't smile anymore, Ms. Rhodes. You okay?"
The question was innocent enough and meant to be kindly
inquiring, but it made Taylor's eyes mist just the same.

"Oh, I'm fine, Nina," she replied to the radio station's
receptionist, as she passed by the front desk and headed
back to her own. She carefully pasted on a phony smile in
an attempt to show she was telling the truth. "Just tired.
Thanks for asking, though."

Nina didn't look the least bit convinced, but she let it
slide, turning her braided head to answer the ringing phone
lines.

Taylor retreated to her desk, shaken up by the question. She thought she'd been hiding things pretty well, but
apparently, people could see right through the façade. No,
she wasn't okay. She hadn't been for several days, and she
had no idea how to pull herself out of this funk the whole
situation with Melanie had put her in. She wasn't eating.
She wasn't sleeping. She was a mess, and she didn't like it
at all. The same thing had happened when she'd finally
realized she and Maggie were never going to survive. Try
as she had, she couldn't consciously pull herself out of

that, either. She'd had to wait it out, something she didn't do well.

She just didn't understand. Or, maybe she did. Taylor liked to think that she knew Melanie pretty well. She didn't think the redhead played mind games or was prone to lying. She seemed straightforward, kind-hearted, and loving. Taylor's best guess was that either Melanie was concerned about the condition of the relationship between Ben and Taylor, or she needed solitude to deal with her new alternative sexuality. Or both. There were no other logical explanations for the way she had just high-tailed it out of the city. Hell, she'd high-tailed it right out of the state. If she had simply been playing, merely been experimenting, she would have just said so, right? She could have said so and just laughed it off. Thanks for the fun time. Have a nice life. Easy, right?

Of course, there was the other possibility Taylor didn't want to acknowledge. The possibility that Melanie regretted the whole incident, that she wished it had never happened. Taylor decided that might actually be worse than the other choices. *Please, don't let that be the case.*

Any attempt at an explanation would have been nice, though, not to mention considerate. A phone call would have been even better. But, the silence was deafening for Taylor. It was Thursday. It had been almost five days since that disastrous Saturday morning, and not hearing from Melanie at all was absolutely breaking her heart.

Her two "angels" were no help. One sat on her shoulder, crying non-stop. The other stood with its arms folded over its chest, shaking its head, a look of "I told you so" plastered glaringly across its face.

"Get lost," Taylor scowled at it. It stuck its tongue out at her.

Why did this keep happening to her? Why did women treat her this way? She felt an unwelcome wave of self-pity wash over her. She was a good girlfriend. She was considerate and sensitive and loving and attentive. Why did she keep getting stepped on? Her feelings were deeply hurt, but part of her was just, simply put, pissed off.

She looked at the list of names she'd pulled off of her voice mail. She hadn't even been able to throw herself into work, which was how she would normally handle a lousy situation. She just didn't want to deal with anybody. More than anything, she wanted to go home, curl up under her goose down comforter, and sleep until the world went away.

Since that was obviously not the healthiest method of dealing with life, she decided she'd better at least pretend she was still paying attention to her job. She glanced at the list on her desk and reached for the handset of her telephone, just as it rang.

She snatched it up. "Taylor Rhodes."

"Hi."

The sound of that one word was magical. Taylor felt all her anxiety slipping away, like a layer of ice melting off of her frozen body. Her throat closed, and she couldn't speak.

"Taylor? It's Melanie." The voice faltered a bit, unsure.

"I know. Hey."

"Hey yourself." The relief was apparent.

"Are you okay?" Taylor asked.

Melanie chuckled. "You are something else, Taylor. You know that?"

"What do you mean?" Taylor asked, honestly puzzled.

"I mean, I take off on you without so much as a backward glance, yet you ask if *I'm* okay. You're amazing."

"Are you?"

"Am I what?"

"Okay. Are you okay?"

There was a pause. "Yeah. I'm okay. And I'm sorry I didn't call. But, I think we need to talk. In person."

Taylor felt anxiety churning in her gut, a sour mix of excitement to see Melanie again and dread over what she might have to say. *We need to talk* rarely meant that something good was about to happen. "Are you back in town?"

"Yeah. Um...are you busy tonight?"

"No," Taylor said, too fast. Melanie chuckled. "No, I'm free tonight. Do you want to meet someplace?"

"Well," Melanie hesitated, not sure how Taylor would take this. "I thought maybe you could...um...come to my apartment."

Taylor blinked in surprise, feeling a bit hurt at this news of which she was unaware. "You have an apartment?"

"Uh huh."

"Wow. That was fast. Um...yeah, okay. Where is it and what time do you want me to be there?"

Melanie gave her directions. "Does seven work for you?"

"Seven's fine. I'll see you then."

"Great."

Taylor hung up the phone slowly, not quite sure what to make of the call. Melanie wanted to talk. She was back in town, and she wanted to talk. This could be good. She also had an apartment. An apartment? When had she secured that, and why hadn't she shared it with Taylor? That was bad.

Contrary to what she'd been telling herself for the past several days, hearing from Melanie hadn't managed to make her feel the slightest bit better. In fact, she felt more anxious than she had all week. She felt her stomach churn, threatening to toss its emptiness up onto her desk.

Chapter
28

Taylor stood outside the huge house, looking up at the windows and trying hard to steady the hammering of her heart.

The house was beautiful. And enormous. Taylor guessed it contained at least five apartments, maybe more. It was an elegant light blue with white trim. The open porch was supported by large, round pillars that Taylor walked between to get to the ornate glass and wood front door, positioned directly in the center. She read the list of names near the doorbells and found the obviously new "Larson" next to number four. Taking a deep, steadying breath, Taylor pushed the button, then raked her fingers through her loose hair, hoping she looked all right.

"Taylor?" the voice crackled over the intercom.

"Uh huh."

"Come on up. Number four."

A buzzer sounded, and Taylor pulled the front door open.

The foyer was as beautiful as the outside of the house. Done in dark wood and burgundy carpeting, it looked very rich, very classy. Taylor walked forward to the large, wide stairwell where the shining banister reflected the evening sunlight back at her in a shimmering burst. She looked up. At the top of the stairs, Melanie peered over the railing, a smile on her face. Taylor smiled back, feeling her whole world slip into place.

"Hi," she called as she climbed.

"Hey, you."

Taylor didn't remember actually reaching the top of the stairs. She suddenly found herself wrapped in Melanie's arms, holding so tightly to her, she thought she might crush the smaller woman's ribs. She smiled into gold-tinted locks as she felt the embrace returned with equal tenacity.

"God, I missed you." She didn't realize she'd said it out loud until Melanie responded to her.

"I missed you, too." She pulled away, clasping Taylor's hand in her own. "Come on in. Are you hungry? I thought we could order a pizza."

"Pizza sounds great," Taylor agreed, immensely enjoying the fact that she was being led by the hand.

"Good, 'cause it's on its way."

Melanie's apartment was small and sparsely furnished, but had great potential. The door opened into a small hallway with a huge closet. Straight ahead was a little half-kitchen lining the left wall. It contained all the essentials: refrigerator, sink and stove, plus a microwave mounted under the oak-colored cabinets. Several boxes were stacked on the counter, a testament to the fact that Melanie hadn't gotten around to unpacking her kitchen stuff.

A small kitchen table with two chairs was placed opposite the kitchen wall. Directly to its right was a large, cozy-looking cream-and-blue striped couch, the pillows giving the appearance of much use. The couch provided a break between the living room and kitchen, since there was no wall separating the two. There was a simple coffee table in front of it, but that was all the furniture in the small living room. In the opposite corner, between the two windows that spilled sunlight into the small space sat a top-of-the-line television and VCR. No table or stand was in sight, and the electronics were stacked on the bare hardwood. No pictures graced the walls. No houseplants stretched toward the plentiful rays of sun. No knick-knacks of any kind were visible.

Melanie carefully watched Taylor's face as she surveyed the apartment. "Kind of sparse, huh?"

"Well, um..." Taylor didn't want to insult her in any way, but she was right. "Yeah, actually. It's a beautiful place, though. I'm just surprised."

"You are? Why?"

"Because this apartment doesn't represent the Melanie that I know," she said simply, shrugging her shoulders. "I suppose it could just be because you haven't finished unpacking."

Melanie scratched her forehead. "Actually, other than the kitchen, I am done unpacking."

They looked at each other for a long minute before breaking into laughter. "Jesus, Melanie. We'd better get you to the housewares section of *Wal-Mart* or something. It still echoes in here, for crying out loud. You need...stuff."

Their bout of laughter eased their moods tremendously, and they fell into the comfortable, easy bantering that they had missed so much during their time apart. The pizza arrived, and Melanie felt more at home sitting in her nearly empty apartment with Taylor on her living room floor than she ever remembered feeling at any other time in her life.

Taylor took a large bite of her pizza, scrutinizing the living room as she sat cross-legged on the floor, using the coffee table to hold her plate. "You know, we could find a couple of colorful prints to put on this wall and that one." She pointed at the largest bare spaces on the white walls. "They'd brighten things up a lot. And plants. You need plants. Look at all the sun in here. It's great. We've got to get you some plants."

Melanie just watched her, loving the apparently growing enthusiasm as she rattled off ideas and suggestions.

The dark eyes crackled with excitement and one side of her mouth curved up into a half-smile.

"Does that mean that you'd want to be around to help me decorate?" Melanie finally asked softly.

Taylor stopped in mid-chew and looked at the older woman thoughtfully. "Of course, I'd want to. Haven't I made that painfully clear by now?" She softened any sting the words may have carried with a playful grin.

"Even after my cowardly display last week?"

Taylor set down her pizza, stood, and moved around the coffee table to sit next to Melanie on the couch. She wet her lips with her tongue while searching for the best way to put her thoughts and feelings into words that wouldn't terrify the woman sitting beside her.

"Melanie," she began slowly, "I have never enjoyed anybody's company like I enjoy yours. These last few weeks have been amazing to me. I know we haven't known each other very long, but you've become a part of me so quickly, it's a little scary."

Melanie chuckled at that, nodding in agreement. "I know what you mean."

Taylor took that as the positive comment it was meant to be and plunged onward. "I didn't know what to do when you left without talking to me. I was worried about you. And I was hurt. You didn't feel safe enough to talk to me about what you were going through. I mean, I know that we really don't know each other all that well, and maybe it's silly of me to expect you to feel comfortable enough to completely open up to me. I'm aware of that, but it doesn't change the fact that it bothered me when you didn't let me help you."

Melanie grasped Taylor's hand. "I know. I'm so sorry. I never wanted to hurt you."

Taylor grimaced at the overused line, gently withdrawing her fingers. "You could have talked to me, you know."

"I don't think I could have talked to anybody at that point."

"You could have tried," Taylor pointed out softly. "We

made love, for Christ's sake. I think I deserved some sort of explanation."

Melanie studied her fingernails, feeling small. "You're right. I could have. I should have." She had hurt Taylor more deeply than she had realized. It was apparent from the tone of her voice. She swallowed, taking a deep breath and deciding it was now or never. Taylor deserved the truth. "I was just so scared by what was happening. Samantha and your dad and you and me...it was so much, and I didn't know how to deal with it. I still don't. I'm not trying to offer excuses. Please don't think I am. What I did was...well, it was a shitty thing to do. I know that. I've never run from anything in my life, but this has floored me. It's just...I just...I've never felt this way before, and I didn't know what to do about it."

Taylor felt the first glimmerings of real hope. "You've never felt what way?" she pressed gently. Melanie half-smiled, half-grimaced and looked away, swallowing hard. Taylor gently cupped her chin, returning the blue-eyed gaze back to her own face. "What way, Melanie?"

"The way I feel when I'm with you," Melanie whispered. "In love."

Taylor had to consciously force her butt to stay put on the couch. Her body was itching to jump up and do a little dance around the room. She smiled widely. "You love me?"

Melanie slapped her arm, trying to allay the heaviness of the subject, unable to believe she had actually admitted her feelings to Taylor and the world hadn't come crashing down around her. "Well, duh. You think I jump in the sack with just anybody?"

"I hope not."

"Well, I don't."

"Good. Melanie?"

"Hmm?"

"I love you, too."

They were quiet for several long minutes, absorbing the words recently spoken, each enjoying the company of the other. Taylor put her arm around Melanie's shoulders, and they sat back on the couch, basking in one another's presence.

"Now what?" Taylor asked, finally breaking the comfort of the silence.

"I'm not sure," Melanie replied. "I'm still dealing with all of this, trying to make some sense of it. It's not every day you fall in love with another woman, you know."

Taylor grinned. "Speak for yourself." That got her a slap. "Hey. I'm kidding."

"I know." Melanie smiled back. "It just takes a little...absorbing." She was quiet for several minutes, then spoke in a very small, childlike voice. "Do you think we could...you know...date? See what happens?"

Date? Hell, I want to marry you, Taylor thought. "I think we could give it a shot," she said instead. "See what happens."

Taylor's answer seemed to come as a big relief to Melanie, and her body visibly relaxed against Taylor's. "Did you think I'd actually say no?" Taylor inquired, surprised.

"You had every right to. I haven't exactly made this easy for you. I've been pretty selfish. I thought that may have turned you off."

Taylor grinned devilishly, nuzzling Melanie's neck. "There is *nothing* about you that could possibly turn me off."

"Hey," Melanie squealed as the nuzzling turned to nibbling. "Now *that* sounds like a challenge."

"You're dealing with some pretty big stuff. I can understand that." She grinned. "I don't have to like it, but I understand it."

"It's big stuff. It's definitely big stuff."

"Are you...okay? With things, I mean?" Taylor treaded lightly on the subject.

Melanie thought for a long moment before she answered. "I think I will be. It definitely makes it easier having you nearby." She rolled her blue eyes. "I realized that once I got back to Chicago."

"You were scared. I know."

Melanie studied Taylor's face. "How did I get you?" she asked quietly.

Taylor shifted to look in the redhead's eyes. In them, and much to her surprise, she saw love, trust, and utter passion. They were the only invitation she needed. She leaned in gently and pressed her lips to Melanie's, savoring the sweet softness of them. They kissed slowly and deeply, drinking from one another as if their very existence depended upon it. Melanie finally extracted herself from Taylor's mouth long enough to wrap her arms around the younger woman and squeeze her tightly, unable to believe they were actually together again, that Taylor still wanted to be a part of her life after everything that had happened. At that very moment in time, and for reasons she couldn't explain, Melanie knew that Taylor was the person with whom she was meant to be. More than that, she accepted it, finally able to push away all the doubts and stumbling blocks hindering the path to the future. She knew that with Taylor by her side, she could deal with anything life could throw her way.

She pulled back to look penetratingly into the depths of the dark, loving eyes before her. They stayed that way for what seemed like eternity, no words spoken. Melanie poured every ounce of love she could muster into that gaze, willing Taylor to see it, to feel it.

"This won't be easy, you know, you and I being together," Melanie told her. "I can be very difficult. Pig-headed, even." She half-grinned at the last statement.

Taylor held her gaze steadily and confidently. "It will be hard at first, but we'll manage. I can handle you." The dark eyes sparkled in challenge.

"Oh, you think so?"

"Oh, I know so."

Melanie stood from the couch and held out her hand. "Let's find out if you're right, shall we?"

Her voice was low and seductive. Taylor felt the tingle of excitement course through her system as she slipped her own hand softly into Melanie's and allowed her love to lead her around the corner and into the bedroom, which was surprisingly roomy for the size of the rest of the apartment. Unlike the living area, the bedroom was completely furnished and decorated in shades of burgundy and rosy pinks. Curtains were hung and matched the bedspread, as well as the round area rug that peeked out from under the queen-size bed. Half a dozen pillows were strewn about the bed, and an aromatic candle burned on each of the nightstands that stood guard on either side of the bed, scenting the air with a soft vanilla. The overall atmosphere was warm and romantic. Taylor looked at Melanie, her eyebrows raised in question.

Melanie smiled, blushing slightly, her confident demeanor wavering just a bit. "I was hoping we might end up in here, and I wanted it to be perfect, so I did a little shopping."

"You did this for me?"

Melanie nodded.

"It's beautiful, Melanie."

"So are you."

"What if things hadn't worked out? What if we didn't end up in here?"

"I'm afraid I might have been calling the fire department by this point."

They both laughed, feeling the final remnants of the previous tensions leave the room completely, leaving only the two of them and their new found world. Their lips met again, more insistent this time, impatient and demanding. Melanie backed Taylor up to the bed, forcing her to sit on it as the backs of her knees touched the soft, flowered fabric. Melanie perched herself in Taylor's lap, a knee on either side of the dark-haired woman's hips, and surprised herself with her own confidence and aggression by taking control of the situation. Taylor allowed her to keep it, sensing it was something she needed.

Being loved by a woman had been an altogether amazing departure from Melanie's usual existence. She had decided that right away. In the same vein, loving a woman was intensely erotic, and a totally new experience for her. She made every effort to take her time, enjoying the new sensations, reveling in them. Once they had removed their clothing and Taylor lay stretched out beneath her, she made a slow, sensual exploration of the gloriously female body she wanted so badly to know.

Although she expected it this time, Melanie was still astounded by the softness of Taylor's skin. That was the biggest physical difference between this lover and the few male ones she'd had in the past. It was like sliding her hands over velvet. She ran her fingertips over Taylor's arm, her shoulder, the side of her neck, her throat, and down the center of her torso to her belly, causing goose bumps to erupt in her wake. She watched and listened, fascinated by the effect she was having. Taylor's breathing quickened at certain times, caught at others. Melanie smiled at this, then replaced her fingers with her lips and tongue, kissing and nibbling along the same path. Taylor's skin was slightly salty, a little sweet, and silky against Melanie's tongue. There was something distinctly Taylor about the taste, and the older woman decided right away that she liked it immensely.

The heavier Taylor's breathing got, and the more she writhed under Melanie, the bolder Melanie became. It wasn't long before she ventured to an ample breast with both her fingers and her mouth. Her fingers discovered that the side of Taylor's breast had the softest skin yet. She swirled her tongue around the cocoa brown nipple several times, watching with rapt attention as it stiffened before her eyes, the flesh around it pebbling as it contracted. She flicked the tip of her tongue over it, then smiled in surprise as Taylor gasped. She felt the dark-haired woman's hand clutching the back of her neck, trying hard to keep from pressing her forward. Excited by the effect she was having on Taylor, she closed her mouth over the protruding nipple and sucked gently.

Both women groaned at the same time, Taylor arching subtly into Melanie, no longer holding back, pressing Melanie's head tightly to her own chest. She could tell by the sounds and shifting of Taylor's body exactly how each movement of Melanie's mouth was making her feel. She pulled firmly from the nipple and felt Taylor's hips push up into her own. She found such control intensely arousing, and warmth flooded her center as she sucked again, a little harder, this time eliciting a soft whimper from the body beneath her. She was surprised to find her actions strangely comforting as well as stimulating. Something about the suckling of a woman's breast—this woman's breast—made her feel safe. Strange, but true.

Melanie took her time in her explorations, shifting to the other breast only after she was sure she had given sufficient attention to the first one. Taylor knew this was Melanie's first time with a woman, and therefore let her find her own way around, trying hard not to direct her in any way. Melanie was surprisingly adept, expectedly gentle, and amazingly arousing in her unabashed exploration. Taylor had a very difficult time keeping herself from taking control. She wanted to flip the smaller woman onto her back and ravish her repeatedly until the only word she could muster was Taylor's name. Instead, she held herself in check, allowing Melanie to keep the lead, repeatedly surprised by how well the redhead seemed to know her and how readily she responded to Melanie's touch.

Melanie was in heaven. Having Taylor in her bed, beneath her fingers and mouth, was a fantasy in itself. She could sense that Taylor was making a conscious effort to give her the time she needed, and it warmed her heart. She was also aware of the effect she was having. Taylor's hips were moving—subtly, as if Taylor didn't want to scare her—and Melanie could feel the brunette's wetness against her thigh. The idea that she was the cause of it aroused her even more, and she felt her own center moisten as a trickle snaked down her leg. She finally, almost regrettably, moved her lips from the breasts and down the smooth, velvety skin of the younger woman's stomach. Taylor's abs flinched, and Melanie smiled as she dipped her tongue playfully into Taylor's bellybutton.

Melanie gently spread Taylor's thighs, inhaling the unfamiliar yet comforting scent that surrounded her. The folds were glistened with proof of Taylor's arousal, and Melanie settled herself between the brunette's legs, gently stroking her inner thighs with feather-light touches of her fingertips. She smiled when she felt the slight quivering of the muscles. She glanced up and met dark eyes watching her. They were filled with such love and devotion that Melanie felt her throat constrict with emotion. Taylor reached down to brush her fingers through the gold-touched red strands, and the two women held one another's gaze for a long, meaningful moment.

"I love you," Taylor whispered.

The simple honesty of the words warmed Melanie from the inside out, and she smiled widely.

Turning her attention back to the subject before her, she was amazed to find that she felt no anxiety whatsoever. She wasn't frightened. She wasn't even nervous. She wanted nothing more than to please this woman she loved, this woman who loved her better than anybody in her life ever had.

She brought a finger to the wet and swollen flesh in front of her, and stroked it gently. Her eyes snapped up when Taylor gasped, then she smiled, thinking what a rush it was to be able to make a woman feel that way. She repeated the move, loving the silky texture of Taylor's skin. Taylor gasped again, her fingers tangling in Melanie's hair. Melanie touched her finger to her own tongue, tasting the essence of this beautiful creature. She was salty and sweet at the same time, with a tang of something...she couldn't narrow it down, but giggled to herself at the realization that Taylor tasted absolutely nothing like tuna.

Rather than the expected gasp, Taylor moaned from deep in her throat at the first touch of Melanie's tongue on her, pushing herself up into the redhead's mouth, waves coursing down her legs, rendering them utterly useless. Melanie explored gently, memorizing every little curve and dip and what kind of effect it had on Taylor when each was stroked or licked or sucked on. She filed it all away, as she decided for certain that she wanted to perform this very act as often as she possibly could. Feeling Taylor gently writhing beneath her, whispering her name, grasping her hair, was incredibly exhilarating. The taste of her, the sounds of her, the feel of her, all combined to create an astoundingly erotic potion, drug-like in its intensity. Melanie had never felt such a sexual rush in her life, and she soaked it in as she stroked and tasted and teased Taylor until the brunette thought she'd explode. Only after her quiet begging, did Melanie release her, pushing her to the top, holding her there, teetering, before giving her one, final nudge to send her over into pure, loving bliss.

"I think I like you this way the best," Melanie commented as she stretched up to give Taylor a peck on the nose.

"Wha—what way?" Taylor asked, trying to steady her breathing. She'd never experienced such a powerful climax, and she felt weak, ecstatic, sated, and exhausted all at once.

"Naked, breathless, and underneath me," Melanie answered. She closed her lips around a swollen nipple, causing Taylor's whole body to jerk.

"Uh oh," Taylor said, grinning. "I think I've created a monster."

"Nah. I was already a monster. You've created a nympho."

"Oh no," Taylor protested weakly, purposely allowing no emotion into her voice. "Not a nympho. How awful for me, to have a girlfriend who's a nympho. My life sucks."

"Funny girl," Melanie said with a smile as she settled herself alongside Taylor's lean body, tucking her head onto the brunette's shoulder. *I just made love to a woman,* she thought. Then she smiled, correcting herself. *I just made love to the woman I'm in love with.*

"I can't feel my legs," Taylor whispered in amusement.

"I think I'll take that as a compliment."

"It is, but...I want to...just give me a minute, okay?" Taylor had never been one for one-sided lovemaking, and she didn't want Melanie to think she had no intention of returning the favor, but the surprising intensity of her orgasm had left her feeling as though her body was made of Jello, and she struggled to lend voice to her thoughts.

Melanie silenced her by laying a finger over her lips. "Shh. Don't worry. We have plenty of time to explore each other. Besides, I owed you, remember?" She felt Taylor's body move beneath her as the brunette chuckled. "Just relax, okay?"

"Yes, ma'am."

Taylor tightened her arms around Melanie and took a slow, deep breath, simply absorbing the other woman's presence. Melanie closed her eyes in contentment when she felt Taylor's breathing even into sleep. *That's a good sign*, she congratulated herself. She watched the sleeping woman for several long minutes, memorizing each angle of her face, mapping each freckle and mole on her perfectly creamy skin, tracing her dark eyebrows with a fingertip. Try as she might, she couldn't remember any other time in her life when she had felt so at home.

"I love you," she whispered as she reached down to pull a light blanket up around their entwined bodies. She snuggled closer to the warm body next to her and allowed sleep to claim her as well.

Chapter
29

The next few days were individual whirlwinds of activity. Taylor had several meetings on Friday and an appointment with a prospective client on Saturday morning, so she was unavailable much of that time. Melanie was so busy getting ready for the grand opening of *The Quill is Mightier*, that she didn't have a chance to miss Taylor nearly as much as she could have. Still, their separation was palpable and neither could wait until the evening, when they would discuss their day with one another over dinner. They spent the second half of the weekend in Melanie's apartment, or more specifically, in Melanie's bed, talking, laughing, learning about each other and loving one another.

It was Monday afternoon, and Melanie casually checked her watch. Five-fifteen. The first day of her new business had gone very well. There were several women milling around among the shelves. A petite, college-age woman with a nose ring sat comfortably in one of the overstuffed chairs, reading *The Empty Closet* and twirling a lock of burgundy hair around her finger.

Melanie had gotten several compliments on the name of the store, all of them fans of Xena, just as Lynda had predicted. The redhead smiled happily at the memory of Taylor seeing the sign for the first time the previous Friday. She had been on her way to an appointment, deciding to drive past the shop simply to beep—she confided later, feeling somewhat childish, that she had spent the previous few days purposely avoiding any route that would take her past the bookstore, in order to save herself the pain of being reminded. She had laughed out loud when she saw the large, cobalt letters, scripted clearly above the front door, parking and popping her head in quickly to let Melanie know what she thought.

"The Quill is Mightier? I love it."

Melanie's head had snapped up at the sudden sound of somebody bursting through the front door, then smiled at the light of her life. "I wanted to surprise you."

"You did. I love it," she'd repeated. She had swooped Melanie up in a big hug, kissed her soundly on the lips, then turned on her heel. "Gotta run, baby, I'm going to be late. Just wanted to tell you I love the name. And I love you."

She'd done the same thing again this morning. She'd breezed in, an hour or two into Melanie's first official day of business, wearing a snappy blue suit and a big grin. She'd quickly set a large cup of steaming coffee in front of the auburn-haired woman and kissed her lightly on the forehead. There had been two customers browsing, so she had kept her voice to a whisper. "Can't stay, sweetheart. I was just driving by, so I thought I'd drop in, bring you some liquid drugs and tell you I love you."

Melanie had smiled in pleasant disbelief. "How did I get you?" This seemed to be her signature question of late.

Taylor had simply smiled and shrugged. "I get a check in the mail every week from an anonymous source." She winked. "I'll see you tonight."

And she was gone.

Her timing was near perfect. Not five minutes later, another surprise guest had popped in.

"Hi, Mellie."

Melanie had been bent over a packing slip at the counter. She had recognized the voice immediately and had taken several seconds to get her bearings before looking up to meet the blue-eyed, buxom blonde who shared the same bloodline as she did.

"Hi, Sam," she'd replied with controlled neutrality.

Sam had fidgeted slightly, shifting her weight from one foot to the other, making a point to look around. "It looks great in here," she'd finally commented.

Melanie nodded. "Thanks."

The silence had been awkward at best, but Melanie had been determined not to give in too easily. She had been sure Sam had come to apologize, or at least to perform the Samantha Richter version of an apology, and the redhead had been determined not to make it easy for her. Sam's reaction to last week's situation and the insults flung at Taylor still stung, and Melanie had no intention of letting her off the hook without a fair bit of groveling.

"You've really fixed it up nice."

"Thanks," Melanie had said again.

Samantha had squirmed visibly at that point, unaccustomed to wallowing in her own guilt, part of her becoming annoyed that her cousin had not been making this easier for her. She had blinked in surprise as Melanie had reached around her to take a book from the hand of the customer who'd appeared soundlessly. Sam had stepped awkwardly to the side at the murmured "excuse me" and had watched her cousin.

"Find everything okay?" Melanie had asked the customer, a young, tomboyish black woman, a cheerful note in her voice.

"I did, thanks," the woman had replied with a friendly nod. "Impressive selection."

"Thank you." Melanie had smiled, enjoying the compliment immensely. She'd handed the woman her change and bag, effectively ignoring her cousin while making the transaction. "Have a great day."

"You, too." She'd smiled apologetically at Samantha

as she'd passed.

Only when the customer was actually out the door and onto the street had Melanie returned her gaze to her cousin expectantly, silently waiting for her to continue.

Samantha had taken a deep, steadying breath and studied her well-manicured, blood-red nails with grave interest.

"You were right," she'd finally said softly.

Melanie had cocked her head, like a puppy listening to a high-pitched sound. "Pardon me? What was that?"

Sam had narrowed her eyes. *So this is how it was going to be.* "I said you were right," she'd repeated through clenched teeth.

"I was right? Right about what, Sam?" Oh, Melanie was enjoying this.

Sam had grimaced. Her baby cousin was going to make her spell the whole thing out. She had sighed, resigned to her fate, and had lowered her eyes to the floor. "It was none of my business that you chose to sleep with Taylor, and I had no right to react the way I did," she'd finally said, her voice barely audible. "I'm sorry."

Melanie had never seen her larger-than-life cousin look quite as vulnerable and young as she had at that moment. Apologies had never been Sam's strong point. As a matter of fact, Melanie had been hard-pressed to think up even one example when she'd heard her cousin admit she'd been wrong. The sight at that moment—Sam standing before her with her proverbial tail tucked between her legs—had pulled at Melanie's heartstrings.

"I didn't just choose to sleep with Taylor," Melanie had corrected gently. "I fell in love with her."

"That, too." Sam had nodded.

Though the redhead hadn't been ready to let her completely off the hook, she had accepted the apology with a hug and a promise to have dinner together the following week. It was only after Samantha had left, her step infinitely more bouncy than when she had arrived, that Melanie realized how deeply the tension between them had been affecting her. She'd felt a weight lift from her shoulders.

Lynda had popped in right around lunchtime, a big smile on her face, food stains on her apron. "I come bearing gifts," she'd announced. She'd placed a plastic container of fruit salad and a foil-wrapped sandwich on the counter in front of Melanie, handing over a peach Snapple as the finishing touch. "Can't have you starving to death on your first day of business, now can we?" She held out a spork.

"You are a goddess, you know that?"

"So I've been told." She had stared openly at Melanie. "Wait a minute. You're glowing."

Melanie had felt her face growing red at the comment.

Lynda had leaned closer, scrutinizing the auburn-haired woman's face carefully, cupping her chin and turning Melanie's face from side to side. "As a matter of fact, I'd say that's more than a happiness glow. Correct me if I'm wrong, but I'd say this glow definitely has the distinct qualities of the I've-been-getting-laid-every-night-since-I-returned-from-Chicago glow."

Melanie had blanched, the redness draining from her face as quickly as it had appeared. "Lynda," she'd hissed, not only worried that a customer might have heard, but astounded that Lynda had read her so easily.

Lynda had merely pinched Melanie's cheek affectionately and laughed. "Relax, babe. I'm happy for you. I've seen Taylor popping in and out of here, and if it makes you feel any better, she's glowing, too."

That had made Melanie feel better. A lot better. Tons better. Lynda had rolled her eyes.

"Oh, wipe that stupid grin off your face and eat your lunch. I've got to get back to work." She had turned on her heel and started for the door.

"Hey, Lynda?"

"Yeah?"

"Thanks. For everything."

They had held one another's gaze for a long beat, Lynda easily catching the intended message in the words.

"That's what friends are for, Mel. Eat."

She'd smiled a satisfied smile and exited the shop, leaving Melanie feeling warm and loved.

"This is a great little shop."

The voice startled Melanie out of her reverie and back to the present. She blinked once and focused on the pleasant-looking woman standing in front of her, three books on the counter between them.

"Thank you very much."

"It's nice to have a decent selection of fiction to choose from. The *Barnes & Noble* down the street has one shelf of lesbian fiction and actually refers to it as a 'section.'" She made quotation marks in the air with her fingers.

Melanie chuckled as she rang up the purchases. "Well, I'm glad we could help you out. I'm going to do my best to keep the inventory plentiful and up-to-date. Those seem to be the biggest complaints."

"Glad to hear it." The woman nodded, as she took her bag from Melanie.

"Have a great night."

"You do the same."

Melanie heard the bell over the door jingle as the woman left. She squatted to straighten the pile of plastic bags on the shelf near her knees, retrieving the handful that had somehow ended up on the floor during the course of the day. She stood back up and was immediately startled by the form standing directly at the counter, barely a foot away.

"Jesus." She placed her hand on her chest, hoping to slow down her racing heart.

"Hi, baby." Dark eyes twinkled at her.

"You scared the hell out of me."

"Sorry. You know, you need to pay more attention to the world around you," Taylor chided, then pointed to her feet, as well as the hardwood floor. "I have heels on. It's not like I could sneak up on you."

Melanie laughed, grudgingly conceding the point.

Besides, she was too happy to see Taylor to be mad at her. She took in the figure before her, mentally nodding in approval at the navy blue, pinstriped pantsuit and navy pumps. The cream-colored silk shell under the jacket had a scooped neck, and Taylor's collarbone peeked out invitingly over the trim. "It's good to see you. You look fabulous."

"Back atcha." Taylor smiled. She leaned forward and gently brushed Melanie's lips with her own. Melanie fought the little voice of panic in the back of her mind, the one that screamed in horror at such a public display of affection with *another woman*. She succeeded in ignoring it, but knew it was something she'd be working on for a while, the whole idea still being new to her. Being in private with Taylor was one thing, but being out in the open, in a public place where other people could see them was something Melanie wasn't sure she was ready for. Taylor seemed to sense her anxiety and drew back a bit.

"You okay?"

Melanie grinned, nodding. "I'm great."

Taylor studied her face for several seconds, before deciding to broach the subject at another time. "How was business on your first day?"

"I have to say, it was pretty damn good. A beautiful woman delivered coffee to me this morning. And you'll be pleased to note that I received in excess of seven compliments on the name."

Taylor clapped her hands in delight. "Excellent."

"I thought you'd like that."

"Are you hungry?"

"Famished. And I'm having a craving."

Taylor raised an eyebrow mischievously. "Really."

Melanie slapped at her, blushing. "For food, you barbarian."

"Oh. Food. Silly me. What would you like?"

"Lynda's been filling me so full of healthy sandwiches and salads that my body is threatening to revolt if I don't feed it some grease soon. Could you stop at *McDonald's* for me?"

Taylor glanced at her watch. "How long you staying open tonight?"

"Seven." Melanie rolled her eyes. "Which may change in the future. This has been a long day."

"Okay. How 'bout I go home and change, hit the drive-thru and come back here to help you with your last hour?"

"You are the best."

"Shh." Taylor put a finger to her lips. "Don't you go spreading that around."

"No way. I'm keeping you all to myself."

The subtle clearing of a throat brought them out of their own private world and into that of everybody else. A tall, woman with graying hair smiled sheepishly at the couple, holding up a book. "Can I pay for this?"

Melanie flushed a deep pink, which made Taylor chuckle. "Sure."

Taylor tucked a strand of auburn hair behind Melanie's ear for her. "I'll see you in a bit."

Chapter
30

This is good, Taylor smiled to herself as she drove home from the bookstore. Things were going well, and she couldn't seem to keep the smile from taking up permanent residence on her face. She turned into the driveway, the sun beating down hotly through the sunroof, the air conditioning blasting on her feet. Her father would roll his eyes at such a contradiction, but that's the way she liked to drive. In the winter, she'd have the sunroof open and the heat scalding her ankles.

Ben's car was nowhere to be seen and Taylor breathed a sigh of relief, then scowled at herself in the rearview mirror. Although the two of them had talked several times, Taylor being startled more than once by her father's sudden openness, she still felt a twinge of guilt, like she had stolen his property. Even though she'd been forgiven, it still didn't feel quite right. She guessed it would be some time before that niggling in her brain disappeared. She had managed to keep Melanie away from the house and Ben— not that it had been difficult, since the redhead was in no hurry to force an awkward situation. But come the holidays, she wanted all her loved ones to be together. She hoped that, by that time, things would be much more comfortable.

She quickly sorted through the mail, noting a letter from Gina, her college roommate, along with a bill for her student loan payment. She chuckled at the fact that she had received reminders of college from two opposite ends of the spectrum. She knew she owed Gina a phone call, not just a letter. On the other hand, she didn't feel she owed the Student Loan Servicing Center anything. They should be retiring on her interest alone. She rolled her eyes and tossed the rest of the mail onto the kitchen table, taking the steps two at a time up to her room.

She picked out her clothes carefully, something she found herself doing almost all the time lately. She'd never been quite as concerned about how she appeared to the outside world before. She knew she was a reasonably attractive woman. After all, her mother had been breathtaking, and everybody Taylor knew told her how much she resembled the woman, so it only figured. It had never been important to Taylor, though, until now. Until this charming, kind-hearted, incredibly sexy redhead had shown up. Now, Taylor found herself spending countless extra minutes picking just the right color shirt, just the right shoes, just the right perfume. She wanted so much to be beautiful for Melanie.

She ran a quick iron over her dark green shorts, thinking how Gina would scoff at the fact. She envisioned her short, butch pal easily, and could almost hear her husky voice in the room. *You're ironing your shorts? What the hell for? They're shorts. They're just gonna wrinkle as soon as you sit in the car anyway. And is that nail polish on your toes? Jesus, you scare me, Rhodes. What the hell kind of dyke are you, anyway?* Then, she'd throw up her hands in disgust and pop open a beer. Taylor smiled at the scenario, so typical of her college life, until she'd met Maggie. She and Gina hadn't exactly gotten along, and the two roommates had drifted apart a bit. But, Gina had always stayed in touch, putting her friendship with Taylor above her opinion of Taylor's choice in women.

Taylor decided they needed to get together before the summer ended. She wanted very much for Gina to meet Melanie.

She ran a brush through her hair, debating about pulling it back in a ponytail and deciding against it, knowing Melanie liked it down, liked tangling her fingers in it. She set her brush on the dresser next to a gold-framed picture of herself and her mother at Taylor's college graduation. They both sported huge smiles, their arms wrapped around one another. Taylor's white cap and gown contrasted beautifully with Anna's simple, forest green dress. Their hair and eyes were exactly the same color. Taylor remembered the moment fondly, with Ben scolding them to stand still long enough for him to snap the damned picture. Anna had been giddy with pride.

Taylor stroked a finger over the glass of the frame, tracing her mother's smiling face, her eyes misting slightly. "I wish you were here, Mom," she whispered aloud. She smiled as she pictured Anna's subtle approval of Melanie. "I think you'd like her."

She sighed softly, tucking a pale yellow T-shirt into the waistband of her neatly pressed shorts, then spritzing a touch of musk at the hollow of her throat. She was still amazed at the way she felt when she thought about Melanie. She knew they had a ways to go before their relationship was perfect, but Taylor was willing to be patient with her new love. She was actually getting to the point where she was pretty sure she could read Melanie with nearly perfect accuracy. After all, the redhead's face was incredibly expressive, and it was very difficult for her to cloak her emotions. Whatever she was feeling was usually plainly apparent in her eyes.

Taylor chuckled. Just the other day, Melanie had whined her disapproval at the fact that Taylor could read her so easily, not believing she was quite as transparent as she actually was.

Slipping on her sunglasses and shifting the car into gear, Taylor headed for the nearest *McDonald's*, still bask-

ing in the glow of thoughts of Melanie, wanting to get back
to her as quickly as possible. Given the haste of their
newly founded relationship, Melanie was doing remarkably well. She was still hesitant about public displays of
affection, unless they were in a gay bar, as evidenced in
the bookshop earlier. Taylor had explained to her over the
weekend that it would probably be a common assumption
that the feminist/lesbian bookstore would be owned by a
lesbian, and nobody would really care if she was seen kissing her partner, but Melanie was still uneasy. Rather than
push, Taylor had chosen to wait the redhead out, certain
that she would become more at ease with that type of situation as she became more comfortable with her own sexuality. It would just take time. If it meant Melanie would
stay with Taylor, Taylor was willing to wait forever.

Melanie was also unsure how to deal with women flirting with her. It had happened more than once at *TJ's*, and
Taylor was sure it would occur at the shop. After all, Melanie was a very attractive woman, and her being oblivious
to that fact only made her more appealing. Taylor was
patiently amused by the redhead's insistence that a woman
flirting with her was completely different than a man flirting with her. A man, she could handle. Women absolutely
flustered her.

"Just tell them you're taken," Taylor had suggested
simply.

"It's not that easy," Melanie had complained.

"Okay, honey." Taylor had patronized with a grin.

"I'm serious," Melanie had insisted, half-laughing and
half-earnest.

"I know." That was precisely what Taylor had found so
entertaining in the first place.

A smile had slowly crept across Melanie's face as Taylor's remark had belatedly penetrated. "I'm taken?"

Taylor had nodded. "You bet you are."

Tucking the Quarter Pounder with cheese and large
fries safely into the passenger seat, Taylor headed for *The
Quill is Mightier*, chuckling with glee once again at the

name. Unable to resist the smell, she dipped into the bag and stole a piping hot French fry, sucking the salt from each finger. Taking a deep breath of the fresh air whipping through the sunroof, she exhaled loudly. Life was good.

Parking the car in the back lot, Taylor entered the shop with the extra key to the rear door with which Melanie had surprised her. She stole quietly into the back office to lay out Melanie's dinner for her, listening to her chat with the customer on whom she was waiting.

"No, unfortunately, I've been so busy getting things ready that I haven't had time to sit and read very many of the new pieces," Melanie was explaining. "I hope to change that as things settle into more of a routine. Not that people will necessarily need to know my opinion on the latest books, but..."

"Oh, I bet you'll get a lot of requests for your input," the customer replied in an unmistakably flirtatious tone. Taylor froze, the French fry box in mid-air, as she recognized the voice.

Melanie chuckled, and Taylor could almost hear her blush. "I don't know about that."

"Well, let me help you out a bit. See this one? This story has an absolutely amazing love scene. It's incredibly romantic and unbelievably erotic without going over the top. Of course, if over the top is your thing, this one here is just one big orgy."

Taylor clenched her teeth, torn between running into the store and running out the back door. She didn't want to interrupt Melanie; she knew the redhead would be furious if Taylor thought she couldn't handle herself. At the same time, she didn't know how much longer she could stand here and listen to the blatant attempts at seducing her girlfriend.

"Uh, no," Melanie was saying nervously. "Over the top is not really my cup of tea. I'm a bit more old-fashioned, I guess."

Taylor could hear the electronic beeping of the computer and could picture Melanie's delicate fingers flying over the keypad, ringing up her customer as quickly as she possibly could.

"Old-fashioned, huh?" The customer's voice hinted at a smile. "Well, how 'bout letting me buy you a good old-fashioned drink, then? You must be closing soon."

"You know what?" Taylor cocked her head and strained her ears as she noted the sudden increase of confidence in her lover's voice. "I really appreciate that, but I'm involved with somebody."

Taylor had no control over the smile that erupted across her face.

The customer lowered her voice conspiratorially. "I'm not asking you to marry me. Just let me buy you a drink. Our secret?"

Taylor could take it no longer. Scooping up the burger and fries, she walked confidently around the doorway of the office and behind the counter to set Melanie's food down, purposely not looking up.

"Here's your dinner, honey." Only then did she raise her eyes to the customer and feign surprise. "Oh. Hi there, Maggie. Doing some shopping?" She made a show of slipping her arm around Melanie, making it very clear to her ex which items were *not* available to her.

Melanie was looking from one woman to the other with a puzzled expression on her face. The realization was evident when it finally hit her.

Maggie's demeanor went from mildly seductive to disgusted. "*This* is who you're involved with?" she asked Melanie, emphasizing the last two words with heavy sarcasm by making quotation marks in the air with her fingers.

"Yes, it is," Melanie nodded simply, not liking the woman's tone. Taylor beamed.

"Can't fault your taste, Tay. She's adorable. No wonder you wouldn't return my calls."

Taylor felt Melanie stiffen next to her and anger well up in her. "God, Maggie, when did you become such a miserable bitch?"

"Oh, I don't know," Maggie sniped back, snatching her bag of books off the counter. "Maybe the day you walked out on me."

"Oh, please. Can't you come up with a new act?"

Maggie turned her fiery green gaze on Melanie, who was watching the exchange with wide-eyed wonder. "I hope the going never gets rough for the two of you." She jerked a thumb in Taylor's direction. "Just when you need her, she disappears." She snapped her fingers to punctuate the point, turning on her heel. "Have a nice life, Taylor."

"Fuck you, Maggie," Taylor murmured at the retreating woman's back.

The bell over the door threatened to crash to the floor from the force of the slam. Melanie silently thanked the gods above that it was closing time and there had been no other customers in the shop to witness the exchange. She could hear Lynda's voice scolding her. *Very bad for business.*

She walked to the front door and locked both the dead bolt and floor bolt, shut the blinds and dimmed the lights on the window displays. She stood quietly for a minute before returning to Taylor, who still stood behind the counter, the redness in her face finally subsiding.

"Well," Melanie said lightly, snagging a fry out of the box and popping it into her mouth. "That was interesting." She pulled herself up onto the counter facing Taylor, her legs dangling. She swung them gently as she bit into her burger and waited for Taylor to say something.

Taylor took a deep breath and studied her hands, which were pressed flat against the counter, supporting her weight. She was afraid to move them, fearing her shaking knees would be unable to hold her up. "Yeah. She certainly knows how to make an exit, doesn't she?"

"It was good," Melanie agreed. A memory quickly flashed into her mind. "Hey, you know something? I've met her. At *TJ's*. She spilled her drink on me."

Taylor rolled her eyes. "Figures."

Melanie studied her partner's face. "You want to talk

about her?"

"Want to? Absolutely not. Need to? Probably."

"I'm all ears." Melanie smiled warmly, and Taylor felt some of her anxiety slip away. She pulled herself up on the counter to sit next to the redhead, stealing a French fry as she tried to find a good starting point.

"I told you that Maggie was my first long-term girl-friend. I also told you that things were good, pretty solid, for the first two years. Then, we were on-again, off-again for a long time. She kept convincing me we could work things out. I finally made a clean break a couple months ago."

"She seems like she could be pretty charming," Melanie commented, nodding. "I mean, she made me a little nervous with how forward she was, but I was intrigued."

"Oh, she's the queen of charm," Taylor chuckled. She turned to Melanie. "You think if you weren't...seeing me...you would have gone out with her?"

Melanie considered the question honestly. "She's attractive. And she just wanted to buy me a drink. I might have."

Taylor nodded, surprisingly not threatened by Melanie's answer. "And she'd have treated you like gold. Maggie's a real sweetheart when she's sober."

"Ah." Melanie remembered the image of Maggie taking in her drink like it was necessary to sustain life and finally understood the problem. "So, what finally happened? Why is she so angry with you?"

Taylor shrugged. "I couldn't do it any more. It was like being with two different people: the Maggie I loved, and the Maggie that scared the hell out of me. It seemed that I got to see the Maggie I loved less and less. The more I tried to keep her around, the more often she'd disappear, replaced by the scary one. I felt like I didn't even know her any more."

"God, that must have been hard."

"It was awful. I didn't know what to do, how to get her back, how to make her see what she was doing to herself.

Her father was an alcoholic and she always vowed it wouldn't happen to her, so whenever I tried to point out that maybe she had a problem, she'd go absolutely ballistic on me. She even gave me a bloody nose once."

Melanie gasped. "Oh my God."

"Oh, no," Taylor said quickly, holding up a hand. "She wasn't abusive. I don't want you to think that about her. Maggie's a really wonderful person deep down. She just needs help, and I couldn't convince her to get it." Her voice had dropped to a whisper, and she scrutinized the French fry in her hand, no longer having the appetite to eat it, feeling the cold weight of failure settling down upon her shoulders. "I tried, but I couldn't make her see it." She sighed heavily. "She says I left her when she needed me the most. According to her version of the story, I walked out on her because I wasn't adult enough to work on our relationship. So now, she just hates me and tells everybody who'll listen what a creep I am."

Melanie put her arm around Taylor's shoulders and pulled her closer. Taylor leaned her dark head on Melanie's shoulder and closed her eyes. "Taylor," Melanie said, her voice radiating quiet strength. "You did what you could. You're right. Maggie has a problem and needs to get herself some help. Sometimes, the person who's the closest is too close to make the other one understand. You tried, but Maggie has to *want* to get help. Nobody can make her. Please, don't feel like you failed her. You loved her."

A silent tear slid its way down Taylor's cheek and Melanie caught it with her thumb. "Oh, baby," she whispered, kissing Taylor's temple. "Don't cry."

"I didn't run out on her when the going got tough," Taylor explained, sounding like a small child. "I didn't disappear." She lifted her head to look into the understanding and loving blue eyes that were watching her. "I would never do that to you."

Melanie smiled, understanding dawning on her. "Is that what you're worried about? That I might believe her? Honey, I'm not giving any credence to what she said. She was angry, and she was trying to hurt you. I'm not worried that you're going to desert me in my time of need. I've never had a more rock-solid force in my life than you. I know you'll be right here, no matter how hard things might get. I trust you."

Taylor laughed out loud at the shocked looked that crossed the redhead's face as she finished talking. Melanie had spoken directly from her heart, the words never even making it to her head to be approved.

"Well." The older woman shrugged, embarrassed by her embarrassment. "There you have it, I guess."

Taylor slipped off the counter to her feet and turned to face Melanie. "Wow." She was pleasantly surprised by the conviction in Melanie's words, and she smiled as she absently drew a pattern on Melanie's knee with her thumb. "You think I'm a rock, huh?"

Melanie wrapped her legs around Taylor's waist and pulled her in, their noses touching, their eyes searching deeply. "Yes. I do."

"I love you," Taylor said simply.

"I love you, too, sweetheart." Melanie knew inside that she still had some things to deal with. After all, coming to terms with your alternative sexuality was not something that occurred every day, and it was not something that most people dealt with unquestioningly, without any turbulence. She would have some trouble for a bit, she knew that; she needed to have several discussions with both family members and friends; she needed to talk to Ben. She also knew that she could think of nobody she'd rather have in her corner during the upcoming battle she would inevitably have with herself than this strong, loving, passionate woman before her. She pressed her lips soundly against Taylor's, kissing her fully and deeply, trying to give all of herself over willingly, gently placing her heart in Taylor's capable hands.

Taylor kissed her back with equal parts passion and promise, vowing to cradle this gift of her lover's heart, to treasure it, to protect it with everything she had. She felt a distinct sense of peace settle over them, warming them like a woolen blanket, keeping them safe and secure in the company of one another.

The kiss became deeper still, Melanie's hands on either side of Taylor's head, her tongue probing the warm wetness of Taylor's mouth, Taylor's hands under Melanie's shirt, kneading the planes of her back.

Taylor pulled away breathlessly, kissing her way to Melanie's ear. "Remember what happened the last time you were sitting on a counter?

Melanie's breath caught in her throat at the memory. With a growl, she brought Taylor's lips back to her own and continued her exploration. Using her right hand, she fumbled along the wall, searching blindly, finally sighing in satisfaction as her palm made contact with the light switch and she plunged the shop into darkness.

Lost Paradise
By Francine Quesnel

Kristina Von Deering is a young, wealthy Austrian stunt-woman working on an Austrian/Canadian film project in Montreal. On location, she meets and eventually falls in love with a young gopher and aspiring camerawoman named Nicole McGrail. Their friendship and love is threatened by Nicole's father who sees their relationship as deviant and unnatural. He does everything in his power to put an end to it.

Meridio's Daughter
By LJ Maas

Tessa (Nikki) Nikolaidis is cold and ruthless, the perfect person to be Karê, the right-hand, to Greek magnate Andreas Meridio. Cassandra (Casey) Meridio has come home after a six-year absence to find that her father's new Karê is a very desirable, but highly dangerous woman.

Set in modern day Greece on the beautiful island of Mýkonos, this novel weaves a tale of emotional intrigue as two women from different worlds struggle with forbidden desires. As the two come closer to the point of no return, Casey begins to wonder if she can really trust the beautiful Karê. Does Nikki's dark past, hide secrets that will eventually bring down the brutal Meridio Empire, or are her actions simply those of a vindictive woman? Will she stop at nothing for vengeance...even seduction?

Other titles to look for in the coming months from
Yellow Rose Books

Prairie Fire
By LJ Maas

Daredevil Hearts
By Francine Quesnel

Heartbroken Love
By Georgio Sicily

Many Roads To Travel
By Karen King and Nann Dunne

Ricochet In Time
By Lori L. Lake

Love's Journey
By Carrie Carr

When not writing, Georgia Beers works as an account executive at an ad specialties firm in Rochester, New York. She lives in the suburbs with Bonnie, her partner of seven years, and their two dogs.

Printed in the United States
47728LVS00006B/191